WAITING FOR tuesday

TAYLOR SULLIVAN

GOOD HOUSE
PUBLISHING

DEDICATION

To my family. The ones I live for, dream with, and who make my life and endless adventure.

CHAPTER ONE

Tuesday

* * *

I moved the mass of hair from my face and pushed myself to the back of the closet. My heart was beating like a drum, but my room looked exactly the same. Desk covered with invoices and partially packed orders, shabby chic furniture from my favorite secondhand shop, and shelves perfectly organized with Simply Tuesday's products. But there was one slight difference. Today there was a man in my bed. A man I both remembered and didn't remember at the same time. His head was barely visible beneath my over-stuffed pillows, but his body was large, naked, and sprawled across the entirety of my queen-sized mattress. I anchored my glasses to my forehead with my thumb and tried to think. He was facing in the opposite direction now, but all he had to do was roll over and he'd see me. Be eye to eye with the crazy woman he slept with last night.

Crap. What was wrong with me? I didn't sleep with men I didn't know. I didn't sleep with *anyone!* How the hell had this happened?

Whiskers stopped at the open door and tilted his head, his large puffy face giving me a look that said he thought I'd lost my mind.

Him.

1

The cat that was in love with his own shadow. He made his way to the back of the closet, purring as though he didn't have a care in the world, while I tried to figure out how to get myself out of this mess.

Clips of last night began playing in my mind like a film, and I pressed my head into the wall. The launch party with Parker Studios, too many glasses of wine, and the stranger with the perfect ass. The ass that was now naked in my bed.

I forced myself farther into the shadows and picked up my phone. I needed to text Becky. Crazy Becky! The Becky who always got me into trouble.

Me: Are you awake?

I knew the answer before I pressed send, but I didn't care. I needed my best friend. Needed her to tell me to calm down. Needed her to help with a plan—and remind me what the hell his name was.

Becky: I am NOW. What happened with Mr. Hottie with the body?

I swallowed. *She knew.*

The phone buzzed with an incoming call but I rejected it.

Me: Can't talk. He's still here. I'm in the closet.

Becky: In the closet? Why are you in the closet?

Me: Yes. Closet. Why did you let me leave with him last night?

Becky: I didn't LET you do anything. Why are you in the closet, Day?

I shook my head and took a deep breath. How was I supposed to answer that? I was being unfair. She wasn't my mother, my keeper, or anything of the sort—but I felt vulnerable and stupid... *so* stupid.

2

I looked down at my phone to text a response, to explain my fight or flight reaction to waking up in bed with a stranger, to explain that *my* response had obviously been to *fly—because I didn't even remember how I got in the closet*—but then a flash of movement shifted in my peripheral vision and I sat up straighter. I put my phone on the ground, pulled a shirt from its hanger, and dragged it over my head. He was awake.

More buzzing sounded from my phone, but I couldn't move. Nor did I want to. My eyes were transfixed on the man I knew I'd slept with last night. The first in over a year. Since Ryan.

He looked around the room, presumably looking for me, and I held my breath. He was beautiful—perfect actually—almost too perfect. He had the type of body that happened only after long hours at the gym. I normally stayed away from men like that, yet somehow he had come home with me last night; somehow we'd ended up naked in my bed.

He pulled on his jeans, muttered something under his breath that I couldn't understand, and grabbed his shoes off the floor. I knew I was running out of time. He was probably wondering where I was. Probably wanting another round of whatever we did last night, but I couldn't even remember it. How was I supposed to know if I wanted to do it again?

Oh God! How would I face him again? How would I get out of this fucking closet and not look like the girl who was sitting in the back of her closet? I sucked in a long breath and pulled my knees up to my chest. I found the braid of feathers in my hair and twirled them between my fingers. They were supposed to bring calmness and peace, but I didn't feel calm at that moment. I felt rather crazy actually. Crazy and naked. I would have laughed if I wasn't terrified he'd hear me, a deep maniacal laugh, fitting of a girl sitting in the back of her own closet.

More buzzing sounded from my phone, and I glanced down to see three messages waiting from Becky.

Becky: Why are you in the closet, Day?

Becky: Answer me.

Becky: I'm calling the cops.

Shit!

Me: Don't call the cops!

Me: I'm fine.

I stared at the screen while I waited for her response.

Becky: WTF? Why are you in the closet?

Me: I'm hiding in here.

Becky: Why?

I pinched the bridge of my nose and shook my head. *No freaking clue.*

Mr. Hottie disappeared from view and I knew I had to go out there.

Me: I have to go. I'll call you back.

I put the phone on the floor, smoothed my hair back from my face, and pushed myself up from the floor.

Quick like a Band-Aid. Just step out there, pretend you've been here the whole time. Easy as pie.

But when I came out of the closet, he was gone. I took a few calming breaths and peeked around the corner to the bathroom—he wasn't there either. My shoulders relaxed and I let out a deep sigh.

"Okay, deep breaths." I looked into the hall leading to the living room. "Pretend you were using the bathroom. Say, Hi, *Mr. Hott*—" Shit! What was his *fucking* name?

I clenched my jaw, balled my hands at my sides, and headed to the living room. He wasn't there either. He also

4

wasn't in the kitchen, dining room, or guest bath either.

Oh. My. God.

I ran to the window and pulled down the blinds. There he was. My *shoeless* one night stand, practically running down the pathway to the front gate. He still had no shirt on, his pants were unbuttoned, and Mrs. Sanders was there to see the whole thing. She stood frozen in shock, hose in hand, watering her gardenias as she did every morning, then slowly turned to face my window.

I flattened my back against the wall, knowing my reputation had been permanently tainted, and let my body sink to the floor. I pulled my glasses from my face and set them to the ground. *He was doing the walk of shame in front of the little old lady who called me baby, who baked cookies for my birthday—and gossiped to every neighbor in a one-mile radius...*

He was leaving without saying goodbye.

I shoved my fingers through my hair and closed my eyes. This was the first time I'd had sex in thirteen months, and I didn't even remember his name. A slow rumble began in the pit of my stomach then grew, until a mixture of laughter and tears escaped my parted mouth. I gripped my aching skull and began rubbing slow circles at my temples with my thumbs.

His hasty departure was probably for the best. I didn't have time for complications. Didn't have time for sex, dating, or men who walked out of my apartment without shoes.

Then why did it hurt so damned much?

I planted my palms firmly on the ground and forced myself to stand. Simply Tuesday's would open in three months. Three months! A relationship was the last thing I needed. I chewed my bottom lip and paced the floor. Becky thought I was jaded, but it wasn't true. I'd been building my Etsy business for three years, and my hard work was about to pay off. I didn't need a man around distracting me—but walking out without saying goodbye?

"Grrrr..." Part of me wanted to chase after him, stand in the middle of the street, and demand an answer. I was a beautiful, intelligent woman. A good catch. Sure, my hair was a little wild, style a little hippie, but it only added to my character. Certainly nothing to be embarrassed about... Though, maybe he'd seen me crawl into the closet. My eyes widened as I walked to the bathroom. Yeah. He must have seen me. He must've thought I was a total nut job!

Something crinkled under my foot and I bent down to pick up a condom wrapper. "Thank fucking Christ!" Even though I'd been too drunk to think clearly, at least I was of sound enough mind to use protection. I flicked on the shower, yanked my top over my head, and stepped under the spray, determined not to let one stupid mistake ruin my day. A man whose name I still couldn't remember.

* * *

Twenty minutes later, toothbrush in my mouth, and hair still damp from my shower, pounding sounded at the front door.

"Tuesday, open up, it's me!"

Becky.

I spit into the sink, rinsed my mouth under the faucet, and then pulled my tunic over my head.

"Hey," I said, yanking open the front door.

She hurried inside, not even waiting for me to move before she peered over my shoulder. "Is he still here? Were you guys in the shower?" Her black hair was piled on top of her head, and her light blue eyes were wild with worry.

"No." I laughed. "He's gone."

"Shit." She hit my shoulder. "Then why didn't you call me back? I was worried about you."

I bit my lip and gestured to my room with my thumb. "Sorry, my phone—" I pinched the bridge of my nose and moved to the kitchen. "It's still in the closet."

I pulled my blender out from the lower cabinet and waited for her to follow. "I've just never been *walk of shamed* before. It kinda threw me."

Her eyes narrowed as she hopped up on the counter and grabbed an orange from the basket. "What do you mean *walk of shamed?*"

"Well, when I came out of the closet he wasn't there, and—"

"Why were you in the closet, again?"

I lifted my shoulders. "I don't know. I was scared, I guess. He was naked, and you know that's not something I wake up to every morning. It freaked me out."

Becky sucked in a breath, ready to give me one of her infamous lectures, but I held my hand up to stop her. I lifted my chin to the front window. "After I couldn't find him in the apartment, I looked out the window. There he was, clear as day, walking out of the front gate half naked. He didn't even have his shoes on, Becks!"

Becky frowned. "I would've never expected that from Austin."

"Austin!" I hit my head, finally remembering. "Do you know him?"

"Just a little. I've seen him around the set a few times. I think he's a model for Frederick Beck."

Visions of Austin's perfect ass flashed through my mind, and I nodded. Made sense. "How could you let me go home with a guy like that? A model, Becky? Do I look like the type of girl who sleeps with models?"

"Listen, I tried to get you to leave with me, but you said you were having a good time. You *looked* like you were having a good time, and Austin said he'd call Uber when you were ready to go. Little did I know his plan was to join you." She smiled then and quirked one eyebrow. "So... was he any good?"

I shrugged. "That's the thing. I don't even *remember*. The first guy I've slept with in thirteen months, and I don't even know if I enjoyed it or not. How sad is that?"

Becky narrowed her eyes and leaned forward. "If you don't remember, then how do you know?"

"I know." I gave her a hard stare. "I found the condom wrapper." I yanked open the fridge, feeling frustrated all over again. "I feel like a slut."

She laughed. "How can you possibly be a slut? You haven't had sex in a year and a half—"

"Thirteen months," I corrected.

"Exactly," Becky uttered. "And who cares if you're a slut, anyway? There are lots of perfectly happy sluts in the world. It could be fun."

I laughed, grabbed a jar of chia seeds and added a couple of spoonfuls to the blender. "Like who?"

"Ummm... Joey Tribbiani. Total slut."

"Yeah, well he's a guy. Guys can be sluts and no one cares."

"Which is bullshit," Becky muttered around a bite of orange. "But okay..." She looked up the ceiling, chewing. "All the women on *Sex and the City*." She nodded. "Mrs. Roper. Blanche Devereaux," she added with wide eyes and an equally wide grin.

I narrowed my gaze. "Are you comparing me to one of the little old ladies from *The Golden Girls*?"

She nodded and bit her lip.

"Great. I'm like Joey Tribbiani and horny old ladies."

She shook her head. "The *Sex and the City* ladies aren't old."

"Yeah but they live in New York, it's different." I slammed a handful of kale into the blender.

"HA! We're in L.A. Nice try!"

I grinned at her, my mood lifting already. I could always count on Becky for that. To defuse the situation and make me realize life was way too short to take this seriously. I grabbed the bottle of Spirulina and twisted off the cap.

"Are you making some of the green crap again?" Becky asked, not waiting for an answer before yanking open a cabinet door. "Don't you have any bread? Chocolate? Anything?"

"It's a smoothie, and that's where my bowls go. You should know that by now."

Becky was my best friend—more like a sister, actually. I spent every summer, every spring break of my childhood with her, and since finally settling back in the town where we'd met, she was the one person in the world who would know stuff like this. "Don't you work today?" I asked, peeling a banana and adding it to the blender.

"Yeah, in an hour." She frowned and closed the door. "Nothing—I'll have to drive-thru somewhere."

I rolled my eyes, knowing nothing I said would sway her from the artery clogging food she adored. "What time are you off? I'm meeting the contractor later this afternoon. I don't want to go alone."

She jumped off the counter and grinned. "I'm off at three." She grabbed another orange before heading for the front door. "And I wouldn't miss it for the world."

CHAPTER TWO

tuesday

* * *

"Well, this is it," I said with bated breath.

It was just past four in the afternoon, still slightly chilly with the onset of fall, and I stood on tiptoes peering into the windows of the run-down building that would soon be my new store. The twelve-hundred-square-foot space didn't look like much, but it was my everything. My life savings, my reputation, my future—broken windows and all.

Becky pushed herself from the side of my truck and came to stand beside me. Just as she'd been doing every day since second grade, when she was the biggest girl in class, and I was the hippie girl destined to be made fun of.

"It's adorable, but why does it look like a bakery?"

"'Cause it was. A long time ago..."

I turned to the dirty windows and cleared a patch big enough to see through with the heel of my hand. The building had been a godsend, nestled in its own small parking lot like a little gingerbread house in the middle of a big city—but it was so worn down it was hard to see past all the mess. I closed my eyes, pressed my back into the warped wooden siding, and took in the sounds of rushing traffic as people made their way home from work.

"Do you think this is a mistake, Becky? I mean, it's all the space I'll ever need, but—"

She touched my arm interrupting me. "Tuesday—it's perfect."

I took a deep breath and exhaled slowly. I hadn't realized until that moment, but I desperately needed to hear those words. My own mother didn't approve. And even though I wanted this more fiercely than anything I'd ever wanted in my life, her fears always gave me pause. "Did I tell you it has a kitchen?"

Becky laughed and shook her head. "So you can make breakfast in the morning?"

"No." I peeked through the cracks in the boarded windows, choking back a ball of emotion I wasn't expecting. "I'll be able to make all my product here: Lotions, lip balms, all my soaps. I'll be able to increase production by at least fifty percent, maybe even host classes eventually."

I was shocked by all the emotions pouring out of me, but this shop was three years in the making, harboring a lifetime of childhood dreams, fears, and my future. It was my first step to finally feeling settled.

"I'll have my own office in the back room." I turned to face her. "No more storage unit, no more renting space from pervy Mr. Chavez. I would even have space for artists to sell their products. I'll have the room, and—"

But then I noticed Becky was crying. I dropped my bag and wrapped my arms around her shoulders. "What's wrong?"

"I'm just... I'm so happy for you." She wiped her eyes. "You've wanted this for so long."

Fighting back tears of my own, I stepped back a little. "Don't cry. You'll make *me* cry, and you'll ruin your mascara."

11

Just then, a red convertible pulled into the parking lot, and we both turned in unison.

"They're here." I wiped my eyes with the back of my hand and squared my shoulders.

It was hard to keep my voice from shaking. Hard to clear the tears from my eyes and hard to breathe. This wasn't just a little adventure for me—this was my everything. If this project failed...

I shook my head. I couldn't let myself think that way. Today was Tuesday. The day I was born, the day I was named after, my *lucky* day. Shoeless Austin flashed into my thoughts, but I quickly dismissed him. Even his walking out that morning was lucky. Had he not, I would have been forced into a conversation where I tried to pretend to remember his name. Yeah, it was lucky he walked out. Today was lucky. The perfect day to sign papers.

Becky squeezed my hand and leaned over to whisper in my ear. "Is that your contractor?"

I turned in the direction of the lot just as my real estate agent, Mark, gathered papers from the top of his car.

"No." I shook my head. "That's my real estate agent. Mark." I glanced over to the passenger seat, hoping I'd find Jake Johnson, but he wasn't there.

I furrowed my brow and picked my bag off the floor. Mark was a consultant for JM Construction, one of the nicest people I'd ever met, but he definitely wasn't Jake.

He waved his hand in the air as he made his way across the lot. "Mr. Johnson isn't able to make it today. I hope that's not a problem."

I hoisted my bag up to my shoulder and frowned. "Is everything okay?"

"Oh yes, yes. He had an OB appointment with his wife." His dimple retreated a little deeper into his cheek. "It's a boy, but don't say you heard it from me."

I laughed and nodded. "That'll be fine."

Mark punched a code into the lockbox and proceeded to open up the building. "We won't need him today anyway." He waved a hand to the inside of the building and stepped aside. "Would you do the honors, Miss Patil?"

I nodded, grabbed hold of Becky's arm, and pulled her in behind me. I'd found JM Construction after endless months of searching. Jake had one of the best reputations in the industry, but his lack of presence left an uneasy feeling in my gut. I stepped onto the cracked, uneven flooring and pulled in a calming breath. Deep down I knew we wouldn't need him today, that all the fear swirling in my head was ridiculous, but I couldn't stop my hands from shaking as I took in the dark, dusty room. Ten years of neglect laid itself at my feet, and I scrunched my nose at the sight of it.

Becky threw her arm around my shoulder and rested her head on top of mine. "It'll all be okay. It's nothing a little soap can't fix."

Mark followed in behind us, running his hand along the wall so damaged it would need to be torn down. "We'll need to get a HAZMAT crew in here before we start the demo. But it shouldn't take more than a week."

I nodded, even though anxiety threatened to steal my breath. He continued opening cabinets and doors, scribbling notes on a large yellow pad, then stopped and placed his briefcase on the dirt-covered counter. "Are you ready, Miss Patil?"

I looked to the old broken tables scattered about the whole shop, knowing it was too late to back out now. "Yes, of course."

We spent the next hour talking about plans. Even though Jake wasn't here in body, his plans were well laid out and precise. His crew would begin tearing everything down— tables, booths, the bar—and put up a solid wall, separating the product floor from the back room. This was the most pivotal part of my plan. It would cause some delay, but I needed the kitchen operational from the start. The two-phase construction was critical to staying on budget. I'd transfer supplies from Mr. Chavez's garage, replenish product in the back room, and when the product floor was complete, everything would switch.

"The crew can start as soon as we have the keys." Mark looked down at his notes and flipped a few pages before looking back at me. "There aren't any complications that I can see—no liens, we have a motivated seller, and a solid offer. We should have the keys in our hands in thirty days." He smiled and pushed the papers across the table before closing his briefcase. "All that's left to do is to sign."

My stomach fluttered as I pulled the papers toward me. I glanced over to Becky, who immediately nodded her approval as I opened the first page. "Do you have a pen?"

CHAPTER THREE

tuesday

ONE MONTH LATER

* * *

"Wait, where are you?" I balanced the phone on one shoulder, leaning back in my chair to open a bottle of Kombucha.

"Just outside of Crescent City—where I met your father."

It was our normal *Tuesday* conversation. The only regular thing in my mother's wild and transient life. I nodded, taking a swig of the pungent tea before turning back to my computer. "Who are you staying with?"

"A woman I met at the art fair. She has a herd of grass-fed goats with the richest, most beautiful milk I've ever tasted. I'll bring you a gallon next time I'm in LA, for your soaps. It would be outstanding."

"That'd be great," I replied, clicking a few buttons on the computer to print another label. "But what are you doing there?"

"Oh, you know me," she said in a singsong voice. "I've moved onto my next adventure... but I miss you, sweet pea. You should come join me."

15

"I miss you too, Mom. But you know I can't..."

Silence.

"Are you still going through with that brick and mortar?"

I leaned back in my chair and pushed my head into the soft upholstered seat. "I pick up the keys tonight." I gripped the bridge of my nose and laughed. "Most parents would be proud, you know."

"Honey," she said, her voice quiet but emotional, "I *am* proud, just... worried. We're travelers, Tuesday. We're cut from the same cloth. I'm worried you'll get wanderlust in a year or two, and you'll be stuck. Tied to a pile of concrete and brick. It'll break my heart."

I pulled in a deep breath and squeezed my fingers around the phone. It was amazing how much self-doubt my mother could instill with so few words. But she was wrong.

"Mom... that's *your way*. Not mine. I want to feel settled. I'm planting roots for the first time in my life, and it feels wonderful. I know you don't understand. It's not the life you'd choose, but it *is* for me. Please just be happy." *I need you to be happy.*

She sighed heavily. "You're acting like you hated your childhood, that you had no friends. Did you hate it, Tuesday? Were you really that unhappy?"

I gripped the bridge of my nose. "Mom... that's not what I'm trying to say. I loved my life. I wouldn't be the person I am without all the things we've done together, and you always made sure I had Becky. I'm just—I'm ready for more now. Don't you understand?"

There was a long pause before she spoke again. "You're right, honey... You're always right. Of course I'm happy for you."

I couldn't help it; my eyes misted over and a lump formed in the back of my throat. My mom and I didn't always see eye to eye, but she was important to me. She was my family. The only one.

Becky's voice called from the living room and I spun around. Well, except for Becky.

"Hey, Mom, Becks just got here. We're gonna go celebrate. Can I call you later?"

"Of course, go have a good time, dear."

I nodded, wiping a few tears with my finger. "Thanks Mom, I love you."

"I love you, too—and Tuesday?"

I nodded.

"I really am proud of you."

The phone went silent before I could answer, and I swallowed to clear the lump in my throat. My emotions were getting the better of me, and I didn't like it. I turned around in my chair, determined not to let myself cry again, and found Becky standing in the doorway watching me. She wore black high-waisted shorts and a crop top, nude heels that made her legs look a mile long, and black waves hanging to her waist. She reminded me of a superhero, and there was one thing for certain—we weren't just going out to dinner.

"Everything okay?" Becky asked, tilting her head to the side as she walked over to the closet.

"It's fine." I forced a smile. "Mom," I stated. As if "Mom" were some kind of magic answer that explained everything. But Becky actually understood.

Determined not to think about it anymore, I turned my attention to Becky and took a slow, deliberate sweep over her outfit. I raised my eyebrows. "Where are you taking me?"

She bit her lip then squeezed between stacks of boxes.

"We're going to dinner, like I said, then we're going to a pub. There's a bartender there I like."

"Mmmhmm..."

"Okay, there's also a band, pool tables, and organic beer. You'll fit right in." She grinned. "Besides, you've been working too hard, you need a break. I mean, look at this mess. Your apartment's exploding with boxes."

I took in the sight of my bedroom, now stacked waist high with product boxes I didn't have room for. "That's only because Mr. Chavez kicked me out of his garage when he heard about the store. This wasn't exactly my plan."

"I know." Becky frowned. "He's such an ass. I still think we should egg his car."

I pushed to stand. "Nah. It'll work out. I'm saving money, which is good. Plus, after the HAZMAT crew is done with the building, all of this will be gone. And guess who's helping me move it all to my new shop?"

"Umm, Popeye?"

"Nope."

"Donald Trump?"

I took another swig of Kombucha. "Try again."

Becky's shoulders sagged. "It's me, isn't it?"

"Bingo."

* * *

A few hours later, parked in the back of Donovan's Irish pub, I pulled down the visor to check my reflection in the mirror. I was tired... too tired to be out this late on a Tuesday, but the face that looked back at me didn't look half bad. I slammed the visor up to the ceiling, jiggled it to make sure it was securely closed, and then climbed out of my truck.

I spotted Becky a few rows over and made my way through the lot.

"I'm still not sure why we couldn't drive together," she called across to me.

"Because," I stated, "you're going to hook up with your bartender, and I have to meet the HAZMAT crew in the morning."

She made a face that said she didn't like my answer, then stopped at my side and looped her arm over my shoulder. "I'm not hooking up with Colin. Not yet anyway. We're still in the foreplay stage."

"Oh yeah,"—I made air quotes in the sky—"the *infamous* foreplay stage." I looked around the lot to the group of college girls streaming into the building in front of us.

"Why didn't you tell me to dress better?" I glanced down at my faded, oversized overalls to prove my point. "These girls make me look like a sixty-year-old homeless person."

Becky laughed and scanned me from head to toe. "First of all, I did, and second, you look *fine*. Better than fine." She tucked the strand of feathers behind my ear and winked. "Like a bohemian hippy goddess."

I raised one eyebrow and wrinkled my nose.

"Okay, a nerdy, bohemian hippy goddess. She grinned. "But I'd do ya."

I laughed and started walking again. "I had enough *doing* last month. In fact, I've decided I'm going back to my ten-date rule. Coffee then lunch, then—"

"Then a G-rated movie, I know... Just because you had a bad night doesn't mean that's going to happen again."

My jaw fell open. "G-rated? I'm not that bad!"

She laughed and kept on walking. "Okay, PG-13."

I pushed my glasses to my forehead with my thumb. "Have you seen him at all? Austin I mean?"

She shook her head and glanced at me out of the corner of her eye. "Let's forget about him. Anyone who walks out on *you* isn't worth the time of day. We'll find you someone better. Someone who knows how to put on his own shoes."

I laughed then pulled the door open and let her enter the pub before me. But when I stepped inside, I immediately regretted letting Becky decide the location tonight. A man was literally standing on the bar. Literally.

He held a bottle of whiskey in one hand, tequila in the other, and at least a dozen women lined the seats in front of him like fangirls at a concert. He smiled down at them, a smile that was guaranteed to break hearts, and walked down the line, filling the glasses of women who couldn't be much over twenty-one.

"I think I know why the parking lot is so full," I whispered.

All the women were desperate for his attention, which made me look a little closer. He was good looking, sure, but it wasn't anything I hadn't seen before. Short, brown hair, almost buzzed, tall, nice build—nothing that warranted women lusting at his feet.

"I hope that's not Colin," I stated.

Becky took my hand and pulled me toward the corner. "No, I don't know who that is, but he sure is popular." She raised one brow then led me to a table at the back of the room.

I hopped up on a stool and glared across at her. "*Organic beer*, she said. *You'll fit right in*, she said."

Becky cringed. "I'm sorry, the atmosphere normally isn't like this. It must be the Toasted Tuesday thing. Dollar shots."

"Must be." I opened the menu, determined to make the best of the night, and scanned their impressive list of organics. "I'm only having one beer, then I really need to get to bed."

Becky sagged a little and frowned. "Come on, you haven't been out since the launch party. Just stay until Colin gets off work. I promise you won't turn into a pumpkin."

I gathered my hair in a ponytail then pulled it over one shoulder. "Okay." I knew I'd been too much of a hermit lately, and Becky didn't ask for much. "But as soon as he's off, I'm going to bed."

Becky clapped. "Yay. I love you."

I smiled then peered over her shoulder as a dark-haired man approached our table. "Is that Colin?"

Becky spun in her seat and smiled. "Hey, handsome!" She looped her arm around his waist then turned to face me again. "Colin, this is my friend Tuesday. Tuesday, this is Colin."

He wiped his fingers on a red towel then held his hand out to shake. "It's nice to meet you."

I nodded, but a commotion at the bar drew my attention. The man who was standing on it earlier now had an even larger crowd as he poured drinks from behind it. Three rows deep, mostly women, all standing around as if they were about to win the lottery.

I thought he might be telling some kind of story, because all the women burst into waves of giggles and squeals. I couldn't help but grin a little myself. He was as animated as a child at Christmas. He kept running his hand over his head, in that boyish sort of way, and his smile was so joyful you'd think he had a pair of toads in his pockets. But as youthful and playful as his expression, his body sent a completely different message. This man was fully-grown: broad shoulders, corded arms, very tall... Suddenly, I could see what all the fuss was about.

"Can I get you ladies a drink?" Colin asked, startling me back to the table.

21

Becky narrowed her gaze at me and grinned. "Give her the healthiest, most disgusting thing on the menu, and I'll have another of those blue things you made me last week."

I rolled my eyes and looked at the menu. "I'll take a pint of your organic stout. And don't listen to Becky. She's just trying to kill herself with food dyes and GMOs."

Becky lifted her shoulders. "Eh, I'll die happy."

Colin nodded, ignoring our banter as he gathered empties at a nearby table. "Organic Stout and a Blue-eyed Blond. You got it." He flashed Becky a look that said he preferred brunettes, gathered his full tray of bottles, and headed for the back room.

"I thought you were in the foreplay stage," I said, as he turned the corner.

"We are," Becky replied, shifting her gaze away.

"Uh huh. Is that why you're waiting for him until—wait, what time is he off?"

"Midnight." She cringed. "But I promise you don't have to stay a minute later than that."

"Famous last words." I laughed. "Wait, don't you have work tomorrow?"

She shrugged, "I'm on hiatus."

"Nice to be you," I replied, pulling a tube of lip balm from my bag and smearing it over my mouth. Becky was a makeup artist for the studios, an excellent one who was highly requested, but her work in production meant she had lots of breaks of employment. This break couldn't have come at a more perfect time.

"So,"—I sat forward in my seat—"the cleaning crew starts tomorrow, construction starts Monday, and I'd really like everything organized before—"

22

But more squeals made me glance back over to the bar. I immediately saw the reason for all the excitement. The man at the bar had pulled off his shirt. But he wasn't just a man; he was the man with that damned smile.

I couldn't pull my eyes away. His chest was broad, his abs defined, and his whole body tapered to a V that led my eyes to a perfect sprinkling of hair at his waistline. He turned his back to the crowd, showing a tattoo that ran from shoulder to shoulder. A large cherry branch with hundreds of delicate flowers. It was both out of place and perfect at the same time.

"And?" Becky asked, following my line of vision. But as quickly as he'd taken it off, his shirt was back in place. "What's wrong with you? Why are you blushing?"

I sat up straighter, pressing the backs of my fingers to my heated cheek. "Am I?"

Her gaze narrowed. "You never finished your thought."

I licked my lips, searching for the last thing I'd been talking about, but then his eyes met mine and I froze. I hadn't even realized I'd been staring. His lips curved into a slight smile, and he lifted his chin. I couldn't look away. His eyes were so dark they were almost black, and his smile... It made me want to throw my ten-date rule out the window. I pulled my eyes back to Becky. "Saturday! I thought we'd rent a truck." I blew out a breath, trying to recover my fluster. "Move everything over to the shop?"

"You and me?" Becky asked.

I nodded.

She leaned forward and examined me with a knowing expression. "You have the hots for that bartender, don't you?"

"What? You're crazy." But my voice pitched a little higher than usual. I looked over my shoulder, sure Colin should be back with our drinks but found nothing.

"Of course I'll help you." She grinned. "Like I have a choice anyway."

I hopped off my chair and looped my bag over my chest. "I owe you big time." I gave her a kiss on the cheek and gestured to the front of the bar. "Now, where's the bathroom?"

She grinned wickedly "Down the hall."

* * *

There was a line a mile long when I got to the hall, and at least a half dozen fan club members stood in it. I took my spot at the very end and pulled my phone out of my pocket. *Dead.* My stomach did a nervous flutter as I stuffed it back inside. I knew there must be twenty orders waiting for me in email, and I was stuck here for at least another hour. Sometimes I hated having friends. I shook my head and pulled in a deep breath. *You'll catch up tomorrow; everything will be fine.*

The line moved again, and I couldn't help but listen in on the conversation in front of me. It was one of the brunettes I'd seen at the bar earlier, and she wasn't trying to be quiet.

"...he said his name was Donovan. Do you think he owns the place?"

Another shrugged. "Who knows? All I care about is him giving me a *ride* home tonight. If you know what I mean."

They both giggled, and I turned my back to the conversation. I'd come to the bathroom to clear my head, and their conversation wasn't helping matters. But the man known as Donovan seemed to be haunting me. My eyes locked on his back as he poured drinks behind the bar. He wasn't even my type. I liked nerdy guys, ones who liked poetry and books. Not the type who had a different woman in his bed every night, which judging from the size of his fan group, he likely had. I wanted stability, commitment, someone to settle down with, but damn was he hard not to look at.

24

He seemed to be growing more and more attractive the longer I stared. But it wasn't just his looks. It was the way he moved. As if he didn't have a care in the world. As if he was just happy to be alive. He reminded me of my mother in a way. The type who never settled down, who enjoyed life a little too much, the type of living I was trying to break away from. Yet, I found myself unable to turn away.

As if he sensed me watching him, he turned around and our eyes locked again. This was the second time, and my cheeks instantly flushed with embarrassment. Warmth crept up my stomach, over my neck, and I knew, knew with everything that was holy, that I was bright red again. But sometimes there was no denying your downfalls, and this was one of them. I grinned slightly, lifted my shoulders, and held up my hands in a *you caught me* motion. "What can you do?" I whispered to myself.

He seemed amused by my admission, and threw his head back with laughter. It was the sexiest thing I'd ever seen. His nose wrinkled up, making him look even more boyish than before, and he bit his bottom lip. The way he looked at me made me breathless. I whipped back in the other direction, thankful the line had moved enough for me to squeeze into the bathroom. I pulled in a gulp of air and slouched against the wall.

What the hell was wrong with me? Maybe Becky was right, and I'd been working too hard. But as much as I tried to convince myself that was the cause, I knew the truth. I was attracted to him in a way I hadn't felt in ages. Since I was the teenaged girl who fell in love with the boys who never noticed me. It scared me a little. The last thing I needed was a replay of my childhood. Or to wake up with another naked man in my bed.

After doing my business, I washed my hands and splashed cold water on my face. I'd only been gone fifteen minutes, but I was certain Becky would come looking for me. I needed to go back out there, to hang out with the best friend I'd been neglecting for weeks, but the thought of running into Donovan again made me blush all over. My reaction was silly really; he was only a man, and I'd only been caught staring, but his smile had infected my brain. *Way* more than *wine* ever could.

When I finally stepped out of the bathroom, the hall was filled with a hoard of people. I tried to squeeze through the crowd, thankful for the camouflage so Donovan wouldn't see me, but everyone was headed the other way, which made it impossible to move. I opened the door to the bathroom again, deciding to wait out it out for a couple more minutes, but someone grabbed my arm and began pulling me in the opposite direction.

"Hey baby, come with us, we have a keg back at the house."

His breath smelled heavily of alcohol, and his eyes were glassy and bloodshot. More alcohol definitely wasn't what this guy needed.

I smiled anyway, remembering my youth all too well, and shook my head. "Thanks, but no thanks." I pulled away, intending to head back to my table, but another man blocked my exit.

"You think you're too good for us, doll?" He stepped closer, eyeing me up and down in a way that made my heart thud.

"I didn't say that."

He bit his lip, his chest millimeters from mine. "You didn't have to." He grabbed the strand of feathers in my hair, wrapping it twice around his finger, and pulled. "Are you some kind of Indian?"

His foul breath washed over my face and I pushed away.

"How 'bout you *pow* my wow tonight."

I stepped backward, looking over my shoulder for an exit, but a deep voice pulled my attention back to the bar.

"Are these guys bothering you?"

Donovan was making his way toward us, his jaw clenched, and his eyes holding none of the lighthearted humor I'd seen at the bar earlier. He looked like a different person...

I nodded.

The man standing in front of me retreated at the sight of him, smashing my sandaled foot with his heavy boot in the process. I doubled over, looked down to the floor to catch my breath, and pressed myself against the wall.

When I glanced up again, the guys were all gone, and the only person left was Donovan. Squatting at my feet, staring up at me with eyes that were dark as coal.

He touched my ankle, causing sparks of awareness to shoot through my body.

"You okay?" he asked, his voice deep and kind.

I swallowed, for some reason terrified. He was bigger than I'd expected—much bigger.

I knew he wasn't angry with me; it was the boys he'd chased away a minute ago, but my heart still hammered inside my chest.

"Are you hurt?" he asked again.

I couldn't make myself answer. I only stood there, my mouth slightly agape, and said nothing.

Without saying another word, he stood and lifted me off my feet. "Let's get you some ice."

I shook my head, finally recovering my voice as he walked with me down the hall. "It's okay. I'm fine."

But he didn't seem to take any notice and continued walking. When he sat me on the bar a minute later, I was blushing again. The gaggle of women sitting there all turned to stare at me. They looked me up and down, and I couldn't help but feel self-conscious.

"I'm okay—really." I wiggled my toes to prove the point, but it was too late. He already had a red towel filled with ice, coming toward my foot.

When the cold cloth touched my skin, I hissed at the sensation. "Thanks for coming to my rescue, but I think I was more surprised than anything."

He nodded but still didn't move. He didn't say anything at all, just looked at me in a way that was both hard and soft at the same time.

He rested a hip against the bar and finally spoke. "Sorry about that. Dollar shots always bring a different kind of crowd."

I chewed my lip, trying to focus on his words instead of the fingers that made tiny movements over my skin.

"What's your name?" he asked when I remained silent. His eyes were intense and so much deeper brown than I originally thought. Like a hot cup of steaming coffee, with only the barest amount of cream inside.

"Tuesday."

He smiled, but it was in that way that said he didn't believe me. I got that reaction a lot. It wasn't like it was a normal name, and it became especially unbelieving when it was said on a *Tuesday*. I opened my mouth to give him my normal spiel, that I was raised by a hippie mother who was convinced everything good in her life happened on a Tuesday. But then the gaggle of women behind the bar began to squawk. "Donovan, come back."

He looked over his shoulder and nodded, then removed the ice from my foot and tossed it into the sink. But he didn't move away. He ran his fingers gently over my toes— feather soft—and I held my breath again.

"Sorry." He cringed, grabbing for the towel again.

I touched his arm, just barely with my fingertips. "It's okay." Our eyes locked, and I could swear he branded my soul. He'd seemed so carefree when I'd first seen him, flirtatious, full of bold confidence, but the eyes that looked back at me now were weighted with pain, shielding a thousand secrets. I couldn't even think with him so close.

He looked away in that moment, as if he felt something too, but then the girls behind us screamed again, and he glanced over his shoulder. "Sorry, I need to get back."

"Of course." I took a breath, eased off the bar, and plastered a smile on my face. It was stupid to be jealous; we'd only met a moment ago, but the feeling that twisted in my gut couldn't have been anything else.

He grinned again, one I felt in my stomach, and I took a step away from the bar.

"Thanks again for your help," I said, walking backward toward our table. "You better get back to your fan club." Then I spun around, hurrying toward the safety of my best friend, and the pint of beer I needed more desperately than anything.

CHAPTER FOUR

tuesday

* * *

When I arrived back at the table a moment later, I didn't hesitate before grabbing my pint and downing half the glass. Becky was talking with Colin and turned in her seat to look at me with an odd expression. "Thirsty?"

I only nodded.

She had a right to be confused. It wasn't like me to drink this quickly. Sure, I'd gotten drunk at the launch party, but that was odd too. I took a few calming breaths and told myself not to look back at the bar.

"Can I get you ladies anything?" Colin stood reluctantly from my seat and began gathering more empties.

I nodded, my nose still buried deep in my glass as I pointed for another. I desperately wanted to look back at the bar, to see if Donovan was watching me, but I didn't dare. A dozen women probably surrounded him by now. *Girls*, I corrected. I wouldn't be surprised if half of them carried fake IDs.

Colin continued to linger at our table, but I was thankful for that. The longer he distracted Becky, the longer I had to pull myself together. She knew me better than anyone.

My deepest thoughts, my hopes and dreams, every secret wish I'd had since I was eight. She was the only one who knew how much I wanted to find my father—

Wait. Where had that come from?

My brows furrowed, and I found the feathers in my hair. He'd been on my mind a lot lately. Maybe because of the changes with the store, or maybe because I no longer traveled to art fairs where I'd forever hoped to find him. That's where he and Mom met. She was only eighteen and he something similar, and through all her stories, she had never once uttered a bad word about him. Never even a twinge of remorse when she told me about the morning she'd woken up and he was gone.

"He was a nomad, he didn't settle."

Just like her. I sighed. I was told over and over that he loved me, but I knew it wasn't true. He'd left before I took my first breath. My mom was eighteen, seven months pregnant, and he left her to raise their baby on her own. What kind of man did that? What kind of *person* did that? What could have been so important that he abandoned us in the middle of the night?

"Hello." Becky waved her hands in front of my face. "Earth to Tuesday."

I gave her an apologetic look and met her eyes. "Sorry."

"What's gotten into you lately?" Colin had finally gone, and Becky was leaning forward, her arms braced on the table. "What's up with you tonight?"

I shrugged. "I was just thinking about my dad."

Her frown deepened and she leaned closer. "Did you ask your mom about him? Is that why you looked so shaken this afternoon?"

"No... but she's in Crescent City again. Isn't that weird? I can't seem to shake him from my thoughts, and she's back in the place where they met."

"That *is* kinda weird."

"I know." I pushed a drop of water around the table with my finger. "But I told you, I already know everything. His name was Forrest, he was the love of her life, and they traveled together for about a year. She never even knew his last name..."

john

* * *

I watched as Colin brought Tuesday another drink, keeping my hands busy as I dried yet another glass. Shit, I wanted to switch places with him. Have Colin do the babysitting so I could go ruffle Tuesday's feathers again— or whatever the hell her name was.

She looked so innocent and wild at the same time. Gorgeous, though a little bit awkward. Her hair was big, almost overwhelming her small frame, a mass of sun-bleached waves. And her skin was flawless, golden brown, beautiful. But her eyes. They were a shade somewhere between hazel and green, trapped behind the black-rimmed glasses that drove me crazy.

I grabbed another glass from the sink and shoved the cloth inside. She gave a whole new twist to the librarian thing, and I found myself wanting to check out a book. Only I knew that was a bad idea. She was the type who would want a relationship, and I was the type who avoided them.

A few college girls lingered at the bar behind me, leaning halfway over the edge to get my attention.

"Donovan," a blond one cooed. "Why aren't you paying attention to us?"

I flashed them a charming smile and leaned against the bar. "What can I get you ladies? Coffee? Tea? A cab?" It was almost midnight and I was done. Ready to have a few beers of my own, ready to hand over the reins to Fred and make my way to Tuesday.

She pushed her boobs against the bar and giggled. "Are you trying to get rid of us, Donovan?"

I laughed at the use of my uncle's name. My fifty-year-old uncle who hadn't been here all night, but of course I played along. "Now Cindy, why would I want to do a thing like that?"

She giggled and snorted. "My name's Susan, but you can call me whatever you want."

I turned around and blew out a breath. These girls were too much—easy or just wasted. Either way, I didn't want any part of it.

My cell began to ring at the register, and I swiped open the call. "Hello?"

"There you are! Where have you been?"

I smiled at the sound of my sister's voice and pressed my back into the counter. "Hey Lisa, isn't it past your bed time?"

"Ha ha. Have you been avoiding my calls?"

I laughed. "No, I've been working. Uncle Don had a few employees call in sick, and I said I'd cover. What's up?"

She pulled in a deep breath, and I heard some of the tension leave her body.

"Good." She cleared her throat. "Now, I need you to be honest with me about something."

I furrowed my brow and grimaced, already anticipating where this conversation would lead. "Of course."

"Did you ever call my friend Jennifer back?"

And there it was. I scratched the back of my head and

began filling another pitcher. "Well... Like I said, Uncle Don—"

"You didn't!" She raised her voice, cutting me off.

"You're right." I shrugged. "I didn't."

"John, she's nice! You deserve nice."

"I'm sure she is, Lis, but I'm not really into nice."

She laughed. "What do you want then? Some witch to tell you what to do?"

I grinned and slid the pitcher across the bar to a customer. "Nah, I already have three of those."

"Oh my God! I'm telling Penny and Margaret you said that."

I laughed.

"Seriously, John. What are you waiting for? What will it take to get you to settle down?"

I glanced across the bar to Tuesday. "I like librarians."

"TMI... Okay, you can stop right there. I'm sorry I asked."

I chuckled, wiped my hands on a rag, and spotted Colin walking through the double doors to the back room. "Go to bed, sis. Your kids are going to be up in a few hours, and you're going to be grumpy."

"I'm never grumpy."

"Bye, Lis." I threw my cloth in the sink, gave the girls a quick nod to say I'd be right back, and hopped over the bar.

"Hey! Colin." I pushed open the doors before they stopped swinging. "How's my favorite co-worker in the world?"

Colin laughed but didn't turn around. "What's up?" He set a tray of empties in the sink then proceeded to fill a couple of pitchers with stout.

"Who are the girls you've been talking to in the corner?"

He grinned. "You'll have to be more specific. There are so many."

I rolled my eyes. "The one sitting with Xena. The one with the glasses. What's her name?"

He grinned at my Xena reference then shrugged his shoulders. "I don't know, man. Tuesday, I think?"

So she *was* telling the truth. Okay. "Is she single?"

"I have no clue. Look, I gotta get back out there. You'll have to grow some balls and figure that one out on your own."

I grinned. "No problem, cover for me at the bar."

Colin laughed. "Nice try."

He pushed through the door to the bar, where he could see one of the girls lying halfway over the counter, helping herself to the bottle of tequila.

"The natives are growing restless," Colin muttered.

I blew out a breath and jogged back to the bar. "Ladies, ladies..."

CHAPTER FIVE

tuesday

* * *

My second beer lasted to the end of the night. Past Becky's endless flirtation with Colin, past all the wayward glances my eyes took to Donovan, and all the way to midnight, when I was finally free to go home.

Colin came toward us—his nametag removed but a wide grin and swagger in its place. *Time to go home.* I took a sip of water, grabbed my bag from the back of my chair, and hopped from my seat. "Well you guys have fun. My fairy godmother is calling my name."

Becky frowned, somehow making her look more beautiful than always, and grabbed my arm. "Did you have any fun at all?"

"Of course I did." I looked down at her. "I was with you, wasn't I?" I scrunched my nose, letting her know I wasn't upset in the slightest, then looked toward the hall. "I'm just going to stop by the ladies' room before I leave. I'm serious, you have fun."

Becky smiled, but I could tell she wasn't buying it. "Let us walk you out?"

I glanced over to Colin, seeing he was definitely ready to

go, and shook my head. "Nah, I'll be fine." I leaned over to whisper in her ear. "Enjoy your foreplay, and call me in the morning."

"Whatever." She laughed.

Hitching my bag over my shoulder, I headed to the hall before she could stop me. I was determined not to look over to the bar again. I was being ridiculous. I wouldn't go out with Donovan if he asked me, yet for some reason, I couldn't stop staring. The last I'd seen, only a few girls remained at the bar, and soon I knew it would dwindle to one. *The one. The fan girl who would win the Donovan prize.* For some reason, I didn't want to know. Didn't want to know if it was the one with the freckles, the redhead, or the blonde with a killer rack. I wanted to go home, crawl between my organic cotton sheets, and fall asleep.

I was so tired. Maybe more exhausted than I'd ever been in my life. There were too many orders to process, too many phone calls to make, and too many papers to sign. After I let the crew in the next morning, I'd head back home, turn my phone on silent, and hibernate until winter.

When I entered the nearest stall, the door to the hallway banged open, and I turned around. A couple of drunken women stumbled into the bathroom, both giggling and unstable. I nodded, recognizing the redhead from the bar, and closed the stall door behind me. I hung my purse on the back hook, pulled down my panties to my knees, and then heard someone mention Donovan's name. I froze. I couldn't help it—I was more interested than I cared to admit and leaned my ear against the door. My heart squeezed in my chest, and my panties still held up by my knees.

"Do you have any condoms? I'm going home with him tonight."

My eyes instinctively closed.

"Shit, Susan, are you serious?"

"YES! I like him. Don't you?"

"Well yes. Everyone does... Are you sure?

"Yes!"

Both girls laughed again, and I sat down on the toilet. All the air left my lungs, and I looked down to my feet. I didn't know why it affected me so much, but it did. I almost felt like crying. The door to the hall eventually opened, and the sound of music filtered in then out again, indicating I was once again alone. I stood slowly, pulling my underwear back into place, but my stomach sank to the floor.

I guess Susan won.

I opened the door, for some reason feeling defeated, and went to wash my hands. It was stupid to be upset. I wouldn't have time for a relationship for another year, he obviously had more women than he could handle, and besides... He wasn't my type. I rubbed my hands together, not bothering to dry, and pushed the bathroom door open with my back.

"Ooof!" I hit a wall. A wall that wore a black t-shirt and smelled like sunshine and hops.

My eyes moved upward. Over a chest that was solid and muscular, to a chin shadowed with the barest amount of stubble, all the way to Donovan's intoxicating eyes that smiled at me. Literally.

"We have to stop meeting like this."

It was the most cliché thing for him to say, something I would have rolled my eyes at normally, but I found myself grinning. I couldn't help myself. He wore a smile that was a mixture of little boy and pure devil at the same time. It was charming to say the least. But I quickly sobered— Donovan was going home with Susan tonight.

I pushed past him without saying a word and headed for the parking lot. I needed to put distance between us—

needed to put myself to bed before this man made me do things I'd regret.

His hand on my arm stopped me. My breath hitched in my throat, and I looked up again. The same concern he'd shown over my toe at the bar was back in his eyes. "Did I say something wrong?"

I knew I was being a silly. He could sleep with whomever he wanted, and I had no right to be upset. "I'm sorry, I've just been under a lot of stress lately." My heart fluttered, and I forced myself to look into his eyes. Eyes that hadn't left my face for a second.

His brows furrowed and he adjusted his stance. "Want to talk about it? I can buy you a beer. Organic stout, right?" His mouth tilted slightly at the corner, and I swallowed.

It was so tempting. *He* was so tempting. He was gorgeous, I was single, and there was no real reason to say no— except I couldn't bear the thought of waking up next to another man I didn't know. I'd been beating myself up about Austin all month, and I knew if had a drink with Donovan it would lead to more. I shook my head, knowing I couldn't handle that again. "Nah, I really gotta go." I turned back to the hall, to the door that would lead me to the parking lot—far, far away from the man I wanted so desperately to touch me again. This time he didn't try to stop me.

When I made it to the parking lot, I pulled in a much-needed breath and spotted my truck right away. "Crap!"

I jogged through the lot, yanked my door open, and twisted the key in the ignition. I sagged against the vinyl seat and prayed. *Please start, please start.* But nothing happened. I looked up to the slightly open visor and slammed it shut. This was the second time this month.

"Damn it!" I slammed my fist into the steering wheel and closed my eyes. *If you didn't shut the thing exactly right...*

I looked around the lot for Becky, but of course, she'd left with Colin. Just as I'd told her to do.

Why was this happening to me? Why now? Tuesday was supposed to be my lucky day, but lately I'd felt cursed by it. Dead phone. Dead battery. What next?

I made my way back through the parking lot, knowing all I needed was a quick jump. That's how it always was with my old Chevy. I'd had her since I was sixteen, and even though she could be a bit finicky at times, she hadn't failed me yet. Sure, I had to deal with a dead battery now and then, but I usually carried jumper cables for that problem. Until I lent them to Mrs. Sanders... and she saw Austin walk out of my apartment without shoes. I was too embarrassed to ask for them back.

I yanked open the glass door and entered the pub, my cheeks heated, though this time more out of frustration than embarrassment, to find Donovan was no longer there. This made me both relieved and disappointed at the same time. I wasn't sure what to make of that reaction. I'd been able to walk away a moment ago, but a part of me worried I wouldn't be strong enough to do it a second time. Regardless, a tall man with red hair had replaced him, and my eyes locked on a nametag that read "Fred." I leaned against the bar, waiting for him to notice me, but the group of women in the corner seemed to be monopolizing all his attention.

I cleared my throat, not even trying to hide my annoyance. "Excuse me, but my truck won't start. Do you have any jumper cables?"

Fred turned around, wiping his hands on a red rag, and grinned. "What was that?"

"My truck. I left the light on. Do you have any jumper cables?" I shouted.

"No, sorry." But then he called over my head. "Hey *Don*, do you have any jumper cables?"

I cringed before turning around. Of course. Of course, it would be Donovan who would come to my rescue. I found him down the hall, coming out of the double doors that read Employees Only. I'd seen him only minutes before, so wasn't quite sure how it was possible, but he looked even better now. His hair was a little messier—as if he'd raked his hands through it a few times, and his shirt was untucked and disheveled. He smiled at me, like he'd won a schoolyard bet, and that's when I realized. He'd probably come back from having his way with Susan.

He leaned his hip against the bar, looking relaxed and confident. "If you changed your mind about the drink, you could've just said so."

My eyes bulged. *The nerve!* I squared my shoulders and decided to ignore him. If I didn't have something nice to say... "I left my lights on. Do you have any jumper cables?"

He bit his lip, and goddammit, I wanted to bite it too. "No, I can't say that I do."

Fred made a noise between a cough and a laugh, and I turned around to face him. *Does he think something is funny?*

"But there's a phone in the office you can use," Donovan added. "I was just heading up there myself."

I glanced back to him, over to Fred, then to the phone by the register, and my heart did a little twisty thing. "Wha— what's wrong with that one?" My head was reeling with panic. He just invited me upstairs. Did I want to go upstairs? Well, my body did. My body was screaming to go upstairs. My body was screaming for a lot of things. My conscience, on the other hand...

He smirked a little, one that lifted his brow at the corner. "What? Is there a problem?"

I didn't know what to say. Yes, there was a problem. The problem was, I didn't quite trust myself or trust him. But the way he looked at me—with a challenge in his eye and a grin that made my stomach do lots of fluttery things—I couldn't resist. "Lead the way."

41

He cocked one eyebrow and shook his head, which made my heart squeeze again but in a different way. Did he not *want* me to go upstairs? He'd asked me. If that's not what he wanted, why did he ask? Then he leaned over the bar, not saying another word, and removed the drawer from the register.

He mouthed something to Fred I didn't understand then gestured down the hall with his chin. "I'll be right behind you."

john

* * *

Fred raised his eyebrows and grinned at me. I hadn't expected her to say yes—not that I was complaining. Spending more time with Tuesday sure beat the hell out of working on the dishwasher again, but she didn't seem the type. She intrigued me. In a way, that hadn't happened in a long time. She was flustered by my flirtation, yet she didn't back down. I liked that—more than I cared to admit.

When we got to the double doors, I held them open, stepping aside to let her enter the kitchen first. The room was empty, clean for the night except for the tools I'd left on the ground earlier. She slipped past me, her wild hair brushing my arm as she clutched the bag that was almost as big as she was.

"Right this way," I said, leading her to a doorway on the left.

She paused when she saw the staircase and glanced over her shoulder. For a second I thought she might change her mind, come to her senses, and realize she was a tiny girl, and I was the man who'd had librarian fantasies about her all night. But she didn't. She lifted her chin, adjusted her bag, and started climbing.

I frowned. I didn't know why, but I didn't like this one bit.

All of a sudden, I wanted to lecture her about strangers. She looked like a strong woman, but I had no doubt I could snap her like a twig. My brows furrowed, and I remembered the guys who'd cornered her in the hall earlier. I followed behind her, my eyes locked on the slight sway of her hips noticeable even from under her baggy overalls, and I shook my head. When we made it to the top of the loft, my jaw ached from clenching so hard. *Of course I have jumper cables. What self-respecting man doesn't have jumper cables?*

I walked past her, set my drawer on the desk, and gestured to the phone. "Do you always follow strange men you just met?" I couldn't quite explain my anger. This was exactly what I wanted, but now I was pissed she wasn't making wiser choices. Why I felt so protective over a woman I just met was beyond me, but there was something primal about how I felt about her. Maybe my response stemmed from finding her cornered by those assholes, or the fact I grew up with three sisters, or maybe it was because she reminded me of Bambi—a deer caught in headlights, who couldn't get out of her own way.

I turned around and met her heated stare. Okay, so maybe she wasn't as much of a Bambi after all. Her stance was wide, her cheeks red, and her eyes were as bright as a brush fire. "Do you always try to bed two women in one night?"

What the hell?

My brows drew together and I grinned. "*Bed* two women?" It shouldn't have been so amusing, but this wasn't the reaction I'd expected. "What are you talking about?"

She hoisted her bag high on her shoulder and half laughed, half scoffed. "It doesn't matter." She picked up the phone and began dialing.

I cringed and gripped the back of my neck. I wanted to laugh at how ridiculous this was, but at the same time, I knew without a doubt that would be the wrong thing to do. I opened the lock bock and tried to focus on my job, but her words bothered me and I couldn't keep quiet. "Is that what you thought? That I was bringing you up here to sleep with you?"

She shrugged then turned to face me. She was beautiful. Maybe even a little hotter when angry.

"Does that mean you wan—" But my question was interrupted by her doubling over with laughter.

Fair enough.

"Are you kidding me? I wouldn't sleep with you now if you were the last man on earth." She pushed her glasses up the bridge of her nose and scowled at me. It was the cutest thing I'd ever seen in my life. Her wild hair, and her big glasses, and that body—

She turned away, speaking into the phone to the tow truck company, and I wanted to cut the fucking cord. I couldn't help my silly grin. Like hell, she didn't want to sleep with me. I'd been angry only a minute ago, but now I was having more fun than I'd had all night. The chemistry between us was about to set the loft on fire.

I turned toward my drawer and busied myself counting the evening till. But her voice distracted me, slightly husky, mixed with a bit of sexy, and a whole lot of sweet. I had to start over three times before I got the count right.

At one point, she asked for the address of the bar. I handed her a card and continued working. But when she set the phone back on its cradle, I couldn't help but mess with her again.

I pushed myself from my chair and braced my legs apart. That got her attention. She turned to face me. Her head held high and shoulders square.

"I think you're a liar, Tuesday."

"What makes you say that?"

"Because if I were the last man on earth, you'd sleep with

me."

She laughed but didn't move. She only stood there. Her eyes focused on mine, her face both innocent and knowing at the same time. "You're wrong."

"In fact, I think you want to sleep with me right now."

Her face pinked and her breath hitched. "What makes you say that?"

I stepped forward. "You're still here, aren't you?"

"What?" Her expression changed in an instant, almost as if she'd woken from a dream. She pushed her glasses up the bridge of her nose and blinked. "Oh my God, what's wrong with me?" she whispered.

She turned around, muttering something under her breath, and rushed toward the stairs.

"I was kidding!"

But she didn't listen. She clasped the banister with both hands and proceeded to run down the steps as though someone was chasing her.

I squeezed my eyes shut and gripped the back of my skull. "Way to go Eaton, you really fucked it up this time."

CHAPTER SIX

tuesday

* * *

I ran down the stairs so fast I almost twisted my ankle, pushed through the back exit, and stumbled two steps into the parking lot before doubling over and gasping in lungs full of frigid air.

"God, I'm SO *stupid!*"

I should have used the phone at the bar like a normal person. The one that was *right there*. Like any self-respecting woman would have done. Instead, I let him wield his seductive ways around my body and pull me in a direction I knew was all wrong. And to make matters worse, he was an ass about it. I buried my hands in my hair, feeling mortified.

Part of me wanted to go back in there and give him a piece of my mind, but I didn't dare. I was afraid he'd be proven right. Afraid that even though his words made me want to punch him in the throat, I wouldn't be able to resist him. The chemistry between us scared the crap out of me. I'd never felt anything like it before. His effect on me was like breathing... Urgent and compulsive, like breathing a lung full of air after suffocating—only it was as scary as doing it for the first time.

The back door opened behind me and I held my breath. I knew it was him before even turning around.

"So there's something you should know about me, Tuesday. Sometimes my jokes aren't funny."

I whipped around. My hands clenched at my sides, every nerve in my body on fire. "You're a jerk!" I shouted, but as soon as the words left my mouth, I'd wished I'd come up with something better. Something that would make Becky proud.

He stood only a few feet away, a grin on his face, and jumper cables slung over his shoulder. "So I've heard."

I backed up a step, shaking my head in disbelief. "You had cables the whole time?"

"Maybe." He shrugged.

I wanted to scream. Both because he infuriated me and because I still couldn't think of a better name to call him. He began walking toward me, and I backed up in the opposite direction. I couldn't help but notice he wasn't smiling any longer. In fact, he looked almost angry now. I clenched my jaw, determined not to lose my shit.

"I'm guessing that one's yours?" he asked.

I looked over to my truck, the doors open and vulnerable... Exactly how I felt in this moment. I wrapped my arms around my belly, wanting to shield some part of my open, exposed, naive self, and I nodded.

I hated the fact that I'd trusted him. Hated that even now I still did. But most of all, I hated the fact that he was right. I was stupid to follow a man I'd just met.

He hopped into a large black truck in the corner then pulled it over to park beside mine. His was new, shiny, and black as his heart, and mine old, rusted, blue, and broken. He rolled down the window and lifted his chin. "Pop your hood."

I hugged myself around the waist and shook my head. "I don't want you jumping me."

He grinned, but it didn't quite meet his eyes. "Not even if I were the last man on earth, I know." He hopped from the cab and stepped toward me. "I canceled your tow truck. Pop your hood."

Heat flooded my face, and I wanted to scream. Never in my life had I wanted to slap someone before, but I wanted to slap the shit out of his smug face. Who canceled someone's tow truck?

"You're a self-righteous asshole," I said to him. I wanted to say more. To tell him to go to hell, to write his mother and tell her to teach her son some manners, to kiss him so hard he felt an ounce of the unbridled desire that coursed through my veins. *Shit!* I flung open the door, climbed into the front seat, and popped the hood. What choice did I have? I couldn't stay here all night with a man who made me hot in every humanly way possible. Not if I wanted to like myself in the morning.

"Look, I can see you're pissed, but I wasn't about to leave a beautiful woman in the damned parking lot alone." He propped the hood then placed a small flashlight between his straight white teeth.

I focused on my breathing, trying to calm the sudden surge in my heart rate. He said I was beautiful. It was probably a throwaway line, used on a thousand women, but tell that to my skipping heart. He had no idea how much he affected me. How close I was to jumping out of my truck and pushing him up against the hood to have my way with him. What the hell was wrong with me?

Calm down, Tuesday. Deep breaths, slow and even, in and out.

The light was dim under the hood, but I could just make out his features as he worked. His jaw was tight—strong— with a scattering of whiskers that shadowed his cheeks. I thought about getting out of the cab to help him—at least hold the flashlight, but then I noticed a scar under his bottom lip. It was about a half inch long, nestled almost perfectly in the crease above his chin. For some reason, it made me curious. It was stupid to care about how he got it, but for some reason, I did. My head fell back to my seat and I closed my eyes. I needed to keep my distance. Maybe it was the stress of the store, but I wasn't my normal self these days. Sure, I was calm enough on the surface, but inside, my legs were kicking like crazy to keep my head afloat. A list of to-dos a mile long waited for me at home. So much to do, and no time for another dead battery or men who looked like *that.*

When I opened my eyes a moment later, I almost frowned. He looked sad in the dim light of night. So much different than he had inside. His brows were creased, his eyes focused, but no smile graced his lips anymore. I couldn't help but watch him. His movements were almost elegant. So natural, as though he'd spent a lifetime just like this. Trapped under a hood. Engine grease on his hands and a flashlight in his mouth.

All of a sudden, he looked up. Our eyes locked, and he took the flashlight from his lips. He said nothing, just walked over to his truck, started his engine, and then came to open my door and lean in over my lap. He nodded for me to turn the key then revved the engine a couple times with his palm. My heart leapt to my throat. What the hell? I was afraid to move. Afraid not to move. Afraid that if I did, I'd pull him closer instead of pushing him away as I knew I should.

We stayed like that a second longer. His engine poured life into mine the way his touch did to my body. I thought for a moment that he felt it too, because he hadn't moved. His soft t-shirt was warm against my bare arm, causing goose bumps to cover my skin. I was a bundle of nerves waiting in anticipation of what would come next. Wanting something to happen, but fearing it at the same time. Then he moved away, causing a chill to run then length of my body where his warmth had been only a second before. He walked to the front of my truck and disconnected the cables.

He shut the hood, and his eyes met mine one last time before he turned away. "Have a good evening, Tuesday."

That's when I realized. To him, I was just another girl in the fan club. Another number.

I nodded, somehow managing to swallow my pride as I watched him unhook his battery, but I said nothing. I shoved the truck into drive, adjusted my seat belt across my lap, and pulled out of the lot, not once glancing in the rearview mirror as I drove away...

CHAPTER SEVEN

tuesday

* * *

"So he had cables the whole time? What an ass..."

It was the next morning when I told Becky about Donovan. We sat criss-cross on the floor of my apartment, packing backlogged orders from my Etsy store, and my blood still boiled over a man I'd spent less than a couple of hours with. He'd gone from rescuing me in the hall, to being the man I needed rescuing from, yet I couldn't stop thinking about him. He'd gotten under my skin—more than I cared to admit—and I didn't like it.

I shoved a bottle of lotion into an open box and grabbed another invoice. Hundreds of orders waited for me on my desk, but all I could think of was *him*.

I needed my system back. Needed my organized shelves, my organized products, and my organized life. But that wouldn't happen for a while.

"Wow. He's really gotten to you, hasn't he?" Becky stared at me, the pile of products between us as she scrunched her brows in examination. "I've never seen you like this before."

I threw another package into the growing pile and shook my head. "Like what?"

"I don't know." She leaned back to analyze me. "Like you want to hurt someone." She grinned.

"Nah, I don't want to hurt anyone." Not really, anyway... What I wanted was for Donovan to get out of my head! I didn't want to think about him anymore: his adorable smile, eyes that haunted my dreams, or how good it felt being held it his arms. It was all too confusing...

"How are things with you and what's-his-name?"

"Colin?" She shrugged. "He's good for now. Not someone I see going anywhere with." She stretched her long legs out in front of her and proceeded to lie back on the floor and close her eyes.

I laughed. Just like always, her guy didn't stick. It was always like that with Becky. If guys were too nice, she thought them a pushover. If they were too agreeable, she got bored. If they were an ass, she didn't give them the time of day. I wasn't sure what she was looking for, but in the twenty years I'd known her, she hadn't come close to finding it. Kind of like me... though my list was never as long as Becky's. I just wanted a man to stay. To hold me tight and never let go, which was proving to be more difficult than I ever imagined.

Donovan's infectious smile popped into my mind. He was exactly the type of man I didn't want; yet, he'd consumed my thoughts all night. Even though he'd pissed me off, I felt more alive with him than I had in years. He'd done a whole lot more than jump my car that night. He turned something on in me I hadn't been able to turn off all week. Which was the reason I could *never* go back to that bar again. I grabbed a trio of soap and shoved it into the envelope before starting on another order.

"Calm down, Tuesday. It's not worth it." Even with her eyes closed, Becky could sense my irritation. She propped herself on her elbows and looked up through sleepy eyes. "Stop worrying about things you have no control over. He's just another asshole at a bar, him and a million others."

"I know... It's just bad timing with the store and all. Plus, I'm tired of always meeting jerks. I want to meet a nice guy for once." I grabbed another invoice and read it two times before actually seeing it. "Maybe we're looking in the wrong places. Maybe we should start golfing or something."

Becky rolled to her stomach and laughed. "Yeah, no thanks.

"I'm serious, Becky! I'm almost thirty."

She raised her brows and pushed herself up from the floor. "First of all, who cares?" She spoke in a calming voice. "Second of all, you turned twenty-nine two months ago, so chill. What does being thirty have anything to do with meeting a nice guy, anyway?"

"Because I want kids! The risks are higher the older I get, and I'm freaking out! What if I never find him?"

"Who? Prince Charming?" She rose to her feet and stretched. "Day," she said with a sigh. "You can't plan every detail of your life. Your guy will find you when he's supposed to. And if he doesn't, you go buy yourself a sperm Popsicle."

I scrunched my nose but smiled at the same time. "You're gross, Becky."

She grinned and walked to the kitchen. "And you love me."

john

* * *

I sat on the edge of my bed, tired from the long night at Donovan's, and scratched Ginger behind the ears. She looked up at me with sad, caramel eyes and whimpered.

"I know girl, I'm getting up, just give me a minute."

It was nearly seven in the morning, an hour past my

normal wake up time, but I still couldn't move. This week at the pub had worn me out, and five hours of sleep wasn't enough time to recover. I pressed my thumb and forefinger to my eyes and tried to convince my lids to open.

Why on earth Jake wanted to put in a garden when there was perfectly good produce at the store was beyond me, but I'd made a promise long ago, and I was determined to keep it. Even if it meant getting up at seven in the morning on a Saturday. I threw the covers to the edge of the bed and rose to my feet. Ginger pranced to the other side of the room, and I knew it would only be a second before she was back with her leash.

We had a thing, Ginger and me. She forgave me all my flaws, and I took her for a run every night after work. Except for this week. This week I went straight to the pub. To eighteen hour days, and women who were more interested in taking selfies than participating in an intelligent conversation. This week had taken its toll on both of us.

I grabbed my running shorts from the foot of my bed, pulled them on, and then stumbled down the hallway to look for my shoes. The living room was a freaking mess. A week's worth of not caring left discarded clothes scattered across the hardwood floor, and I didn't even give a shit. I plopped down to the edge of the couch and found my shoes under the coffee table.

My phone vibrated beside me and I cringed. *Who the hell was calling at this hour?* I leaned over to get a better look and rolled my eyes.

Lisa. My youngest sister, and the one the other two always sent to do their dirty work. I sent the call to voicemail and bent over to pull on my shoes, but the phone immediately buzzed again.

Ginger plopped her leash down at my feet, and I shook my head. "Just like every other woman in my life, you're trying to rush me." I stood up and swiped open the call.

"Hello"

"Thank God, John! Where have you been?"

I yawned and stretched a little. "What do you mean, where have I been? It's the butt crack of dawn on a Saturday. I was sleeping." I walked to the kitchen, pulled a jug of OJ from the top shelf, and chugged a good mouthful. "What has your panties in a bunch?"

She was quiet a moment, which wasn't like her, and I walked toward the sink and set the jug on the counter. "Lisa?"

"You haven't heard..."

My chest constricted at the tone of her voice, and I shook my head. "Heard what?"

She hesitated. "John—Jake's wife is in the ER. He just called, trying to find you."

I pushed myself from the counter, unable to speak. I saw Jake and Katie less than twelve hours ago. "Wha—what happened?"

"I don't know," she whispered. "I think it's something to do with the baby."

I gripped the phone so hard I heard a crack. "Shit!"

"You-you should go, John. Jake sounded really upset."

I turned to the window and looked out without seeing. "Where are they?"

"Holy Cross."

* * *

It was only ten minutes later when I pushed through the door to the waiting room of Holy Cross Memorial Hospital, but it felt like a thousand. It was early, eerily quiet, but the stench of antiseptic and tragedy left me tense with claustrophobia.

I found Em right away in the corner of the room. Her short hair plastered to her face like she'd just rolled out of bed, her body absent of the fashion she normally prided herself on, replaced with sweats and a t-shirt I knew she'd fallen asleep in.

"What happened? Where's Jake?"

She shook her head and looked over her shoulders to the closed double doors. "I don't know. Jake called this morning in near hysterics and told me Katie was bleeding. That's all I know."

I turned to face the door, needing the limited privacy as I took in the news. I raked my hand through my hair, trying to make some sense of it all. *I saw them only hours ago and everything was fine.* "Do you think she's losing the baby?"

"I don't know," she whispered.

My head began to pound at the thought of it. Jake and Katie didn't deserve this. They were newly married, just finding themselves after a lifetime of hurt, and there was only so much loss one could take. This would break them. Both of them.

Em touched my shoulder, and I forced myself to turn and face her. She was close to losing it—I could see that the moment I walked through the door. I clenched my jaw and pulled her into my chest. She was normally so strong, unaffected by life's mishaps, but this obviously shook her. I hadn't seen her like this in twenty-four years. Since we were kids. "She'll be fine, Em. Everything is going to be fine." Though I wasn't sure I believed it.

* * *

A half hour later, I pushed myself from the red vinyl seat and forced myself to the vending machine. I wasn't hungry, not in the slightest, but I couldn't stand to look at Em's face any longer. It was one of defeat, sadness, and loss. I could practically see her building stone walls around herself, brick by brick. An armor of protection that didn't offer any protection at all.

I punched in my order for a cup of coffee and glanced over my shoulder. "Want anything?"

She only shook her head, not meeting my eyes as she continued to stare at the double doors.

We both startled some time later when Jake pushed the doors open. He walked toward us, his eyes dark and sunken, his clothes disheveled in a way that said he'd been wearing them all night.

"How is she?" I asked, even though the question made my stomach roll with fear.

Jake inhaled slowly then looked over his shoulder. "She's resting." He nodded, as though the action convinced him *resting* was all she needed. "The baby's fine. The doctor said we'll get to go home in a few hours."

Em let out an audible sigh, and Jake turned around to face us again.

"What happened?" Em asked.

Jake raked his hands through his hair and shook his head. "Her placenta's too low." He sat down on a nearby seat and pushed his head back to the wall. "She's on bedrest. She was working too hard... Dammit! I knew I should I have said something!" He hit the arms of his chair, causing the security guard to look over from his post in the corner.

Em and I glanced at each other before she sat down beside him. "Placenta previa?" she asked, taking Jake's hand and squeezing it between her two.

He nodded but kept his head pushed back to the wall. "Yeah, I think so.".

"She'll be fine," Em whispered. "Katie's strong, your baby's strong, and everything will be okay."

Jake nodded, but remained quiet as we all sat there, truly breathing for the first time in hours, composing his nerves and working things out. He sat up a moment later and turned to look at me. His stance was determined, as though he'd finally decided something that has been eating at him for way too long.

He furrowed his brow and nodded his head. "I need your help."

I braced my legs apart and shoved my hands in my pockets. "Anything."

And I meant it.

CHAPTER EIGHT

tuesday

* * *

Adrenalin pumped through my veins as the sounds of construction filled my ears. I took a few cleansing breaths, twisted off the ignition, and inhaled the day I'd waited for three long years. Even from thirty feet away, I could see the transformation of the shop already taking place. Large trucks were already parked throughout the lot, men on lifts were tearing down sheets of warped, rotted siding, and my dreams were starting to take form. I closed my eyes, closed them super tight and focused on my vision. I could just make it out, the shop that reminded me of a little gingerbread house when I first saw it, a place that would be my home away from home, my future. I looped my arm through the wooden handle of my toolbox and grabbed my smoothie and box of donuts from the center console.

Work awaited me in the back room, and I was anxious to get started. I'd done my best at running my business out of boxes, but it was time to get caught up. I jogged across the lot, pushed through the plastic tarp that covered the front entrance, and somehow managed to set the donuts on a small table in the corner of the room without dropping anything. The men were already busy at work, but I called out to the only man who paid me any attention and lifted my chin. "For you." I waved in the direction of the donuts. "Come eat while they're still warm."

He smiled, and I knew what I offered was total bribery, but I was okay with that. My dream was finally coming true. If I had to tempt men with sweet pastries to make that dream come faster, I was going to do it.

I continued on to the back room, pushed my way through a plastic tarp that was the temporary divider, and stopped. I knew they'd be there, but for some reason, they looked more daunting this morning. Stacks and stacks of product boxes lined the floor like soldiers ready to attack me. My stomach twisted into uncomfortable knots. *It didn't seem like this much a few days ago.*

Becky and I had moved everything earlier in the week. We'd planned to get organized, but it ended up being a bigger job than we'd both anticipated. The shop as a whole had turned into more than I anticipated, but I was in waist deep and didn't have a paddle with me.

I looked around the room, overwhelmed by how much stuff there was to do. It seemed insignificant when spread out over a thousand places, but with it all condensed in one spot, I could finally see how much of a mess my life had become. My transient past finally contained in one place. Just looking at the haphazard room made me want to go to sleep. Forget about the whole thing and go back to my apartment. But I wasn't a quitter—like hell, I would start now.

A tall box rested in the far corner of the room, and I knew that was where I needed to begin. I plopped my toolbox on the counter, took a long sip of smoothie, and pulled the instructions from the front envelope. But just as I started to read, voices down the hall pulled my attention. *Jake.*

I grabbed my smoothie, set the instructions on the top of the box, and rounded the corner.

Just as I'd anticipated, Jake and one of his crew were

already engrossed in work. I rested a hip against the doorframe and watched them. They were both bent over, tool belts at their hips, and blueprints spread across the wide surface of my desk. It was like a scene from a romance movie. They were both tall, well built and strong..

I cleared my throat, needing to get their attention before my imagination did naughty things with them.

Both men turned in unison, Jake Johnson, his eyes bright blue but tired, and *Donovan*!

I held my breath.

"Ms. Patil," Jake said. "We were just talking about you. I'd like you to meet my new project manager, John."

Cold smoothie splattered at my feet as I locked eyes with the man who'd haunted my dreams all week. The man Jake had referred to as John. *My project manager?*

Jake handed me a rag to clean up the mess, but I couldn't even move, let alone form a proper thought..

"There are some paper towels in the other room. I'll be right back."

Jake ducked out of the room, and I knew green smoothie covered my feet, but all I could do was blink. This was a dream. I was sure of it. Pretty soon, John would kiss me as he'd done in my dreams all week, and I'd wake up. But he wasn't kissing me, and I wasn't waking up. We stared at each other in silence as I twisted the rag in my hands, finally finding my voice. "What are you doing here?" I forcefully whispered.

He stepped toward me, took another rag from his belt, and dropped down to squat at my feet. "It seems I'm your new project manager." He grinned.

I stepped backward and violently shook my head. "Like hell you are."

He only shrugged and stood up again.

"I thought your name was Donovan?"

"It's not."

"I thought you owned the bar?"

"Wrong there, too."

"Are you even a bartender?"

He sat on the desk, somehow looking as natural in a tool belt as he did standing on a bar. "Well, that part is true. I'm a man of many talents, Ms. Patil." He raised one brow, and my mouth dropped open.

Jake walked back into the office, completely oblivious to the whole situation, and dropped down to clean up the mess. I squatted next to him, a thousand questions lingering on my tongue, but I only asked the one that was most urgent. "I thought *you* were the project manager?"

Jake frowned and tossed the soiled towels into the trash. "Don't worry, Ms. Patil. John is my best man. I can guarantee you're in good hands."

John cleared his throat, and I knew without a doubt his grin had widened. I wanted to scream, to grab hold of his tool belt, and drag him to the exit where he belonged. "I'm sorry, but I hired *you*. I want you!" I said to Jake.

Jake gripped the back of his neck and looked to the floor. "There's been a family emergency." He widened his stance and looked me in the eye. "Don't worry, I'll be overlooking the project every step of the way, but John will be the lead on this job."

I looked from him to John, who was still smiling, and shook my head. "I'm sorry. I'm sorry you're going through a hard time, but this won't work."

Jake furrowed his brows. "I'm sorry, but what won't work?"

I glanced between the two men, one smiling, the other not,

and I didn't know what to say. I was already behind on work, stressed out beyond belief, and *needed* construction to start. Today! I felt the room around me spin, all my plans sink to a pit of sand at my feet, and there was nothing I could do about it. Not one little thing.

It was too much to take all at once. I turned around and walked out of the room. "I have to think."

I continued down the hall, around my abandoned shelving boxes, and didn't stop until I pushed through the back door leading to the alley. I squatted down, pressed my back against the wall, and buried my hands in my hair.

What was I going to do? I couldn't work with him, work with a man who smiled like that—looked like that—who I'd seen naked in my dreams! But I couldn't afford *not* to work with him either. I pulled my phone out of my pocket and began typing a message to Becky.

Me: The ASSHOLE is my project manager.

I sent the message and began counting backward in my head in an attempt to stay calm.

Becky: What asshole?

I swallowed.

Me: Jumper cable guy.

Becky: OMG! Are you kidding?

My phone rang with an incoming call and I answered it.

"What do you mean, he's your project manager? I thought it was Mr. Tall Dark and Married?"

"So did I." My butt fell to the pavement and I stretched my legs out in front of me. "What am I going to do?"

"What do you mean? Is there anything you *can* do?"

I shrugged. "Hire someone else?" I wanted to cry, to kick

my arms and legs and have a big old fit in the middle of the alley.

"How long would *that* take you?" Becky asked.

I whimpered. It had taken months to find Jake, to track down his references and make sure he was the man I wanted for the job. And he was. My breathing quickened.

"Okay," Becky said in a calming voice. "The first thing you need to do is *stay calm.*"

I blew out a breath and nodded. She was right. Panicking now would only lead to more trouble. "I'm trying..."

* * *

Jake turned to me and raised one brow. "Do you know anything about this?"

I crossed my arms, adjusted my feet, and leaned my back into the desk. "I may have an idea."

Jake braced his legs apart and stroked his chin between thumb and forefinger. "Did you sleep with her?"

"No." I shook my head.

"Are you sure?"

"Look." I grinned, cleared my throat, and pushed myself to stand. "It was a misunderstanding."

"A misunderstanding?"

I nodded and scratched the back of my head. "I'll go smooth things over. Don't even worry about it." I held up my hand, telling him to give me five minutes, and headed for the doorway. The truth was I'd been as shocked as she was. Never in my wildest dreams had I expected to see her again. Never in my wildest dreams had she looked so pissed, either. I laughed, even though the situation I found myself in wasn't the least bit funny.

The guys were all busy at work when I pushed through the tarp to the product floor. "Eddie!" I shouted. "Hey, Eddie!"

He turned around and lifted his chin.

"Did Ms. Patil come through here?"

He placed his sledgehammer on the counter before facing me. "You mean that cute thing with the hair? She went back there ten minutes ago. Carrying a little pink toolbox with her."

I frowned. "She didn't come back here just now?"

He shook his head. "No, not that I noticed." His grin widened. "She left us donuts, though."

I nodded, glancing down to the flakes of sugar that covered the front of his shirt. "Thanks, man."

I pushed my way to the back room, wondering where the hell she'd gone, and spotted her little pink toolbox on the counter. I scratched my head and opened the box. A little saw, hammer, a few screwdrivers, and a bottle of lotion. *What the hell she was thinking?* She'd hired a whole construction crew to work for her, yet she'd brought her own toolbox with her to work. I wasn't sure if that made me like her more or think she was completely crazy.

I finally found her in the back alley a minute later. She was sitting on the dirty pavement, her legs splayed out in front of her, her hand gripping her phone so tight her knuckles were white.

Without saying a word, I adjusted my tool belt and sat beside her. Judging by the way her back stiffened, she wasn't happy about it.

She straightened up, pulled one knee to her chest, and spoke into the phone. "Becks, I gotta go." She cleared her throat then threw her phone into the same oversized bag I remembered.

She remained silent, just tapped her foot repeatedly until I eventually had enough.

"So... I guess you're still pissed about the other night."

"Yeah." She laughed. "I guess I am."

I turned to face her.. "Come on, it wasn't that ba—" But her stare alone stopped me mid-sentence. I gripped the bridge of my nose and closed my eyes.

"You treated me like I was a child."

Our eyes locked, and I shook my head. "Well,"—my brows furrowed as I looked into her vivid green eyes—"you shouldn't follow strangers. And you shouldn't hang out in dirty alleys, either." I dusted off my legs and pushed myself to stand. "Didn't your father ever teach you anything?"

She rose to her feet and stepped toward me, our bodies only half a foot apart. "Didn't your *mother* teach you manners?"

I shrugged, my eyes narrowed as my blood instantly heated. I didn't know why she affected me so quickly. I was always the calm one in my family, but something about this woman sent me over the edge.

She turned away again and pressed her back against the wall.

I almost laughed. I'd come out here to apologize, but for some reason, she pushed all the wrong buttons. Jake's wife Katie was on bed rest from almost losing their baby, Jake was more stressed than I'd ever seen him, and here I sat with a woman who was throwing a fit over something that happened in a bar.

"So what's the solution, Tuesday?" I gripped my skull and began rubbing. "Am I fired or what?"

Her head fell back against the bricks and she blew out a breath. "I don't know. I don't think I have a choice."

"You always have a choice." I met her eyes and held my ground. "The way I see it, you have two of them. We can go back inside, and I can work my ass off for the next three months. You do your thing, and I'll do mine. Or I get my crew, and we walk out that door right now."

Her chest was heaving as she stood in front of me, but she didn't look away. She looked up and down my body as if she was making her mind up about something. "I thought maybe I'd been overreacting. But I was right, you're an asshole."

I chuckled. "I never said you had to like me, Tuesday."

"Well I don't." She lifted her chin but didn't look away.

I nodded. "You can let me go, hope to find someone on short notice—one who won't do half the job I will—or we can walk inside and forget this conversation ever happened. Just so you know, I prefer the latter."

She looked toward the door, her shoulders rising and falling with each breath. She picked her bag up off the ground and threw it over her shoulder. "Fine." She opened the door. "But if you piss me off *one time*, you're out of here."

She slammed the door closed behind her, causing the whole doorframe to shake with the impact. I gripped the back of my neck and let my shoulders fall. I'd grown up with three older sisters, all of whom required a lot of patience, but Tuesday may have just outdone them all. I pushed my back against the wall and inhaled through my nose. I needed a minute to compose myself before going inside—and if my instincts were right, so did she.

CHAPTER NINE

tuesday

* * *

"Insert post A into slot X. That's what it says." Becky sat on the counter, reading the shelving instructions for the fourth time and chewing a piece of gum so loudly it made me cringe. She'd come to the shop early that morning to help me unpack, which we'd done all afternoon, but for the last two hours, we'd been stuck trying to put this stupid shelving unit together.

"But I don't see a slot X." I looked down to the row of pieces alphabetized on the floor. "Where's slot X? Are you sure that's what it says?"

She shook her head and laughed. "Yes, I'm sure. You read it if you don't believe me." She thrust the papers toward me and hopped from the counter.

"No, I believe you." I scratched the top of my head. "It must be missing."

"Maybe." She gathered her bag off the counter before turning around. "I still don't understand why you don't have one of *them* helping you."

She was referring to John and his crew, which I had to admit would have been much more convenient, but they weren't my employees. Not really.

"Because I need them out *there*"—I lifted my chin to the product floor—"so I can open this shop and hope to make my money back. I don't want any delays. Not even the couple of hours it would take to put this thing together." I inhaled, letting my shoulders rise up then fall again with a huge sense of defeat.

I leaned against the counter and glanced to the product floor. I hadn't stepped foot out there a second more than necessary. Not a second longer than it took for me to drop off the donuts I hoped would fuel their motivation and then head to the back door. I told myself it was because I didn't want to get in their way, but the truth was I couldn't stand the thought of asking John for anything. His smug grin would push me over the edge.

She raised her brow. "Well, good luck then." She kissed me on the cheek and gave me a little side hug. "I gotta go. I have a bride consult in an hour."

I tilted my head. "I thought you gave up weddings?"

She shrugged and backed toward the plastic sheet that now served as a door. "Friend of a friend."

I laughed and watched as she squeezed herself through the plastic divider. My plan for the evening was to unpack all my chemicals so I could start replenishing product, but then *this* happened. The shelving catastrophe I didn't have time for. Yet another delay, another day where inventory went out but didn't come in. I was determined not to let the whole evening go to waste.

I made my way to my office, sat at my desk, and stretched my legs in front of me. It had been forty-eight hours since my altercation with John, and we'd done exactly what he'd said. Kept our distance. He did his thing, and I did mine, which was exactly how I wanted it.

I'd only seen him a handful of times. When I left each night, and when I arrived each morning. On occasion, I'd catch a glimpse of him through the plastic divider.

Covered in filth, dirt, and sawdust... and an expression that looked so sad it made my heart hurt. I'd only just met him, but it looked all wrong. He was the *happy to be alive* guy at the bar, and I couldn't help but feel a bit responsible for the change.

I shook my head, telling myself I was being dramatic for no good reason, which I was doing a lot lately. The stress of the store was getting to me. I was emotional, cranky, and PMSing like nobody's business. I opened my office drawer and pulled out a stack of product boxes, determined to do the only thing that didn't make me panic. Work. The desk was cleared, drawers organized, and everything was in its proper place. Including the light blue sofa I'd picked up on a whim with the shelving unit— the only reason that furniture store was still in my good graces today.

My body begged for a nap. To curl up on the soft, corduroy upholstery and forget about everything. But it was amazing how quickly I'd gotten behind. I had two large orders to ship, one being from my number one client Mrs. Tuso, and I tried to focus on the positive.

I hit the button on my oil diffuser, causing a billow of lavender mist to wash across my face. I inhaled, taking in the earthy, floral scent that would normally ease my worries. But not today. Today it would take more than a few drops of oil to cure the knots embedded a mile deep inside each of my shoulders. I needed to get some work done. More than a little. I flipped open my computer and pulled up this week's invoices. I pressed print, and the low ink button began to blink immediately.

"Perfect." I pushed myself off the desk, pulled a new ink cartridge out of the drawer, and threw the top of my printer open.

Of course the printer was out of ink. Of course! Nothing had gone smoothly since I'd purchased this damned shop. Nothing.

After finally printing the invoices, I headed to the back

room with my pile of shipping supplies. Becky and I had organized the best we could under my current circumstances, but that only consisted of boxes stacked shoulder high against the far wall.

I placed the invoice next to the sink, propped my fulfillment box open on the floor, and began searching for Mrs. Tuso's order.

Three boxes of Lemonade Girl body scrub. Check.

Two cases of Pour Some Sugar lotion. Check.

This was larger than her typical order, one she'd be using in swag bags for clients. I was thrilled when she sent in the order, even though it couldn't have come at a more inconvenient time.

I read the next item on the list, searched the labels, and added more lotions to the order.

"Okay... one case Cream In My Coffee lip balm." My finger ran down the line, and I stopped at the pink cursive marks encircled by my best friend. I opened the case, immediately scrunched my brows together, and checked the box again. It was supposed to be lip balm, but the case was filled with body butter. I took the oval tubs out of the box, placed them one by one on the floor until it was empty.

I closed my eyes and forced in a breath. "Don't panic. You made it—I remember it like it was yesterday..." I spotted another box across the room and rushed over to pull it open. Maybe I put them in the wrong box? I pulled the cardboard flaps wide, opening it all the way so I could see inside, but they weren't there either.

My heart began to pound and I ripped open another box, not even bothering to check labels this time.

Your Body's A Wonderland bath bars, Slow Like Honey massage lotion—nothing that I needed. I'd had the order for three months, promised it wasn't too much for me to handle, but her favorite scent, the one that made my store famous, was missing.

How could I let myself lose something so important? Not only would I lose potential clients—clients I needed desperately with my new expenses—but I'd also be letting down one of my favorite people. The woman who almost single-handedly spread the word about my shop.

By the time I got to the fifteenth box open, packing peanuts littered the floor, and empty boxes were discarded at my feet. I couldn't even imagine confessing to Mrs. Tuso that I'd let her down. That I'd let myself down. That I was in over my head with this whole fucking shop.

With each discarded box, the claws of desperation around my throat tightened, but I didn't slow down. I was determined to find them. I needed to find them.

I'd once witnessed a woman at a bus stop, kicking and screaming, her hair wild and disheveled, her eyes sunken and feral. I'd wondered how someone could get to that point—to lose all self-control, to be so desperate they didn't care about the repercussions of their actions. But standing there, surrounded by discarded products, cardboard, and paper, I didn't care about anything but finding those damned lip balms.

I opened another box, dumped the contents on the floor, and moved to another. When I got to what must have been my twentieth box, I found them, nestled in a mislabeled box, safe and sound.

Four cases of Cream In My Coffee lip balm.

I sank to the floor, my nose burning with unshed tears, and I let myself go. Huge tears began to stream down my cheeks, and I didn't try and stop them. I let myself cry, hard, sloppy, and wet. Tears of frustration, desperation, uncertainty, and *fear*. I was so damned scared. Afraid of losing everything I'd been trying to create my whole life. My stability...

* * *

I glanced from my phone to the back room, growing more impatient with each second. It was already seven thirty, an hour and a half past our normal cut off time, but here Eddie and I waited.

Tuesday hadn't come out all night, and I couldn't hide the fact that I was pissed. Her friend had left hours ago, yet Tuesday continued to pound away in the back room, doing God knows what.

I flipped open my laptop and began writing an update for Jake. My family was expecting me a half hour ago. Part of me didn't mind the delay. I knew Lisa was itching to hound me about her friend again, but when I spoke to my mom this afternoon, she'd sounded *strange*. Even when I'd stayed on the phone five minutes longer than usual, she didn't say what was wrong. For that reason alone, I was anxious to get going.

I looked down to my cell and shook my head. "Okay, we're done." I ripped my tool belt from my body and threw it in a pile on the counter. As much as I hated leaving her alone, I couldn't stick around all night. Especially a woman who hadn't said a word to me in two days.

"Start packing up, Eddie, you win. I'll go tell Ms. Patil we're leaving." *And give her one last opportunity to go with us.* But when I pushed through the plastic to the back room, I stopped.

She was crying. Not loud—but not quiet either. The sounds caused my heart to clench. A reaction fostered from being raised with three sisters, no doubt. I couldn't stand the sound of it. Not any tears, but especially not from her. Tuesday's cry was different. Lonely, desperate—hollow.

The back room was a mess. Open boxes and packing peanuts littered the floor, and she sat in the middle of all of it, her head down, a lap filled with a handful of small brown boxes, and her shoulders shaking so hard I could almost feel the vibration from fifteen feet away. I retreated back through the plastic.

Shit!

She didn't like me. She'd stated as much, and proven it over and over by not speaking to me for the last twenty-four hours. I knew the last thing she'd want was my awkward consolation... but I couldn't leave her alone. I squeezed my eyes shut, trying to figure out what to do then turned around.

"Sorry Eddie, but there's something I'm going to need you to do."

His brows pinched together and he muttered under his breath. "Ahh fuck..."

"Ms. Patil has had a rough night," I began. "I need you to escort her to her car when she's ready to leave."

He retrieved his tool belt from the top of the counter and began fastening it around his waist again. He nodded. "Sure thing, boss." Then he patted me on the shoulder and gestured his chin toward the exit. "Go, I'll take care of her. Go see your family."

It was exactly what I wanted him say. Exactly what I wanted him to do—but for some reason, I didn't like his answer one bit.

Not one little bit.

CHAPTER TEN

john

* * *

It was five after eight when I pulled in front of my parents' house. I knew they'd already eaten. Just as I was sure a plate would be waiting for me in the microwave. My family was like that, which was what made it so nice to come home. There were no expectations, no complications, just a family who was happy to see me walk through the door. No matter how late I was.

I jogged up the front steps of the two-story house, past the cherry tree in the front yard that had been my safe haven, and the brick pedestals I'd carved my name into when I was six. I took a deep breath, pushed open the front door, and stepped inside. The sounds of my family carried down the long hall, the familiar sound filling me with a sense of peace. Voices big and small echoed in the foyer from ceiling to wooden floor. And when I walked around the corner, the sight of them all together still made me smile. Mom was in the kitchen doing the dishes with Penny and Margaret. Dad was watching baseball in his favorite chair with a couple grandkids curled up on his lap, and Lisa was sitting on the couch with my niece and nephew.

"It's about time," she said, taking my niece Frances and placing her back on the couch cushions.

"Sorry, I got tied up at work."

She nodded and tucked the blanket back around her kids' shoulders before moving toward the kitchen.

Mom turned around and smiled at me, her hands covered with yellow plastic gloves. "There's a plate of food for you in the microwave."

I smiled, patted my nephew Johnny on the head, and then made my way across the kitchen to heat up my food.

Lisa came to lean against the counter and frowned. "How's Katie?"

"She's good. She's home, seems to be doing well, but Jake's a mess... He hates not being on site, but there's no way he's ready to leave her alone just yet."

She nodded. "I'm glad she's okay. How's the new job?"

I lifted my shoulders and pulled a fork out of the drawer. "Good."

Lisa tilted her head and examined me, surely sensing my frustration with the whole situation. It was thirty minutes later, and my shoulders were still rigid like rocks from seeing Tuesday like that. I was pissed at myself. Pissed for my actions the first night we'd met. Pissed at *her* for being so damned stubborn she couldn't just forget about the whole thing. Maybe if things had gone differently it wouldn't be like this between us now. Maybe her tears would have landed on my shoulders instead of her sweet, little hands.

Mom came to stand by my side and touched my arm. "You tell Jake I'm bringing him a lasagna tomorrow, okay?"

I nodded, smiling at how thoughtful she always was, then leaned over to give her a kiss on the cheek. "I'll tell him. I'm sure Katie will appreciate a home cooked meal."

Mom smiled and turned back to the sink to finish washing dishes. "I'm praying for them all the time."

Lisa parked herself against the counter between us and

started talking to Mom about Katie's condition. Lisa had gone through something similar a few years ago when she was pregnant with my niece Frances. We all knew how scary the whole thing could be, how until you were out of the woods it was completely thought-consuming, but when she started talking about Katie's placenta, I turned around. Even though I'd grown up with three sisters, there was only so much I was willing to handle.

My dad lifted his chin from his spot under the grandchildren and waved for me to come join him in the living room.

I took my hot plate off the counter, filled a glass with water, and came to sit on the couch. "What's the score?" I whispered, hoping not to wake any sleeping kids.

"Ten–ten, Dodgers," he replied.

I chuckled then set my glass on the coffee table and leaned back in my seat. "Ten–ten Dodgers, huh?"

Even though it was a tie, my father was the eternal optimist. Every year he was sure that "this year" they'd go to the World Series. "This year" they had a chance.

He made some sort of grumbling noise, dismissing my amusement and turned back to the TV. "You'll see."

I leaned back in my seat even farther and took another fork full of food, but my thoughts filled instantly with Tuesday. She hadn't spoken a word to me since the day we started work. This bothered me more than I cared to admit. I wasn't used to people not liking me. I was a funny guy. Easy going, easy to get along with. It shouldn't have bothered me so much that she didn't see that, but it did. She was too damned stubborn. If she wasn't so stubborn, I'd still be there right now instead of here, wondering what in God's name was going on with her.

I took my phone out of my pocket to see if I'd missed any calls from Eddie, but there was nothing. I frowned and shoved another bite of meatloaf into my mouth. Aside from my sisters, no other woman had ever given me the cold shoulder for this long. Even Lisa, who was the worst of all three.

Lisa sat down on the couch beside me, leaned over my shoulder, and scooped a piece of mashed potato off my plate with her finger. "So what's going on? Why are you acting so weird?" She popped it in her mouth and began chewing.

I turned toward her and lifted my brown. "Seriously? Didn't you just eat?"

She laughed and took another finger full. "No, seriously. Are you okay? You look... I don't know... upset about something?" She paused, as if suddenly remembering something that caused her voice to lower. "Did Mom tell you—" She stopped. "You know what, it's none of my business."

I set my plate on the coffee table and took a long drink of water. "Did Mom tell me what?"

Mom came into the living room just then, wiping her hands on a kitchen cloth, and looking from me to Lisa.

"Did Mom tell me *what*?" I said, loud enough for her to hear. They were obviously keeping something from me, and my stomach clenched at the fear I saw in my mother's eyes.

She gave Lisa a hard look before turning back to me and shaking her head. "It's nothing, I was going to tell you after dessert." She paused for a long time, so long that adrenaline began to pump through my veins. "Another letter came," she finally confessed.

I stood up and looked from Lisa to my mom, wondering how long they'd kept this secret from me. I couldn't help the sense of betrayal that washed over my body. "Burn it," I said in a low, distant voice.

"John," my mother protested. "Maybe you should—"

"Burn it," I said again, picking up my plate, not wanting to hear another word. It had been years since I thought about him, *years*. I thought it was all behind me, but it obviously wasn't. I placed my plate in the sink, braced my arms on the counter, and tried to calm the surge of aggression that ached in my limbs.

Why after all these years? What could he possibly want from me that he didn't already have?

Mom rested her hand on my shoulder and gently squeezed. I could barely feel it, but I knew she was there. I turned around, finding her eyes red-rimmed with emotion, almost overflowing with unshed tears. She looked into my eyes, searching for something I wished I could give her, then she turned around and pulled open the drawer under the spice cabinet. She took a folded envelope from a pile of bills, came toward me, and laid it down on the counter. Without a word, she turned around, leaving me in the kitchen alone.

I looked down at the letter, his elegant scrawl, and the name I'd tried so hard to forget for as long as I could remember. Gabriel.

I picked it up off the counter, shoved it in my pocket, and then ran my hand through my hair. Mom was only the innocent bystander in all this. I knew it was hard on her, and I wouldn't make her do my dirty work. I'd burn the fucking letter myself.

tuesday

* * *

It was just after dawn when I arrived back at the shop. The store smelled like sawdust, which was a vast improvement from last week—though the smell still stirred in my nose, causing my already aching head to pound. I deposited my usual box of donuts onto the empty counter, then walked back to the parking lot and filled my lungs with the brisk morning air before I unlatched the tailgate of my truck. I needed to grab the new shelving unit I'd exchanged before work.

I was exhausted, caused by too little sleep and too much worry about the shop. But every time I drifted at night, thoughts of all I had to do the next day would spark new life into my body. I'd lie there—restless—for hours. Better to make some progress if I was going to be awake than lie there being miserable.

The shelving unit was heavy, so I pulled the large box to the edge of my tailgate and let one end drop to the ground. Then holding one end at my waist, I began to walk backward, shimmying it through the lot and inching it across the pavement. I cringed halfway to the front door when I saw the headlights.

"Perfect," I muttered under my breath. "Just perfect."

John hopped down from his truck a moment later and began walking toward me.

Damn, he looked good when he walked. Though to be fair, he looked good when he was doing just about anything. Like standing, or leaning, or breathing.

"Need help?" he asked.

I shook my head. Mostly because his presence stirred the same reaction in my stomach I got before tests, like an anxiously excited feeling—like I was about to jump out of a damned airplane. "Nah, I got it."

He came to stand beside me, frowned, and then turned around to walk backward beside me.

"You sure?" His head tilted to the side and his deep voice lowered. He wasn't smiling at all, and there wasn't a hint of humor in his eyes. I didn't like it at all. Didn't like this new, sad man who hadn't smiled in days.

My throat tightened, and I looked over my shoulder. I couldn't stand the thought of him seeing me cry. Seeing how weak I'd become, when I always prided myself on being strong. "Yeah, actually." I dropped the box to the pavement, not caring if the whole thing shattered to a million pieces. My only thought was for self-preservation, to get away from him before tears began streaming down my cheeks again. "You can bring it to the back room." I pushed my glasses up the bridge of my nose and walked across the lot, without bothering to wait for his reply.

I hurried past the pile of boxes in the back room, knowing he'd see them but not having the time to care. I opened the door to the bathroom, closed it as quickly as I could, and sat on the toilet. I put my head between my knees and forced myself to breathe. "You can do this, Tuesday. You can do anything."

But the tears came anyway.

* * *

When I came out of the bathroom a while later, the shelving unit was propped against the wall beside my mess. I chewed my inner cheek and glanced to the plastic door. I could hear the rhythmic hum of the air compressor and knew he'd seen it all. Seen the evidence left behind from my weakest moment. John was the last person I wanted to see something like that, and I began making up excuses in my head. Excuses that were stupid. That I was reorganizing, that I'd seen a rat, but then I forced myself to stop. I didn't need excuses. I didn't need to defend myself for something that was none of his concern. I squared my shoulders and went to work, picking up the pieces of my crazy life, one box at a time.

I heard Eddie's voice from the front room a while later and knew he must have arrived for work. I kept my head down and continued cleaning. Last night had been interesting. It had been just after eight when I finally pried myself off the floor. I'd contemplated staying later to clean up, but I was too overwhelmed to think straight. When I'd pushed through the plastic tarp to the front room, I found Eddie sitting on the counter, waiting. He didn't say anything. Just jumped to the floor, nodded his head to the front door, and walked with me out to my truck.

I shook my head and thought about my puffy face. The face he'd been gentlemanly enough to pretend he hadn't seen.

I snatched random soaps from the floor and began organizing them inside a box. Luckily, in my frantic search for lip balm, nothing was permanently damaged. Just disorganized in a way that took me four hours to sift through. Just enough time for Becky to miss the whole ordeal. She strolled into the back room late that morning, her hair in long braids, and she placed a brown grocery bag of food on the counter. "So what's on the agenda for today?"

"More orders, what else?" I said, resting my hip against the counter.

She frowned. "You look like shit, Day. How long were you here last night?" She nodded to the shelving unit and lifted a brow. "I guess you never found slot X?"

I laughed—a real laugh that felt good after my long night— and I smoothed my hair away from my face. "No, I exchanged it this morning. I'll work on it again later, once I get the rest of my orders shipped."

She nodded and began pulling containers of food out of the bag. She threw a tub of seaweed salad onto the counter and made a face. "Here, it looked disgusting, so I knew you'd love it."

I rolled my eyes and snatched the fork from her hand. "You'd be right. Because it's delicious, you should try it. You may live longer."

She shook her head. "Nah. My goal in life is to die at sixty-nine."

She raised her brows, and I hit her on the shoulder with a

napkin.

"You're such a perv."

CHAPTER ELEVEN

john

* * *

I flicked the switch on the air compressor, causing the room to fall into silence, and I looked over to the door leading to the back room. *She was late again.*

Eddie raised his eyebrows from a few feet away, silently asking me what we wanted to do, and I gave him the sign to cut it. I wouldn't make him stick around another night, and I wasn't going to either. Not when she dropped boxes at my feet and didn't even thank me for hauling her stuff to the back room.

I had my own shit to deal with.

I tossed the nail gun to the corner of the room and unfastened my tool belt. Tonight was the first get-together since Katie got out of the hospital, and everyone was already waiting on me.

I gripped the back of my neck and closed my eyes. A happy as I was that Jake and Katie were finding their new normal after the scare, I'd rather go home. I hadn't opened the letter, but I held it in my hands all night, unable to muster enough guts to burn it. I hated the fact that his name affected me so much. Hated that even now, as a grown man, it still gave me nightmares.

My keys were on the edge of the counter, and I snatched them up before heading to the back room. I nodded to Eddie to go ahead and pack up then pushed myself through the plastic divider to let Tuesday know we were taking off.

I stopped when I saw her laughing. She was sitting on the floor with that girl who'd been helping her all week, and I leaned against the doorframe to watch them, my feet crossed in front of me. Tuesday's smile was beautiful—wide and honest. It brightened the whole room and warmth spread through my chest. It was good to see her smile, and for some reason, I longed for more of it.

She doubled over, gripping her stomach with more laughter, and started to wheeze. "Oh my God! You didn't!" Her words were coming on gasps of air between each giggle. I shook my head in amusement.

The scene reminded me of one of my sisters' slumber parties when I was young. And just like all those days, I knew if I stuck around too long, I'd be caught.

I pushed myself from the wall and cleared my throat.

Tuesday turned to face me and instantly sobered. Her eyes locked on my chest, and she pushed her friend's leg to get her attention.

Her reaction bothered me. I wanted her to look at me like the night we met. Before I screwed everything up. "I just wanted to let you know we're packing up." I threw my chin toward the product floor. "Eddie's already gone."

Her friend smiled at me and Tuesday nodded, but they both remained silent. I gripped the back of my neck and nodded to the other room. "I'll lock the door behind me."

Again, they both remained silent, and I eventually turned around to leave. The sound of Tuesday's laughter hit the minute I stepped foot on the product floor.

"Oh my God, he's SO hot!" the brunette shouted.

"Shhh..." Tuesday whisper yelled, and I shook my head as I walked across the room to gather my stuff, unable to stop myself from chuckling.

I still didn't know how I felt about leaving. There were always vagrants hanging around the alley at night, mostly just looking for a safe place to huddle down for the evening, but it still worried me. The fact she had her friend with her eased that a bit.

I climbed into my F150 a moment later, noticing Tuesday's old truck parked by the trash cans. Her friend's brand new sports car parked right beside it. They were a mismatched pair if I ever did see one. But it was obvious they loved each other.

* * *

The gang was on the back deck when I got there. Jake stood at the grill, Katie and Em sat in front of the fire, and the smell of smoke filtered through the night air. I tilted my head up and inhaled. I hadn't been sure if I wanted to be here tonight, but now that I was, it felt good to be around friends.

Em waved before pushing herself from her seat and coming toward me. The sway in her step indicated she'd already had too much to drink. I tilted my head and looked at Katie. This wasn't the norm for Em. She could drink like a sailor and still hold her ground. She must have had a lot.

Katie shrugged at my silent question, obviously having taken notice of Em's condition. Truth be told, I was surprised to see Katie out and about, and that Jake looked so relaxed beside her.

Em came toward me, throwing her arms around my neck as she exhaled. "I missed you," she whispered. Her words were soft but filled with a heaviness that wasn't like her.

My brow furrowed, and I gave her a tight squeeze. "Back at you, kid."

She leaned back to smile at me, but her walls were still up, and I raised my eyebrows, silently asking her what was going on. Her eyes glassed over, and I realized maybe she was drunker than I initially thought. She moved away, staggering a little as she pushed her hands through her short messy hair.

"Woah! How much have you had?" I asked.

She shrugged indifferently and looked over at Katie. "I'm drinking for two."

Katie gave a slight shake of her head, and Em continued to the back door where she walked back into the kitchen.

"She okay?" I asked, coming to stand beside Jake at the grill.

Katie gently rose to her feet, waving off Jake as he eyed her cautiously. "It's been a slow progression. She got here around four and has been drinking ever since. I'm a bit worried."

Jake's jaw tightened, obviously concerned with what had been going on. "Something's up with her tonight, but she hasn't said anything."

Katie's hand came to rest on her belly, and she looked toward the kitchen. "Do you think something's happened?"

I looked back over my shoulder. "I don't know." I grabbed a beer from the bucket of ice and cracked it open before going into the house to find Em.

She sat slumped over on the couch, her legs spread wide, and her head resting in her hands.

I took the chair at her side and pulled it over so I was sitting right in front of her. "You okay?"

She shook her head but didn't look up. "I'm drunk." Then her shoulders began to shake with laughter. "Drunk as a skunk."

87

I lifted her chin with one finger and stared at her, not stopping until she looked me in the eye. "Are you *okay?*"

Her eyes met mine as if it was difficult for her to focus, and her lips began to quiver. She shook her head again. "No."

Em was normally confident, strong, and I'd never actually seen her cry before; it broke my heart. I hugged her to my chest, causing her drunken body to sag against me.

"It's those damned demons." Her voice was sloppy, raw, but the words so real.

I nodded, knowing all too well what she was talking about. We both had them, Em and I. Demons that were buried deep, embedded in our bones. "You want to talk about it?" I squeezed her tighter, wanting to protect the girl who was like my first sister.

"No." She buried her face into my chest and sniffed.

"Are you sure?"

She pushed against my chest and looked me in the eye once more. "Will you just take me home? I don't want to be here tonight."

Her eyes were barely open, and I pushed my fingers through her short hair, wondering what had rocked her so hard she'd let herself go like this. "Of course."

* * *

It was just after nine when I locked her apartment door and pulled it shut behind me. Rain poured from the eaves of the building, and I rushed toward the stairs, taking them two at a time on my way to the parking lot.

Seeing Em like that brought back memories. Things I spent a lifetime trying to forget. Things I wished I could shield her from ever thinking of again.

Memories of Em and I huddled under the kitchen table at the Clarks' home flashed through my mind. She'd only been three years older than me, an eight-year-old girl, but her arms squeezed me tighter than anyone had in my whole life. Seeing her like this—broken, hollow—shook me.

I hopped into my truck as rain pinged on the ceiling of the cab. The sound stirred memories of Mrs. Clark's heels clicking on the hard ceramic tile; the sounds as clear in my mind now as they were twenty some years earlier. She was the woman who was supposed to provide us a stable home, but Em and I were huddled under a damned table, hoping it would offer protection. We only spent three months together in that house, three months of never being able to please the family who should have loved us— but Em had become my sister.

I flicked on my headlights and turned out of the lot. Visions of being pulled out of Em's arms entered my mind. Her screams, my tears... I didn't want to leave her. She was all I had...

I forced out an emotional breath and rubbed my eyes. *I needed a drink.* To settle my mind before the memories took over. I turned my truck down Parker Road, intending to stop by Donovan's for a pint, but as I passed the parking lot of the shop, Tuesday's truck was still parked by the dumpsters, only now it sat all alone.

"Shit!" I shook my head and kept on going. She wasn't my problem. I had too much shit to deal with to worry about a girl who obviously wasn't worried about herself.

But I only made it a half a mile before my conscience took over, and my hands flipped a U-turn of their own accord. Five minutes. That's it. I'd check on her, tell her she was crazy for being in the building alone, and then I'd leave.

CHAPTER TWELVE

tuesday

* * *

The rain was coming hard and fast as I stood in the middle of the shop. Row after row of pieces were laid out on the floor in front of me like a puzzle, all alphabetized, just as I'd done before. And just like last time, slot X was missing. I grabbed the box and held it upside down, shaking it a few times, praying that somewhere, slot X was hidden inside. Nothing. It was empty. Completely empty.

I lifted my glasses and rubbed my eyes. Hard. *This wasn't happening.* This *really* wasn't happening. I could feel the blood boiling under the surface of my skin, and I took a calming breath. *You can go back to the warehouse in the morning, get a totally different unit. Or better yet, try to find something already assembled.* The pressure of the last few days was crushing me. I needed sleep, I needed a vacation, a day at the beach with a mojito in my hand. But... the shop hadn't even opened yet.

Then I heard a loud *ping* from behind me, echoing through the silence of the empty back room. It was a sound I'd heard a few other times in my life, but one that was never welcomed. I turned around, just in time to hear it again. The sound of water—dripping. Another drop of rain hit the metal counter in the middle of the room, and I closed my eyes. This was a nightmare. There was no way I could handle this. I was out of money, running out of product, and out of time. I could handle going to the warehouse in the morning. I could handle losing another day of work, but a leak in the roof was something I just couldn't take.

Then it came again, the sound barely audible, but one that caused every cell in my body to explode. I picked up a piece of shelving from the floor and slammed it as hard as I could against the counter. I let out a cry, the impact so heavy it caused my palms to ache—but the shelf remained perfectly intact. I wanted to scream. I needed it broken. I *needed* something to take the pressure from my life. Tears fell to my cheeks, and my whole body began to shake. I lifted the shelf over my head and slammed it down again. Harder. Then again, and again, and—and someone grabbed me from behind and hauled me against their chest.

"Shhh... It's okay, you're okay."

John wrapped his arms around my waist, pulling me backward, holding my shaking body firm against his. I lowered my arms, letting the solid board fall in one piece to the ground. Defeated.

"You're okay. Shhh..."

I wrapped my arms around my waist, trying to hide that part of me away. To shield the evidence of my pain. This was all I ever wanted, the thing I'd been dreaming of since I was eight years old. To own something that was mine. But every day I could feel it slipping, and I didn't have it in me to hold on any longer. My body sagged, and he held me closer, harder, causing the vibrations in my limbs to sink into his.

I didn't know why he was doing this. Or even why he was here. But most of all, I didn't know why I was letting him. Things would be awkward in the morning, I knew that, but for some reason, I couldn't pull away. I was weak and he was strong. I needed strength. I didn't even care at what cost.

"You're okay."

I shook my head, feeling another tear slip into the corner of my mouth. "How do you know?" My voice was broken, hoarse. "Everything is falling apart."

I pushed myself away, turning around so I could face him. The heaviness I saw in his eyes was not what I expected. My chin began to quiver, and I hugged myself with both arms. "Everything is falling apart." I was repeating myself, but I needed to say it; I needed to yell it, but I didn't.

He looked to the row of pieces on the ground, still organized in alphabetical order.

An ache of frustration rose in my chest and let out a sob. "Except that." Tears rolled down my face. Fat tears of exhaustion and stress. But of relief too—relief from finally sharing my burden with someone else.

He stepped closer, brushing a thumb across my cheek. "You look tired. You should go home and get some sleep."

I laughed, but the sound was hollow. "How do you know? How do you know what I need? You hardly know me."

His face remained serious, and he looked into my eyes. "Because I see you."

I held my breath, his words stilling me. I didn't know if it was the gentle way he said it, or something else, but it made my heart constrict in my chest.

"Go home and get some sleep."

I glanced at him and gestured to the roof, where water still dripped periodically onto the metal counter. "I can't."

He didn't seem to listen and turned me around to face the exit. "I've got it. Go get some sleep. You'll feel better in the morning."

He gave me another shove in the direction of the plastic divider, but this time I didn't resist. I didn't even stop by my office to grab my bag. I went to the car, somehow feeling lighter than I had in days. I wasn't alone in this.

John was there to help me.

I wasn't alone.

CHAPTER THIRTEEN

tuesday

* * *

It was still drizzling when I got to work the next day, though I didn't feel better. I felt worse. My throat was sore, and my whole body ached. I'd worked myself to breaking point and was finally sick.

I rested my head on the steering wheel, trying to convince myself to go inside. I was thankful for John last night, but now warmth flooded my cheeks at the thought of facing him again. He'd seen the part of me I hid from even my best friend, and now I had to go in there and pretend he hadn't witnessed me having a nervous breakdown in the back room.

The door to my truck creaked open, resisting movement as much as my limbs. I hopped down from the cab, and moisture instantly seeped through my lambskin boots. I looked down to my feet and the deep puddle I now stood in. Fantastic. Fan-fucking-tastic.

Ignoring the squish in my step, I rushed toward the shop. Somehow feeling naked even though I wore my thickest sweats, the ones I wore during that time of the month when I wanted to hide from the world. Which was exactly what I wanted today. I wanted to stay home, read a romance novel, maybe make a batch of homemade bone broth to warm the chill that had invaded my bones. But a day off was a luxury I couldn't afford. At least not for another month or two.

To my relief, when I pulled open the door, the shop was empty. Metal buckets filled with water were littered across the floor, and the sound of hammers on the tile roof echoed through the barren room. I looked up at the ceiling, wondering how many men were up there working. My chest tightened with anxiety as dollar signs flashed through my thoughts. I had no idea what a new roof would cost, but whatever it was, I couldn't afford it. I couldn't afford anything extra at the moment.

I blew out a breath and pushed through the plastic sheet to the back room. I needed to take off my boots. I needed to find money I didn't have. Even if it killed me.

My purse sat on the desk in my office, right where I'd left it.. I plopped down in my seat, pulled off one boot at a time, and set them upside down on the heating vent. I rubbed my fingers back and forth over my lips before pulling my wallet from the bag.

The American Express I'd never used sat inside. The sticker still on, still perfect, the line of credit untouched. I'd gotten it in case of emergencies. For things a normal person would go to their parents for. Like my truck breaking down, a broken bone, or God forbid, something more serious. But all I had was my hippie mom, with this biggest heart, but no sense of responsibility. Everyone knew I was the stable one in the family.

More pounding came from the ceiling, and I let my head sag to my shoulders. I needed to find out what this would all cost before I started to panic.

I pushed myself from my seat, opened the office door, and froze. There, on the other side of the room was the shelving unit. Light maple, beautiful, exactly like the picture on the box. I didn't know why, but it took my breath away. Not only had he been my savior last night, but he'd also put my shelving unit together.

Just then, a gust of wind blew in from the alley, and John

walked through the door. He wore a yellow poncho covered with rain and his hair had beads of water resting on its ends. Stubble slightly longer than his normal shadow covered his face, but he looked—amazing.

He shook his head, causing the drops to fly in every direction, then turned to me.

I swallowed, remembering his arms wrapped around me last night, how gentle he'd been. How hard he'd hugged me. How sweet, even though I'd practically ignored him all week.

His eyes found mine but he didn't speak. He didn't smile either.

"Y-you put my shelving unit together. Thank you." I wrapped my arms around my waist, sure it was the chill in the air that caused my stutter. "You didn't have to."

His brows furrowed and he nodded—once. Then he moved toward me, his boots leaving puddles of water on the plywood floor, and I instinctively took a step backward. "Where did you find slot X?"

The corner of his mouth lifted, not quite a smile but not a frown either, then he shifted his poncho to the side, exposing a power drill on the holster of his belt. "I made one."

I grinned. "I can't even tell you how relieved that makes me."

He nodded but kept moving forward.

My heartbeat quickened and I touched a hand to my throat. "You probably don't want to get too close, I'm might be contagious," I croaked.

But he kept on coming, ignoring my warning, moving with the confidence of a stallion. I wasn't sure what I expected him to do, but at the same time, I craved whatever it was. My body tightened, already anticipating his touch—then he stopped at the nearby table and grabbed a set of towels from the surface.

Oh.

He braced his legs apart and began drying his hair as I watched him. In truth, I don't know if I could have pulled my eyes away if I tried. He was incredibly attractive, maybe even more so because he was all wet, and I was too damned tired to stop myself.

"If you're sick, why are you here?"

I tucked my hair behind my ear and leaned against the doorframe. "Because I have work to do."

He dropped the towel to his neck and leaned against the counter. "It'll still be here on Monday."

"Yeah." I shifted my weight to the other foot, slightly turned on by his deep, sultry voice. "But I like self-torture."

He grinned then. Something I hadn't seen in weeks, and it caused a longing to form in my gut. "Me too."

I laughed. "That doesn't surprise me."

"Oh yeah? Why's that?"

I looked up to the ceiling. "'Cause I'm pretty sure you were here all night." I swallowed, looking into his deep, brown eyes and remembering how good it had felt to be held against him.

He didn't look away. Just smiled at me. His lips barely lifted at the corners, as his eyes heated my whole body.

I adjusted my stance and looked up to the ceiling again, finally breaking the stare that had left me steaming. "How much is it going to cost me?"

He shook his head then placed the towel on the table. "Don't worry about it."

I straightened, pushing my glasses up the bridge of my nose. "What do you mean?"

He turned his back to me, crossing the room to the product floor. "It's covered, Tuesday. It won't cost you a thing."

I swallowed, watching him push through the plastic divider, and I held back the protest that settled on my tongue. He was doing me a favor, a huge one that I had no right to accept. I'd been nothing but rude to him all week, but he'd sent me home to sleep, while he stayed up all night fixing my roof... for free.

I turned back to my office, stuffing my wallet back into my bag and feeling like the shittiest person in the world. The memory of the jumper cables smug asshole was now replaced with something different. A man who had come to my rescue more times than I could count on one hand.

* * *

I worked hard that afternoon, filling orders, making products, and not giving the slightest thought to the roof. I even set a couple of batches of Sweater Weather bath bar to cure on my new shelves. But John was all I thought about. I was pretty sure he was flirting with me this afternoon, and I flirted back, which was equally concerning.

I knew better than to get involved with someone I worked with, but this was worse; he was under my employment.

I wasn't positive, but I was pretty sure I could be charged with sexual harassment if this continued. The thought amused me. Me, the nerdy soap maker with too much hair, harassing the hot construction worker who could make a living doing photo shoots for calendars. I grinned and set the double boiler to the top of the range, and then began measuring ingredients for lip balm.

By the end of the day, I'd replenished my stock of Cream In My Coffee, Kiss You All Over, and Lemonade Girl. It felt good getting some products on the shelves, and in spite of my sore throat, I wasn't feeling half bad once I got into it.

When I placed the full boxes of product on the shelves, I noticed for the first time the evidence of my temper. Little nicks in the maple wood from where I'd slammed it on the counter last night. My stomach tightened, as visions of John's arms wrapped around my waist entered my thoughts. He'd left hours earlier, so why had he come back that night? I looked over my shoulder in the direction of the front room. He'd stayed up all night, drenched on top of the roof—for me. Aside from Becky, I wasn't sure if anyone had gone to such trouble for me before. Ever.

CHAPTER FOURTEEN

tuesday

* * *

The whole next week was uneventful. I worked in back, catching up on my orders and replenishing product, while John and his crew made good progress on the store. But when I came to work the following Monday, John was sitting on the tailgate of his truck in the parking lot. Alone.

I'd never seen him just sitting there before, and my eyes immediately scanned the front of the shop, looking for something wrong. But everything looked normal. Better than normal. The shop was starting to take shape. The siding, which had been splintered and broken only weeks before, was now sanded, painted a crisp white, and framing a set of windows where I could see Eddie in the back room prepping the walls for paint. I pulled into my habitual spot by the dumpsters, shifted to park, and looked over at John.

He smiled at me. That adorable grin that was getting harder and harder to resist. He pushed off the side of his truck and walked toward me, setting at least a dozen butterflies loose in my stomach. He was wearing his usual jeans and t-shirt; the jeans cut low, the t-shirt tight enough to show off his broad chest. And his face. His face was clean-shaven and wore a smile as sweet as a child.

But he didn't stop at my window as I'd expected; he walked around the side of my truck, opened the passenger door, and lifted the box of donuts from the seat to climb in beside me.

I didn't move, just looked at him then back to the shop. "What are you doing? What happened?"

He took a donut from the box and took a bite. "We're going to pick out flooring."

I was confused, and it took me a minute to understand. The way he said it seemed so intimate, not like an employee to an employer, but something more. Something closer. "I thought we already did that?"

He shrugged and glanced out the window. "I have an idea, but I thought you'd like to pick it out in person."

I swallowed. Mostly because I really wanted to lick the bits of sugar from his bottom lip. I couldn't do that. No matter how tempting it was. I shook my head to clear it and turned to look at the front of the store. "Why aren't we taking your truck?"

My eyes shifted to his brand new F150—one I was sure had air conditioning that didn't require rolling down the window.

"Eddie needs to go to the dump later."

My brows furrowed, but I nodded anyway. This was a bad idea. I could feel it all the way to my toes, but how could I explain the reason? "Put your seatbelt on," I said, then I shifted to reverse, pretending not to notice him watching me as I pulled out of the parking lot.

* * *

He directed me to the freeway a couple miles away, programed the address into my phone, but after that, we didn't speak. This was the first I'd been alone with him since the storm, and I wasn't sure what to say. Every time he'd walked through the back room this week, my heart would constrict uncomfortably. And now, sitting so close, it was doing it again. But worse.

"Are you sure you don't want one?" he asked, holding a glazed donut under my nose.

It was the third time he'd offered, and I shook my head. "No thanks." I turned my gaze back to the road.

He braced his back against the upholstery and turned to stare at me. "Now that I think about it, you bring these in every morning, yet I don't think I've ever seen you eat one."

"So?" I glanced at him out of the corner of my eye, wondering where he was going with this.

"Why do you do it? Why go to the trouble?" He wasn't laughing now; he wasn't smiling either. He was looking at me dead serious. As if this were a mystery he was determined to figure out.

I shifted in my seat, feeling slightly uncomfortable. "Bribery." I smiled a little. "I figure if I treat you guys well enough, you'll work harder."

His brows furrowed. "That's what you're *paying* us for."

I grabbed one of my pigtails and began twisting it with my figures. He looked offended, and that's not what I meant to do at all. "I know."

He looked up at the ceiling then back at me again. "There's only one thing we can do to make this right." He paused. "You're going to have to eat one."

I shook my head, not understanding his meaning, but then he held it up to my mouth, and I started to laugh. "How does that make any sense?"

"Because I've been eating your donuts, and you haven't, so if you eat one, I'll feel better."

"But I don't even like donuts."

He made a face and leaned farther back against the door. "Everyone likes donuts."

"I don't, I swear. They're processed and disgusting."

He narrowed his eyes. "You *must* be joking."

"I'm not," I said, hardly able to keep my face serious.

He sat up straighter, took a glazed donut from the box, and held it to my mouth. "Take a bite."

I turned my head and shoved his hand away. "No," I said with a laugh.

"Take a bite, and I'll leave you alone."

I glanced over at him, glaring playfully. "There's a name for this, you know."

He laughed. "Yeah, intervention."

"You think I need an intervention because I won't take a bite of your donut?"

He shrugged, but the playful grin was almost my undoing.

Without saying a word, I opened my mouth. The action was instinctive, something I would have done had it been an argument with Becky, but I immediately regretted it. John was not Becky, and I shouldn't expect him to feed me. But right when I was about to close it again, crisp, sweet icing hit my tongue. My breath hitched in my throat and I bit down, filling my mouth with the warm, soft pastry.

The donut was better than I remembered, buttery, and delicate. Then his thumb gently brushed across my lower lip, and my stomach came alive with tiny flutters. I didn't dare look over at him. It was such a slight touch, one that could have been on accident if it hadn't lingered a bit too long. He pulled his hand away, stopping for a second before sucking the sugar from his fingers. I forced myself to swallow.

The whole mood in the cab changed in a second. We'd gone from playfulness and laughter, to serious and... And I didn't want to admit what this was.

"Did you like it?" His voice was low and caused my stomach to tighten all over.

I shook my head. "Not one bit."

Siri's voice broke the silence, guiding me to our destination and making me relax a bit. No matter how good it felt, or how much I wanted John, I couldn't let this happen. I kept my eyes locked straight ahead, focused on the instructions coming from my phone and the life I'd been building for years.

CHAPTER FIFTEEN

john

* * *

She walked ahead of me through the parking lot, her pigtails swaying against her back. Her overalls much too large, and her cheeks flushed as red as her lips. Yet she could have been the most beautiful thing I'd ever seen in my life.

Inviting her along had been a last minute decision, one I was pretty sure was a mistake. But when her eyes met mine in front of the shop, eyes as bright as the sun, I couldn't resist.

I pulled a flatbed from the front of the warehouse and gestured for her to go ahead of me. She wasn't the type of girl I normally went for, and I wasn't sure what I wanted to do about it.

Actually... that was a lie. I knew exactly what I wanted to do about it, but I couldn't. Not while I was under her employment anyway.

My brows furrowed as I followed behind her. She was a mystery to me—witty, beautiful, and a hard worker. The fact that I wanted her made me feel like shit. I wanted her for selfish reasons—because the tension between us was insane, because every time we touched she melted, but mostly, because she made me forget. Forget about the fear that took hold of my stomach, forget about the man who still gave me nightmares to this day.

But in the short amount of time we'd known each other, I was sure of two things. One, she wasn't a woman you wanted; she was a woman you kept. And two, in spite of her confident exterior, there was a part of her that was fragile. The part of her that lost it in the back room, a piece that cried alone in the dark.

We made it to the flooring aisle before she finally turned to face me, her head slightly tilted, eyes wide, and lips parted. "Wow," she said, taking in the various wood, marble, and slate that were stacked three stories high.

Her excitement caused warmth to spread across my chest. "You have a lot to choose from, that's for sure."

She bit her bottom lip and continued walking. "Is this like a contractor's version of a wet dream?"

I chuckled somewhat shocked by her choice of words and nodded. "Something like that."

She placed one finger on the top of a large marble slab, and proceeded to drag it across the surface as she moved down the aisle. "How long have you been doing this?"

I leaned into the handle of the flatbed, feeling some of the walls between us start to crumble as I followed her. "Doing what?"

"Construction."

I blew out a breath and looked up to the ceiling. "Four years."

She glanced over her shoulder and lifted a brow. "That's it?

"Yep, that's it. You sound disappointed."

She shook her head. "Not disappointed, impressed. You're really good at what you do."

I smiled and continued to follow her. "Thanks."

She moved down the aisle a few more feet before I spoke again. "What about you?" I almost regretted the question as it crossed my lips, but then I didn't. I was curious about her, had been for a long time.

She moved to another flooring display and paused. I thought she might close up as she'd always done, but she didn't. She traced a slab of marble with her finger then looked over her shoulder.

"I've been making soap since I was ten years old." She pushed her glasses up the bridge of her nose and lifted her shoulders. "That's what happens when your mom's a hippie."

I laughed. "You learn how to make soap?"

She nodded. "Among other things."

"Oh yeah? What other things?"

She began walking again, stopping at various displays to check prices before answering. "Let's see... I know a dance that will make it rain. I can plant just about anything and make it grow. I know a home remedy for anything that ails you."

She stopped, and her chest rose and fell with a deep breath. "I know how to pack a lifetime of possessions in a single night."

She shook her head as if regretting her words, then looked back over her shoulder again, her grass-colored eyes serious and wounded.

"But I wouldn't be where I am without it. I learned something from every place I've been. I've met a million people. Crazy people, beautiful ones—all *different*."

She turned around again and continued walking. "I've worked every farmers market from coast to coast... By the time I was eighteen, I was making enough money from my wares to venture out on my own."

She stopped at a display and our eyes locked. I wasn't sure what made her open up like this, but I didn't want it to stop. Something was exchanging between us. A connection that didn't come with just any person.

"My mom did the best she could with what she had, but I've never really felt settled." Her brows creased slightly. "That's why I'm opening the shop. That's why it means so much to me. That's why it all makes me so insane sometimes."

She was explaining her actions from the other night, telling me the reason she'd lost it in the back room. I wished I could tell her it wasn't needed. That she didn't need to explain herself to me because I was more fucked up than anyone. But for some reason, I didn't want her to know that. I wanted her to go on looking at me like the hard piece of stone her hand rested on.

Unbreakable.

tuesday

* * *

Feeling like an idiot, I closed my eyes and chewed my inner cheek. He was my contractor, and here I was spilling my guts as if he were my best friend. I turned away and pressed my hand against another display. "What do you think of this one?"

I wished I could retrace my steps and start over again—but the words were already out there, floating in the air like a cloud of vulnerability.

Wanting to apologize, excuse him from having to respond to my silly admissions, I turned around, but he was right behind me.

"I like it." His voice was soft, deep, textured—so close—and made me forget what I was going to say.

I stared at his chest, just inches from my face. "Like what?"

"The tile."

"Yeah, it's nice, isn't it?"

He didn't speak, he didn't move, and I finally built up the nerve to look up again. "I'm sorry□"

But he shook his head, stopping my words. "We all have our shit, Tuesday. You don't have to explain yours to me."

My throat went dry, and I swallowed to clear it. The understanding in his voice was almost my undoing. "Even so,"—I looked down—"I'm sure you weren't asking for my life story."

"What makes you say that?"

I looked up again, finding he watched me, his expression so serious it made my breath quicken.

"I liked hearing about your life. It actually cleared up a few things."

I furrowed my brow. "Like what?"

He lifted the strand of feathers in my hair and rubbed them between his calloused fingers. "Like these."

I backed away, my breath coming harder, faster, but my eyes betrayed me and came to rest on his mouth. "They're supposed to keep me calm," I whispered. "But they aren't working. They haven't been working for weeks..."

He stepped closer, his hand resting on the wall of the display behind me.

I looked up into his eyes. Eyes that were so deep I could see my own reflection. "What are you doing?"

His body leaned toward me, his breath lingering a little too close. "Something I shouldn't."

My throat hitched, and I knew I should step away, but his mouth, his beautiful mouth settled on mine. Firm, like the pressure to an open wound. A wound I didn't even know was bleeding. But in an instant, his lips, warm and seductive, soothed a part of me.

All evidence of thought left me as I stood there. His arms caged me in on either side of my body, his chest so close I could feel his heat, but our lips the only things touching. I wanted to grab hold of his t-shirt and pull him closer, to lose myself completely in this intoxicating man. Then his tongue, whisper soft, brushed across my lips. Sexy, inviting, and completely irresistible. My whole being surrendered to his request. My mouth, body, even my throat let out a soft groan of submission. All I could do was focus on the taste of him. The smell of him. More enticing and erotic than the most potent pheromone. I didn't care that we were in the middle of the aisle, or that someone could walk by at any moment. I was wanton with my desires, and couldn't care less what people thought of me.

I wrapped my arms around his neck and lifted up on my toes. My heart was pounding so hard I was sure he could feel it, but I didn't care. I'd wanted his lips from the moment I met him, had dreams about them, yet their reality was so much sweeter.

My hands traveled to the back of his head, to the baby soft skin of his jaw, and I held his face between my hands. This man, a man I had no reason to care about, was seducing the panties right off me in the middle of the hardware store. And he hadn't even tried to touch me.

I moved closer, wanting to press my body against his, but his hands came up between us, holding me back. His lips pulled from mine and his head fell back to his shoulders. "*Fuck!*"

I stilled, my heart running harder and faster than it had in a long time, and I turned away. "That shouldn't have happened. This can never happen again." My words were soft, staggered between gasps of air. I took a couple of steps, needed to put some distance between us, needed some time to clear my head so I could think.

"Tuesday, I didn't mean☐"

"Don't." I squeezed my eyes shut. I didn't know why, but I didn't want excuses, I didn't want to hear that he was sorry. All I wanted was to pick some tile and get the hell out of there.

I turned toward the white distressed wood where he'd kissed me. A kiss that put every other kiss in my life to shame. A kiss that I would remember the rest of my life. I lifted my chin toward the display before I turned around. "I want that one," I whispered, then wrapped my arms around my waist, and turned to leave. "I'll go wait in the truck."

* * *

I sat in front of my pickup, fingers running over my mouth where the memory of his kiss still lingered. It had been five whole minutes since our lips parted, yet I was more turned on than ever. His kiss was perfect. His mouth demanding, rough, passionate, yet soft and coaxing at the same time.

I didn't know what I would have done had he not pulled away. I was lost, almost certain I would have let him take me on the concrete slab of the warehouse floor. But his mouth, his tongue, they moved with mine, giving me what I needed, exactly where I needed them. A piece of me wished he would come out here and kiss me again. I pressed my head against the upholstery of the seat. Why did he have to work for me? Why did he have to kiss so damned good?

The passenger door opened, and I instantly straightened, barely glancing over to ensure it was John before twisting the key in the ignition to start my truck.

"Where's the flooring?" I asked, keeping my eyes fixed on the steering wheel.

The engine sputtered and groaned, not wanting to cooperate, so I turned the key harder, giving it a little nudge with the gas pedal.

"It's being delivered tomorrow."

"Oh," I said, giving the engine a bit more gas, causing it to roll more but produce nothing. "Shit!" I slammed my hand hard on the steering wheel then tried again, but John's hand covered mine, preventing me from trying again.

"Give it a second, or you'll flood the engine."

I snatched my hand away and turned to the window, frustrated by how quickly his touch affected me. But he was right. I was pushing the engine too hard, too fast. If I didn't give it the time it needed, we'd end up stranded here all day, and that was something I couldn't handle. I began to count. One, two, three, four—

"Do you want to talk about it?" His voice was gruff, flat, filled with an edge that cut into my heart.

He sounded pissed off, but I had no idea why. How could he possibly be upset? Because I gave him what he wanted? What a dozen women did on a weekly basis? Because I'd lost myself and looked like a fool? "No, I don't." I picked at a nick in the steering wheel with my finger.

"Suit yourself," he muttered.

I looked over at him, to his eyes fixed out the front window. "How can you possibly be mad at me? I didn't kiss you, you kissed me, remember?"

His eyes never wavered from the window as he shook his head. "I'm not mad at you."

"You could have fooled me."

"I'm pissed at myself!" He turned toward me. "I'm pissed because I should be able to resist you, but I can't. I've wanted you since the moment I met you, and I caved—that's it. It won't happen again."

My heart picked up speed, causing my chest to tighten with uncertainty, but I didn't blink. I didn't know what to say. Knowing he wanted me too, scared me to death. "You're right." I moistened my lips and forced myself to look away. "It won't." I turned the key in the ignition, and my truck roared to life. I took my phone from the center console, programmed the shop into navigation, and waited for Siri's voice to fill the cab. I didn't say a word the whole way back to Simply Tuesday's, and neither did he.

CHAPTER SIXTEEN

john

* * *

"What's wrong with you?" Lisa whispered, poking me in the ribs as I took another scoop of potato salad from the bar. The rest of the family was already seated in the dining room, and only Lisa and I lingered behind in the kitchen.

I continued filling my plate, ignoring her question before heading to the dining room to join the others. My mind had been consumed all afternoon by what happened with Tuesday. I shouldn't have kissed her. I knew I shouldn't have kissed her, but damn, I wanted to do it again. She was so responsive, so real... so damned sweet!

Lisa sat down on my other side and plopped her plate on the table. "You're *hiding something*," she whispered. "You've been moody since you walked through the door. I haven't seen you like this since Tabetha Swanson."

My brows furrowed and I pulled back to look at her. "You mean from second grade?"

"Yeah. From second grade." She laughed. "That's how ridiculous you're being."

I took a forkful of steak and shoved it in my mouth. "Thanks, sis. Love you too."

"I'm not trying to be a nag. I just worry about you." She leaned forward, her hand touching my shoulder as she whispered, "It's not the letter is it? Because you have no control over that, you know that, right?"

I glanced down at the table at my parents. For the first time all week, I hadn't thought about the letter. Somehow, the one thing that had consumed my thoughts for seven days was replaced with Tuesday in a single afternoon. Her lips, her smile, the way she looked so damned cute in those overalls.

I turned back to Lisa and rested my forehead on one elbow. "Have you ever told a guy no, when you really meant yes?"

She choked on her glass of tea and raised a brow. "No, John." She laughed. "No means no. Always. Why the hell did you ask that question?"

I scratched the back of my neck then jabbed another piece of steak with my fork. "That's not what I meant." I took a bite. "You know what, never mind."

She quickly sobered then wiped her mouth with her napkin. "I'm sorry, that was shitty of me. Are you okay? Did something happen?"

I knew I shouldn't say another word, but for some reason, the words still poured right out of me. "I kissed the woman I'm working for today."

Lisa took in a sharp breath and moved closer. "What? Your boss?"

My brows furrowed and I made a face. "No, she's not my boss. Jake's my boss. She just... hired us. It's different."

She made a motion of dismissal with her hands. "Doesn't matter. What matters is..." Her voice softened even further. "You kissed your *boss*."

I rolled my eyes as Penny leaned across the back of my chair to talk to Lisa. "What are you guys talking about?"

she whispered.

"John kissed his boss," Lisa whispered back.

"What!" she whisper-yelled. "When did this happen?"

I closed my eyes. *I shouldn't have said anything. I REALLY shouldn't have said anything.*

"He wants to know if no sometimes means yes."

Penny hit my arm. "No always means no, John. Have we not taught you anything?"

I shoved back from the table and rose from my seat. "You know what, I'm suddenly not hungry."

Lisa grabbed my arm, trying to get me to stay, but I shook her off and picked my plate up from the table. Mom glanced up from her conversation with my niece Ashley and eyed me warily. I looked away and walked out of the room.

I placed my plate on the counter and raked both hands through my hair. Normally I had no problem shaking off their teasing, but for some reason, I couldn't find the humor in the situation. I promised Tuesday I would never kiss her again, but it was a promise I wasn't sure I could fulfill. Not when she looked at me like that, when she smiled like that...

Lisa came from behind me a minute later and put one hand on my shoulder. "You know I love you, right?"

I laughed and shook my head. "You have the worst possible way of showing it."

She hugged me at my side and rested her head on my upper arm. "You really like this one, don't you?"

I pinched the bridge of my nose, suddenly having a headache. "Fuck—I don't know."

She swallowed, and I could tell she was a bit emotional,

but she laughed at the same time. "You do. Come to think of it, I haven't heard you talk about anyone like this in I don't know how long."

I nodded, knowing she was right—but relationships were hard for me. They required trust, and that was something I gave only a handful of people in my life. If I couldn't trust her... I sighed heavily. "It doesn't matter anyway. She doesn't want anything to do with me."

Lisa moved to lean against the counter and crossed her arms over her chest. "What happened?"

I glanced over, knowing I was making a mistake, but I told her everything. But I didn't stop at this afternoon. I told her about our altercation with the jumper cables, the night we first met. About our heated conversation when she found out I was her project manager... about her breaking down in the back room.

"And today..." She paused and tilted her head. "She kissed you back?"

I leaned my head on my shoulders and blew out a breath. "Yeah."

She turned to stand in front of me, her face intense and serious. "Are you sure?"

I made a face. "Yes, Lisa, I'm sure. She's not the first woman I've kissed."

"I know that, *John*." She moved to lean against the counter again and was silent a moment. "So I take it back."

I lifted one brow and looked over at her. "Take what back?"

She cleared her throat and chewed her bottom lip. "I think in this case, 'no' might actually mean, 'convince me'."

* * *

I tipped my head up, glancing to the solid brown door that replaced the plastic I'd become accustomed to. It was only the second day since the switch, when the crew moved to work on the back room, and the shop became mine for the taking. But even though the product floor had turned out more beautiful than I could have ever imagined, my enjoyment was minimal because my thoughts were forever consumed with John.

We didn't speak the rest of the way home that day. Actually, we still hadn't spoken since our conversation in the truck. I knew it was probably for the best. We had four more weeks left to tolerate each other, and when he was gone, life would continue on like every other day before him. But for some reason, my stomach twisted in knots every time I thought about it. Thought about how honest he looked the moment he told me he wanted me. Thought about the possibility of never seeing him again.

I turned back to the box of lotion I'd been working on, determined not to obsess for a second longer, and climbed up another step on the ladder. The herbal scent of rosemary and lavender hit my nose, and I looked to the moss-covered basket that hung from the ceiling —one of four that graced each corner of the room. Everything was crisp and clean, the perfect offset for the rustic brown paper of the Simply Tuesday's packaging. Exactly what I'd wanted. So why wasn't I happy?

My head sagged a little as I pulled a bottle of lotion from the box. My heart knew the reason, even though my mind was having a hard time keeping up. The kiss from John made me realize I'd been selling myself short for a long time. Possibly my whole life. His kiss brought to life the feelings that came with fairy tales, romance novels, and dreams of little girls. Something I'd convinced myself didn't exist. So why did it have to come from a man I knew couldn't give me a happy ending? A man who was a player, one who had multiple women in a single night?

I placed the bottle of lotion firmly on the shelf and hastily grabbed another. It slipped from my hand, landed on the step of the ladder, and then finally hit the hardwood floor with a thud.

"You okay?" Becky asked, startling me from my thoughts.

"Yeah, I'm fine." I climbed down the steps and snatched the bottle of lotion from the white distressed flooring. The fucking floor where he'd kissed me. "Damn it!" It had been three days since his mouth had been on mine, yet my lips still burned from the touch.

Becky sat on the other side of the room on the floor, her brows knit together as she peered at me. "You sure?"

I forced a smile. "Yeah." But my insides twinged with guilt from not telling her what was going on. In the twenty years we'd known each other, John was the first man I'd ever kissed that she didn't know about.

"What should I do next?" she asked, and I glanced over my shoulder before climbing up the ladder again.

"How about the cold-pressed soaps? There are a couple of cases over in the corner."

She nodded and pushed herself off the floor.

It felt wrong keeping secrets from Becky, but at the same time, I didn't want the questions. Not while John still worked under the same roof. I'd eventually tell her as I always did. I just wanted to do it when he was a safe distance away, so she didn't fill my thoughts with dreams.

She grabbed a box from the corner and carried it over to the two-tiered display in the center of the shop. "Anyone coming to interview today?"

I turned my back to her and began stacking lotions on the highest shelf. "The lady who does placenta encapsulations. She's coming at noon."

Becky made a gagging noise behind me and I grinned.

"That's so gross, Tuesday. Why would people do that?"

I laughed, finally finding the comic relief I needed, and looked over my shoulder, but my eyes locked on John standing in the doorway.

I instantly sobered. My heart flip-flopped in my chest, and I forced my eyes over to Becky. "They help replenish the mother's hormones after birth." My voice was flat, my cheeks incredibly heated, and I hadn't realized until that moment, but I'd missed him. I knew nothing about him, but seeing his face just now was like breathing air for the first time after a long tunnel... and having your wish come true.

Becky narrowed her eyes, obviously noticing my fluster. "I don't care what it does." She rose to her feet. "I wouldn't take placenta pills if you paid me." She turned to John and lifted her chin. "How about you? Are you into placenta?"

He stepped forward and held out his hand. "I don't think we've met. I'm John Eaton."

She smiled. "Becky. And you didn't answer the question."

He grinned a little and glanced at me. "No, I'm not into placenta." But the way he said it, with his voice lowered a little, and his eyes searching mine—I couldn't breathe.

I swallowed then turned to my display and continued stocking lotions on the shelf. I hated that he could affect me like this. He was a player, someone I needed to stay away from, yet my body wasn't listening to what I was throwing down. It wanted him, and the tiny flutters all the way to my toes were only one of the signals.

He moved to lean against the counter next to me, his tool belt resting perfectly over his narrow hips, and his forearm flexing as he braced himself there. He grabbed a cookie from the plate and took a bite.

I cleared my throat and looked over. "Did you need something?"

He shook his head. "Just expecting a friend."

"Oh." I nodded and continued to work. But I was irritated—and it was becoming increasingly difficult to swallow. He hadn't come out here in two days, yet here he was with the gall to show himself looking like *that*. His t-shirt stretching across his broad chest, his beard all shadowy and accenting his manly jaw, and his lips—a shade of pink that would make any girl jealous, but somehow looking absolutely perfect on him. The way he looked every day.

I peered at him, frustrated by all of it. "Those are lactation cookies," I muttered.

His face contorted with disgust, and I couldn't help but smirk with satisfaction. I wasn't being fair. I was mad at myself, not him.

He spit the contents of the cookie into his napkin and coughed slightly. "Did I just eat placenta?"

I giggled at the thought then attempted to stifle the growing laughter with my hand. "N-no. Just oatmeal and brewer's yeast." But it wasn't working.

He grinned slightly, wiping his face with the back of his hand, then picked up another cookie.

The bell at the front door jingled and I turned around. A tall brunette with short hair walked inside, and I instantly began climbing down the ladder.

"Can I help you?" I asked. But John pushed himself off the counter and walked toward her. Her smile widened as he pulled her into his big, strong arms. My lungs deflated and I leaned against the shelf for support.

Her figure was stunning, curvaceous, held with the confidence I'd only seen from movie stars. She wore big Hollywood glasses, a pencil skirt, and reminded me of

Marilyn Monroe. And there was one thing that was certain: she wasn't the placenta lady.

He turned around to face me. "Em, this is Tuesday Patil. Miss Patil, this is my friend Em..." But his voice trailed off a bit, and he looked at me with uncertainty.

I cleared my throat, suddenly feeling sick, but held my hand out to shake anyway. "Nice to meet you," I said, but I could barely hear my own voice, barely hear hers as she repeated my words and shook my hand.

We made small talk for a few minutes. She asked about my products and complimented me on the shop, but I couldn't focus beyond the fact that John had kissed me only days before. Yet, here he was, with another woman in *my* shop, flaunting her in front of my face.

"So where are you two off to?" Becky asked, coming to stand by my side.

"Probably Donovan's. I've been craving their fries for weeks," Em replied. "Have you ever had them?"

Becky smiled and shook her head. "No, but I'll put them on my list."

We stood there a minute longer, all four of us, and said nothing. The air became thick as a fog, and John eventually took his tool belt off and placed it on the counter. "Well, I guess we should get out of here. Then he turned to me, his eyes asking a thousand questions. "I'll be back in a few hours."

"Have fun." I turned back to the shelf and started working.

"It was nice meeting you," Em said, but I only nodded, too shaken to turn around again.

The door jingled at their exit. Becky walked over to me and rested her hand on the small of my back. "Okay, tell me what's going on. And start at the beginning."

* * *

When he came back later that afternoon, I was in my office, wasted. I'd spent over an hour spilling my guts to Becky, filling her in on every moment, every touch that John and I shared that I'd kept a secret... And I cried.

I don't know if it was because of stress from everything going on, or the relief of finally sharing it with her, but it was something I swore I wouldn't do, yet I found myself blubbering on the shoulder of my best friend as I confessed to her about a boy. A boy who had kissed me so good I almost believed in fairy tales again. Almost.

To my surprise, she hadn't given me advice as she usually did. She asked me what I wanted—which would normally be the response I craved—yet I couldn't form an answer. I didn't *want* to figure this out on my own, but she was no help at all.

She'd left over an hour earlier, and still, I didn't know what the hell I was going to do.

I stared at the screen on my desk, tapping my fingers on the hard surface, searching my mind for answers... but I found nothing. I knew I didn't have time for a relationship, nor the energy... but I still wanted him. I wanted him to be mine, but it was like trying to make a home for a whale inside a bathtub. He didn't fit the mold I had for him. He was too big, too much, too... I didn't have the words for it.

When John entered the room, I didn't even look up. I didn't acknowledge his presence at all, just continued typing at my computer, hoping he'd eventually take the hint and leave.

He didn't. He didn't seem bothered by my ignoring him at all and leaned against the doorway, examining his fingernails.

I clenched my jaw and continued adding items to my online cart. He was irritating, and even though I desperately wanted to give him the cold shoulder, he was making it impossible to work.

I pushed my glasses to the bridge of my nose and cleared

my throat. "Can I help you with something?" My tone held an inflection you'd expect of a sales clerk.

He glanced over, taking his sweet ass time before answering. "I was just wondering when we were going to address the elephant in the room."

My heart hitched and I moistened my lips. "If you're talking about the cookies□"

He smirked. "You know God damn well it's not about the cookies." He turned to face me, his legs braced apart and face sober. "I'm talking about the fact you've been giving me the cold shoulder ever since I kissed you two days ago."

His voice was deep, layered with an urgency I didn't understand. A thousand excuses tickled my tongue, but none of them convincing enough. I pushed myself from my seat, crossed the room before I knew what I was doing, and stood in front of him. Practically nose to nose. "How can you kiss me like that one day, and bring another woman into my shop the next?"

I hadn't meant to ask the question. It let on too much about how I felt, but it was too late. His brow lifted and his eyes bored into mine. He didn't speak for a moment, just searched my face, causing all the insecurities inside me to shake.

"Is that what this was about?" His voice was softer, kinder, but held a hint of gravel that twisted my stomach.

I shook my head and tried to leave the room, realizing this conversation was going nowhere good, but his hand on my arm stilled me.

"She's just a friend, Tuesday."

His eyes were deep and searching, causing my hopeful heart to squeeze. "Did you bring her here to make me jealous?"

One of his brows lifted. "Are you?"

It was a ridiculous question; one there was no point in answering. I turned to leave again, but he held me tighter.

"She's a friend who needed someone to talk to. That's it." Then he dropped his hand, allowing me to leave, but there was an edge to his voice that made me look up.

Here was my chance to go, to put the distance between us, but my heart was caught in quicksand—uncontrollably sinking. I found myself wanting to help, even though I didn't know what was wrong. "Is everything okay?" My voice wavered, but for once I didn't care.

He shook his head and looked up to the ceiling. "It's her story to tell, not mine." Then his gaze settled on me again. "You haven't answered my question."

I backed up a step, finding the wall at my feet. "What question?"

"Are you jealous?"

I looked away, annoyed by the fact he was pushing me like this. "Why do you even care?" My chest heaved as I pulled in a breath. "Does it give you pleasure, knowing I want you? That everyone does? So you can add another notch to your bedpost?"

His jaw constricted, but he didn't speak.

"My being jealous has nothing to do with us. How I feel about the women you go out with doesn't matter. You're my employee, that's it."

He stepped toward me, causing the air to deflate from my lungs. "I'm not your employee." His voice was firm, filled with a gravel that overwhelmed my stomach with tiny flutters. "And how you feel has everything to do with this." His eyes raked over my face, down to my mouth, and then up to my eyes again. "If my working here is a problem, I'll walk out that door right now and tell Jake to find someone else."

A knot formed in my throat. All of a sudden, the one thing

I thought I wanted sounded like my worst idea ever. I didn't want him to stop working for me. I couldn't stand the thought of never seeing him again. "W-why would you do that?"

He looked at me for a second, not moving, then he took a step backward. "Because." He paused for so long I thought he was finished, but then he spoke again. "Because there's something between us, Tuesday. Something I haven't felt in a long time. And judging by the way you kissed me, you feel it too."

I shook my head and swallowed. "I didn't kiss you. You kissed me."

The corner of his mouth lifted in a smile. His voice lowered, soft and rough at the same time... A voice just for me. "You kissed me, Tuesday. You kissed me so good I haven't been able to stop thinking about it. Not with your mouth, but your whole body. Every part of you was in that kiss, and I want more. "

My eyes widened. Never in my life had I been spoken to like that. So brazenly honest, not hiding an ounce of the truth. It did something to my insides that made me want to kiss him again. "What do you want from me?"

I wasn't sure what I wanted to hear, but I needed more time. I needed time to think, time to figure out how to get out of this mess...or decide if I wanted out at all.

He leaned against the counter, crossing his feet out in front of him. "I think you know what I want."

I swallowed. I knew I should leave, but my feet were glued to the floor— and my eyes, they were transfixed on a man who just admitted, not for the first time, that he wanted me. Blood rushed to every part of my body, and my mouth fell open.

"The way I see it," he continued, "I can walk out of this office, and we can never talk about this again, or"—his eyes held onto mine, taking them captive in his deep, seductive gaze—"we can stop denying this attraction, and you can meet me after work tonight. But I'll warn you Tuesday, if you were one of my sisters, I'd tell you to run. You deserve better than I'll ever be able to give you, but the thing is, I'm too goddamned selfish not to ask."

His eyes never left mine, his face serious as he watched for my reaction.

On the one hand, I was pretty sure I should be offended. He just admitted he wanted me—maybe only for sex. But on the other hand, maybe it wasn't the worst idea in the world. I had needs, needs I was certain he could take care of, and he was offering himself to me on a golden platter.

One of the guys called from the back room, and my heart jumped to my throat. In the midst of this heated conversation, I forgot we weren't alone. Which was a good thing in the moment... I didn't know what would happen if we were. John looked over his shoulder, calling back that he'd be there in a minute then met my eyes again.

"Yes or no, Tuesday?"

Every nerve in my body was on fire, but my brain must've been full of cotton wool, as the only word I could think of was, "Yes."

He nodded then but didn't smile, just pushed himself off the counter again and headed for the back room. "I'll pick you up at your place at seven."

I shook my head and fisted my hands at my sides. "I'll meet you here."

His brows furrowed, seeming bothered by my reluctance to invite him home, but eventually he nodded. "Seven."

Then he walked out of the room, closing my office door behind him, and I hid my face in both hands. "What did

you just do, Tuesday? What have you done?"

CHAPTER SEVENTEEN

tuesday

* * *

Whiskers weaved in and out of my legs by my closet, causing me to stumble as I pulled a long, bohemian skirt from its hanger. "Ooof!" He fell to his side, looked up with pathetic green eyes, and mewed.

I frowned and crouched down to my haunches to scratch him behind the ears. "I'm sorry, buddy."

He began to purr, rolled to his back, and started rubbing himself against the carpeted floor, ignoring me.

I pushed myself to stand, feeling guilty about rushing out of the house so quickly when Whiskers had been left alone all week. But he'd always been a loner, and I wasn't sure he'd notice my absence anyway.

Which reminded me. I grabbed a dark brown halter from the top of my dresser and pulled it over my head before I walked down the hall, sliding my skirt to my hips. The best thing about wearing only a B cup was that a nice cotton spandex was all the support I needed.

Whiskers' bowl sat on the mat by the breakfast table, and I filled it with two scoops of kibble. Then out of guilt, I opened the fridge and added a few pieces of tofu on top. John would be back at the shop any minute, so I really had to go, but already my stomach was filled with nervous flutters.

I should have said no, but I couldn't. All the reasons and excuses I'd come up with since I met him weren't good enough anymore. I wanted him. I wanted this, and as hard as it was for me to admit, there was something between us that was beyond my understanding. Even though I'd never done anything like this before in my life, a part of me knew I'd regret it if we didn't explore it.

I leaned against the wall to pull on my sandals, thinking about that afternoon. The fact that he would walk out on work because of how I felt about the situation still rocked me. I searched my mind for any man who'd ever cared that much, was willing to give up something—*anything*—like that for me... but I couldn't, not even my own father.

Something pulled at my heart strings a little bit. Something I didn't have a name for. I only met him six weeks ago, and for half of that I couldn't even stand him. Yet here I was, getting ready for a night that was pretty much guaranteed to lead to sex. I wasn't sure how I felt about that. All I knew was the thought of seeing him again sent a shiver up my spine and caused goose bumps to cover my whole body.

I grabbed my bag and keys from the top of the bar, and Whiskers turned to look at me.

"It's just a date. I'll be back in a few hours."

He tilted his head slightly, as if knowing that wasn't the full truth. I paused at the couch and scratched him behind the ears before opening the door. "It's nothing. It'll be fine."

* * *

John was sitting in the bed of his truck when I pulled into the lot. Exactly as he had the afternoon he kissed me, but this time he was waiting for me. I was ten minutes late, which already had my nerves on edge, but the sight of him wasn't helping matters. Seeing him again was like pulling in a lung full of crisp clean air after climbing a tall mountain. It sent goose bumps to run the length of my body but filled me with a sense of satisfaction that overwhelmed me. It didn't seem possible, but he was becoming more and more attractive the longer I knew him.

He wore the same style of jeans I'd seen him in almost every day, though these were a little darker. Maybe a little newer. His face was clean-shaven, his hair freshly styled, and his soft, blue button-up shirt was stretched across his broad shoulders and rolled up to his forearms.

I took a deep breath and climbed out of my cab. My heart was beating harder and faster with every step, but I kept moving toward him.

His eyes raked over me, taking me in, then came to a stop on my face. "I was beginning to think you changed your mind."

A knot formed in my throat, tight and constricting. "It was touch and go for a while, but I didn't want to make things awkward between us in the morning."

He laughed then shook his head and looked down to his feet. He was beautiful, sinfully good looking—maybe more so because he got my sense of humor. He was the type of guy I would normally deny myself. But here I was with my heart in my throat as I walked toward the devil, and it felt amazing. I inhaled deeply as I came to stand in front of him. The smell of him, even though faint, left me intoxicated. I loved the scent of him. So clean, masculine, and raw.

I came to rest on the tailgate, not sure what was supposed to happen next. I'd never had a relationship like this before. One that was purely about enjoying each other and nothing more.

"So, how do you feel about animals?" he asked.

I turned to him. "That depends, what kind?"

His chin tipped up as he looked over at me. "Lions, tigers,

bears. That kind of thing."

"Do you want to watch the Wizard of Oz?" I laughed.

"Nah." He rose to his feet and stood in front of me. "I have a buddy who works at the zoo and they need some help. I thought maybe you'd like to go with me?"

I cleared my throat, then waved my finger between the two of us and shook my head. "We can do this later... I mean, if you have to help your friend."

He grabbed my hands and pulled me to my feet. "I want you to go." His voice was soft but didn't waver in the slightest.

I chewed on my inner cheek and nodded. "Okay."

The corner of his mouth lifted, and he began to walk backward, pulling me in the direction of the passenger side of his truck. "Good," he said. His thumbs brushed softly over my knuckles before he opened the door. He took my arm and helped me get settled in my seat, then pulled down the seat belt and leaned over my lap to fasten it.

He looked at me. "I was afraid that if I let you leave tonight, I'd never get you out here again." His voice was low, almost a whisper, and sent goose bumps down my legs.

He finally closed the door, and I took a long, calming breath before placing my keys in the side pocket of my bag. He climbed in beside me then threw his arm over the back of my seat and looked over his shoulder to back out of his space.

"So," he asked, finally pulling out to the street, "what do you do for fun, Tuesday Patil?"

I grinned at his use of my last name and turned to face him. "Let's see." I pressed one finger to my lips. "I make soap, lotions, body butters, and when I'm feeling especially daring, I go to the post office at closing time with my truck full of packages." I met his eyes in the rearview mirror. "Really... work is my life." I shrugged. "What about you?"

His brows furrowed, and he glanced over at me. "You don't do anything for fun?"

I shrugged. "Not really. Not what normal people think is fun anyway." I looked out the window. "But I love what I do."

"Why's that?"

I shifted in my seat, feeling slightly uncomfortable. "Are we playing twenty questions?"

"I just want to get to know you, that's all."

His eyes met mine, and the honesty I saw there made my breath hitch. He genuinely looked interested, which surprised me. He admitted to wanting me for sex, which was pretty clear, so why would he bother with this? It was something you'd ask of someone you cared about, not someone you planned to leave behind in a couple of weeks.

He lifted one brow, and I realized I hadn't answered.

I looked out the window again. "I've loved the smell of things since I was a little girl. That's how it all started. The smell of concrete after a storm, laundry drying in the summer sun, fresh cut grass, and children covered in dirt."

He laughed, and I grinned a little at how ridiculous it all sounded.

"And I've always had a more sensitive nose than everyone else. I can tell the variety of an apple without cutting its skin. I can tell you who walks in the door without opening my eyes... In wine tasting, I would be called a sommelier. In life... I'm pretty much a freak." I grinned. "But just like wine, everything has its own unique scent." *Like you, for instance.*

I closed my eyes and tried to concentrate on my story. "When I was five, I used to sit in my mother's bathroom in our RV and mix up all the different oils and lotions I could find. First, it was out of curiosity, but then I realized that by blending two scents together I could make something altogether new. For a while, my mother got angry and told me not to do it anymore. But eventually, when she realized I wasn't going to stop, she began teaching me how to use them.

"I started blending my own formulas by ten, mixing things my mom said wouldn't work—but I did it anyway—because it made sense to me. Sometimes, when two polar opposites meet, it creates magic ..." I looked over at him, wondering if it could be the same for us. He was all wrong for me... but under the right circumstances, circumstances like these... I turned back to look out the window again.

"Eventually, my formulas started selling more than my mother's." I shrugged. "Customers began asking for me at markets, and my business took off from there. Five years ago, I began selling on Etsy. Mom didn't approve, so we went our different ways. She's always hated technology. She doesn't even have a cell phone, no TV, no Internet.

"But one thing she warned me against was true. Selling online took the person out of the product... the face away from my customers. In a way, the absence of a face is the reason I'm opening my shop. It got kind of lonely working from home after a while."

I cringed, realizing I'd spilled my guts again, and I looked down to my hands. "So now that you know about my whole childhood, want to tell me about yours?"

He glanced over, one brow arching. "Absolutely not."

I took the strand of my feathers in my hair and started fiddling. "Why not?"

His eyes shifted back to the road and he grinned slightly. "I was nothing but trouble, Tuesday, I can tell you that much." He sighed then glanced over at me. "Okay, what do you want to know?"

I chewed my lip, charmed by his easy way. "You said you had sisters?"

"Three." He looked over. "And when did I tell you that?"

I laughed. "When you warned me to run away from you."

The corner of his mouth lifted, and he turned back to the road. "You didn't listen."

I lifted one shoulder. "I rarely do."

"I noticed that about you."

"Noticed what?"

"You're stubborn."

I arched one brow. "There are people in this world who would agree with you." I cleared my throat. "So are you close?"

He met my gaze out of the corner of his eye. "Me and my sisters? Yeah, I guess we are."

"Are you the oldest?"

He shook his head. "No. Youngest."

I made a face and looked at him again. "That's surprising."

"Why's that?"

"Because you seem so protective."

He laughed but didn't say more, and I didn't either.

We rode the rest of the trip in silence, but surprisingly, it wasn't so bad. Well, besides the heart-pounding, blood-rushing, spine-tingling thing he did to my body, but I was getting used to it... kind of.

When we pulled into the zoo parking lot ten minutes later, we were one of only five cars in the lot. We pulled into a space in the very front, and he shoved the truck in park and came around to open my door. I took his offered arm and jumped down to the pavement. "So what kind of job are you doing here, anyway?"

He took my hand and began leading me to the entrance before he spoke. "Jake and I worked a job here a few years ago. They're having some kind of issue with a gate at the elephant exhibit. It shouldn't take too long." He was walking so fast I had a hard time keeping up, but I couldn't help my smile. This was kind of exciting. An elephant exhibit? It sounded like something out of a movie.

The entrance was just as I remembered it. Enormous stone steps, palm trees, and a, three-story high metal gate, with the words "Los Angeles Zoo" lit up on the top like a Christmas tree.

The security guard nodded and smiled as we approached the gate, but didn't ask any questions before opening the door to letting us enter.

"Do you know that guy?" I asked, slightly awed by our red carpet entrance.

He laughed. "I told you I used to work here."

But I knew it was more than that. John left an impression wherever he went. People liked him. No, people flocked to him... and I was starting to realize why. He was fun to be around—addicting.

John never slowed as he led me up two flights of stairs to the main level, past the sea otters and an alligator named Reggie, then finally to the very heart of the zoo. A man in khaki clothing was waiting for us.

"John." He came toward us to shake our hands. "I know this was last minute, but we didn't know who else to call on such short notice. I hope we didn't ruin your evening." He looked me up and down and frowned.

"Nah." John squeezed my hand. "But I did promise her dinner. If Marco could fire up the grill when we're done, I'd sure appreciate it."

The other man nodded. "If you can help us with this problem, we'll give you anything you want."

Ten minutes later, practically out of breath from moving so fast, we made it to the lookout of the elephant exhibit. A crew of people was huddled around talking, and John turned to me. "I'm going to go get filled in. Will you be okay over here?"

I straightened, taking in the sight of the large elephant enclosure I'd never seen before. "Yeah, I'll be fine."

He left me over by the info booth, and I settled in, resting my back against a support beam of the bamboo arbor. The exhibit was huge, spanning what I guessed to be five acres wide in both directions. Large eucalyptus trees grew along the edge of the exhibit, and play structures with tires and other elephant things were scattered around the ground. But in the far corner of the large space was a lone elephant, crying into the night as it pushed against a far gate.

I looked over at John, wondering what was going on, and found him in a group of at least ten others. He was dressed so differently but fit in nevertheless—as though he was supposed to be there. His hands were stuffed deep into his pockets, and his brows were creased with profound concentration.

I couldn't pick up on all that was being said, but it appeared the gate to the west of the lot was stuck, separating the mother elephant from her baby calf. Even from a mile away, trumpeting cries from the mother could be heard echoing across the dirt-covered lot, causing my heart to ache.

I bit my lip, listening from afar about all that had been tried. John was their last option before tranquilization, and from all their talk, it seemed large mammals didn't handle anesthesia well. They discussed various options for at least ten minutes, then finally, John turned to me and held up one finger, letting me know he'd be right back. He climbed into a nearby jeep with some of the crew and headed in the direction of the closed gate.

I twisted the strap of my bag at my shoulder, feeling anxious as I watched the mother try to push open the gate with her large body. Her cries shook me with their desperation, and I closed my eyes briefly.

One of the crew who'd been talking to John a moment before must have noticed my distress, because when I opened my eyes again, he was standing by my side.

"They'll get it open, don't you worry."

I bit my lip again, blinking back the tears that threatened to spill over. "It's heartbreaking, isn't it?"

He looked about sixty, and between his teeth, he held a sprig of fresh grass. He turned around in the direction of the exhibit and leaned against the post opposite me. "She'd kill herself trying to get to that calf." He pulled the stalk of grass from his mouth and used it to point toward the enclosure. "That's why it's such an emergency. That baby is fine. There are people behind that gate who'll take care of her, but that mama won't stop. Even if it means her own demise." He made a clicking sound with his tongue. "A mother's love is an extraordinary thing..."

His voice trailed off, and I found myself nodding in agreement, but I was barely listening. My eyes were locked on the mother as she pushed on the gate. I wiped my hands over my eyes, my throat tightening, and my nose beginning to burn. I'd never seen anything more devastating in my life.

A few minutes later, the man with the grass in his mouth gestured to the exhibit with his chin. "Isn't that your boy out there?"

I turned around, and clear as day, saw John walking along the cement wall at the back of the exhibit. The one that flanked the side of the gate that was stuck. Another man mirrored him on the other side and both scaled slowly closer until they lowered to their bellies and began working at the hinges of the gate.

But whatever they were doing wasn't working, and the mama elephant was growing increasingly anxious. She was almost in a frenzy with their being so close to her baby, and all I wanted to do was call to John and tell him to come back. This was far too dangerous. That mother was out of her mind, and John looked so tiny out there next to her.

Then he threw his legs over the back of the wall and climbed along the opposite side of the gate. The mother began to push and push from the other side. Harder and harder, causing him to shake. I clenched my jaw, gripped my hands tighter on my strap, but there was nothing I could do but watch. I wasn't even sure he'd hear me if I called out a warning.

The mother continued to ram into the gate, harder and harder, then all of a sudden the gate sprang free and slammed against the far wall. John never lost his grip. His head whipped back at the impact of the door opening, but he didn't fall.

The baby calf ran out to her mother, pressing her small body against large, protective legs. Cries from both of them mingled in the air as John climbed up the gate again and seated himself at the top of the cement wall.

I wiped at the fat tears that landed on my cheeks and let out a shaky breath, still recovering from the adrenaline rush. That had to have been one of the most emotional things I'd ever witnessed. I turned around, meeting the eyes of the crew member, the blade of grass still pressed between his teeth as he nodded.

He lifted his chin to the other side of the exhibit and nodded. "Some guy you got there."

I turned around and my eyes found John. He waved to me

across the exhibit, and I nodded. "Yeah. He really is."

CHAPTER EIGHTEEN

tuesday

* * *

An hour later, we walked down the large, paved hill to the main level of the zoo. But John didn't hold my hand this time. We walked side by side, a little slower than before, and occasionally his arm hit the fabric of my skirt. I wasn't sure if he did it on purpose, or if it was by accident that he touched me, but after witnessing all that happened with the elephants, I was ten times more aware of every move he made.

He looked over at me and smiled, the expression on his face sending a shiver all the way to my toes. "I'm so high right now." He raked both hands over his face and bit his lip. "I almost cried when that calf made it back to her mama."

I took a deep breath and nodded. "I *did* actually." I didn't usually share things like this with others, but for some reason, after all that, I felt closer to him than ever.

He looked at me sideways, his nose wrinkling slightly at my admission. "Are you in a hurry to get back?" He moved in front of me then spun around and walked backward, waiting for my answer.

I shook my head, adrenaline mixed with sexual tension burning my skin. "No, I'm in no hurry."

"Good." He grabbed my hand, and before I knew what he was doing, he ducked under an overhanging branch and began leading me down a narrow, darkened path. "Let's go see who's awake."

I laughed and ducked down after him. This wasn't at all what I was expecting. "Are we even allowed to do this? Aren't they going to get mad at us?"

He shook his head and kept moving. "Nah, they owe me... Besides, I already told them I'd be giving you a tour." He looked over his shoulder and winked at me, but all I could focus on was keeping my skirt from tangling up my feet and moving fast enough to keep up with John and his incredibly long legs.

Soon we came out to a main path again, where the overhead lights illuminated the lush, tropical foliage that surrounded us. "Do you even know where you're going?" I asked, following after the man who was as joyful as a Peter Pan. His whole being oozed with a sense of life, and I wanted to suck it all in, bottle it, and save some for later.

He turned down a little alcove, and I followed after him, realizing before long that we'd entered the gorilla habitat. We came to stand in front of the large window, and his hand that wasn't holding mine came up to press against the surface of the glass. "I wonder if he's awake."

"Who?" I asked in a soft, hushed voice.

He put a finger to his lips but didn't answer, just kept searching the dark enclosure for something.

I examined his profile in the dim lighting. One that was hard, chiseled, beautiful. Yet beyond that manly exterior was a much softer side to him. The side that wanted to cry at the reunion of a mother and her baby, that ran through the zoo with the excitement of a child. The man who stood beside me, his hand pressed to the glass, waiting...

My heart squeezed in my chest, and a ball of emotion rushed to my gut. I'd expected to be intimate with him tonight, but this was a whole different kind of intimacy. I didn't think I was ready for it.

He tugged me closer, put his arm around my waist, and then turned me until my back was against his chest. His head rested on the soft space between my neck and shoulder. "There, in the far corner," he whispered.

My heart was pounding so hard.

He was so close I could feel the vibrations of his voice, feel the soft whispers of his words as they brushed my ear. It was difficult to breathe with him so close, but in the distance, I could just make out the silver fur of one of the gorillas in the back of the exhibit. "I see him," I whispered. I wasn't quite sure why we were whispering, other than this was a purely magical moment, and I didn't want to mess it up.

His cheek came to rest next to mine. "That's George," he said.

I smiled slightly, though my eyes brimmed with tears at the way he said the name. Maybe because I felt he was sharing a piece of himself with me, and I wasn't exactly sure why. "How do you know that?" Goosebumps covered my body, and he pulled me closer, wrapping me in the warmth of his embrace. I inhaled, breathing in his intoxicating scent and going with it, even though my instincts were telling me to run. Just as he told me to in my office earlier.

"I spent every lunch break for an entire year right here, watching him."

I nodded, wondering how I had ever thought him shallow. How I ever thought he was just another asshole at a bar, when he was so much more than that.

Eventually, we made our way back to the front of the zoo, and the security guard handed us boxes of food he had waiting for us at his station. We carried them back to the parking lot, climbed into the cab of John's truck, and drove back to my shop in silence—but he held my hand the whole way.

* * *

A half hour later, parked in the very front of Simply Tuesday's, John unpacked the boxes on the bed of his truck. A veggie burger for me, and a double cheeseburger for himself.

He handed me a carton filled with my sandwich and an extra large order of fries. "I figured since you haven't had a donut in a year, a hamburger was out of the question."

I laughed, knowing he was completely right, and headed for the back of his truck. I pushed myself up to the tailgate, my heart twisting at the realization we were completely alone, and I let my legs dangle from the side as I unwrapped my burger.

I took a large bite, horrified when the whole leaf of lettuce came with it. It spilled from the corner of my mouth, and I pushed back just as John came around to the front of his truck to join me. He leaned against the tailgate, his brows lifted as I pushed the last bits of offensive greenery in my mouth. "Sorry," I said around a mouth full of food.

He arched one brow, and his shoulders began to shake.

I frowned, covered my lips with one hand, and put my burger down in the box. "Are you laughing at me?"

He shook his head and made a coughing noise before he finally gave in, gripped his stomach, and let his head fall back to his shoulders. "I'm sorry, I just wasn't expecting that."

"Expecting what?"

"For you to eat like a man," he said, throwing his head back with laughter.

I couldn't help it. I grabbed a fry out of my box and shoved it into his mouth.

"Hey!" he protested, but then I took another handful of fries and crammed them into his mouth again. We were both laughing now, and he pushed me to the bed of the truck, got on top of me, and held my hands over my head. His body straddled mine and he grinned like the devil, chewing and swallowing as he looked down at me.

My heart constricted, and my body tightened beneath him—neither of us was laughing anymore. I couldn't help but think about his kiss, what it did to my body, what his body was doing to me now. I wanted more of him. More than a night at the zoo. More than one heated kiss in a hardware store. I was ready.

His eyes shifted to my mouth and my lips parted. He was going to kiss me. My heart was in my throat, screaming for him to do it already. For him to kiss me again. But this time, I wouldn't stop it. I'd welcome it with open arms and take in every bit of him I could get my hands on.

His eyes remained on my mouth, as if he was trying to make his mind up about something. "Thanks for coming with me tonight," he finally whispered, then his eyes lifted, meeting mine once again.

My hair rubbed up and down against the bed of his truck as I nodded. "No, thank *you*. I wouldn't have missed that for the world."

He rolled off me then, causing confusion to surge over my body, leaving me chilled where his warmth had just been. I wasn't sure what was going on. He grabbed his food from the bed of the truck and started eating again, this time a good yard away from the truck. I tentatively sat on the edge of the tailgate, unsure what was happening between us, and took another bite of my burger.

We both ate quietly for the rest of our meal, bathed in an awkwardness that consumed the dark night, but I only finished a quarter of my burger. I was too nervous, too confused to eat more than that. He packed up his empty boxes in the brown bag then pulled his cell phone from his pocket. "Well, it's pretty late." He turned in the direction of my truck, and I couldn't help my heart from squeezing with rejection.

"Did I do something wrong?" I asked.

He shook his head, keeping his back turned while I searched my brain for what he'd said in the office, wondering if I had made the whole thing up. He shoved his hands deep into his pockets and glanced over his shoulder. "We both have work in the morning, Tuesday. It's almost midnight."

I hopped from the bed of his truck and turned my back. I closed the tailgate, unable to keep the words from spilling from my mouth. "Less than twelve hours ago you were telling me to run from you, and now you're running from me?" Why I felt so vulnerable I didn't know, but my voice shook with it. I felt it in my bones, in the blood that rushed to my neck and cheeks; there was no way I could hide it from him now.

He grabbed my arms, his touch the last thing I expected, and he turned me around to face him. "You did too much right, that's the problem."

Tears pooled in my eyes, but I forced my chin up to meet him. "I don't understand."

He looked back at me, his jaw clenched as his eyes bored into my soul. "I like you too much to just sleep with you."

I inhaled, my breath shaky. "Is that what this was to you?"

He looked away, over my shoulder to the dark empty lot. "I don't know what this was."

"Why?"

He shook his head, chuckling as he pulled me against his chest again. "Why do you need all the answers right now?"

My body tensed and I pushed away. I was tired of the

mixed signals. Tired of being some amusing little woman for him to laugh at. Yes, I was emotional, yes, I cried too damned much, but the last thing I wanted was him laughing at me. I turned away, deciding that maybe he was right, and we both needed to go to sleep. Separately!

I walked around to the side of his truck and yanked open the passenger door.

"Don't laugh at me, John. This may be funny to you, but it's not funny to me." I grabbed my purse from the floor and slammed the door, realizing too late that his hand had taken the full force of the blow.

"Oh my God!" I opened the door as quickly as I'd shut it, but John doubled over, holding his hand to his chest as he walked a couple of steps away.

"Fuck." He muttered under his breath.

I covered my mouth with my hand, completely disappointed in my lack of control. "I didn't mean to do that. I didn't mean—" I came closer. "Are you okay?"

He scrunched up his face and nodded, then leaned against the side of his truck, his head held back on his shoulders in pain.

I stood in front of him, my lip between my teeth as I took his hand in mine. "Here, let me."

He hesitated, but finally relaxed and let me turn it over.

I cringed at the sight of his bloody knuckles, already bruising and starting to swell. "I'm so sorry... I didn't mean—" I stopped because my guilt wasn't helping anything. "I have a first aid kit in the shop."

He looked into my eyes, and for whatever reason, something shifted between us. A mutual trust I wasn't quite ready to acknowledge. I turned around, hoping he would follow, and he did.

My heart leapt to my throat as I pulled my keys from the

zippered pocket of my purse, and my hands trembled as I unlocked the door and turned on the lights. I made my way to my office, John right behind me, and pulled the kit from the bottom drawer of my desk.

"Wait here," I said, patting the top of the desk before hurrying to the product floor. I grabbed a container of antiseptic salve then stopped by the kitchen and filled a small bowl with warm water. When I got back to the office he was still waiting for me, sitting on top of my desk in the relaxed way he did everything.

I opened up my kit and examined his hand again. The wound wasn't as deep as I had thought in the dark but still looked incredibly painful. I took a dampened cloth from the bowl and began to clean it. He didn't make a sound.

"I'm so sorry," I said again, my muscles tightening involuntarily as I dabbed his wound over and over. I was reminded of that first night at the bar, when he'd taken care of my foot and I'd run away, but now the roles were reversed.

I opened the tin of salve, took a small bit with my finger, and began spreading it across his knuckles. I could feel his eyes on me, and the same sexual tension that always floated between us filled the room. His other hand settled on my waist, gently pulling me toward him.

I knew I shouldn't let this happen, that I should run away as I had that night, but I didn't have the strength this time, and I let him pull me closer until his muscular thigh settled between the two of mine. My breathing deepened, but I kept my eyes focused on my task. I pulled a spool of gauze from the first aid kit and began to wrap it around his hand, while his other hand traveled down to rest on the small of my back. It was such a tiny movement, so subtle, but my whole body ignited like a torch.

I fastened the gauze with a bit of tape, closed my eyes, and pressed his bandaged knuckles to my lips. I could feel him watching me, knew we were crossing a line that could never be uncrossed, but I didn't care. I did it again, this time letting my lips linger a little longer than the last. I swallowed, fighting back an emotion that overwhelmed me, and then I stepped away.

He caught me at my waist and lifted my chin with his finger. He tilted my face up until we were both nose to nose, and there was no avoiding his gaze. "You're too good for me, Tuesday." His voice was gruff, but this time he didn't push me away. His lips came down on mine, hard and passionate, crushing my mouth with a beautiful pressure that floored me. His arms wrapped around my body, and he pulled me against his chest, supporting all my weight.

I wound my arms around his neck and didn't hold anything back. I gave him everything, wanting to take everything of his in return.

His tongue pushed into my mouth, filling me with the delicious taste I longed for. He felt so good, smelled so good, tasted so good...

I stepped closer, wanting every part of my body pressed against him, every part of his body pressed against me. He pulled away, just enough for his mouth to trail down my cheek.

"What are we doing?" he said between kisses.

I shook my head, letting my head fall back to give him better access to my neck. "What do you think?"

He groaned. "I don't want to hurt you."

I swallowed, not exactly sure what he meant, and pushed back so I could look into his eyes. "Why do you think you'll hurt me?"

"I don't know." He stared at me, his breath as heavy as mine.

I looked into his eyes, sensing a confusion I wished I knew more about. It may have been selfish, but I wanted a piece of him. Even if it was only one night, I wanted it. "Just be honest with me, John. That's all I want from you."

"Promise?" His eyes grew darker, searching my face with uncertainty.

I swallowed. "I promise."

He pressed his forehead to mine, but I felt his reservations. I trailed my hands down his back, causing his muscles to flex in reaction to my touch. "Maybe you'll be the one who's hurt by me. Did you ever think of that?"

His shoulders fell forward, and his lips came to rest at the crook of my neck.

I pulled in a breath and repeated the words he'd said to me in the office. "I want to stop fighting this. You make me feel good, and I make you feel good. We don't have to think about more than that."

He remained quiet, but I could feel him begin to relax. "Tuesday..."

I pushed my finger up to his lips, not wanting to hear another word. "Shhh..." I wrapped my arms around his neck and replaced my fingers with my mouth. "I don't want to talk anymore."

A deep groan filled the back of his throat, and he picked me up, flipping me around until my backside hit the top of the desk.

He shoved a stack of papers to the floor then pushed me backward until my shoulders were pinned to the hard surface. My hair spilled over the side, and his eyes bored into mine.

He only stared at me, while his hand trailed down the center of my body, lifted the hem of my shirt, and pulled it slowly up my abdomen and over my head. He bent down, pressing his lips against my collarbone, and I gasped. My body quivered with the sensation I'd wanted from the moment we met.

His kisses were like torture. A sweet, incredibly seductive torture I wanted more of. I let my head fall back, taking in the feel of his mouth against my skin. I couldn't believe I was letting this happen. That I was entering a relationship with no guidelines, with a man who was all wrong for me.

My hands trailed up and down his back, my chest rising and falling quickly as his warm breath found my mouth. His kiss was firm, his heavy body hard against mine, and I lifted my hips to shove my underwear and skirt to the floor.

I was ready to end this torture, ready to have him inside me. I reached to the buckles of my shoes, but quickly decided against it. I didn't have time for straps. I didn't have time for buttons either. I took both sides of his shirt and pulled as hard as I could. Buttons flew in every direction, and he stopped moving. He met my eyes again and lifted his brow. I pushed his shirt over his shoulders, completely turned on by the way he watched me. I yanked his sleeves down his arms until he was free of them, pressed my lips to his chest, and began working on the fastening of his pants. Before long, I had shoved them to the ground.

He took a condom from his wallet and rolled it over his length. He pushed me back to the desk, looking down at me with an expression that was both hard and soft. "You should be made love to on a bed of fucking roses." He yanked me down to the edge of the desk, his face heated. "But for some reason, you chose me."

He pushed inside me, and the force of his entry made me hold onto the desk. I knew when we stopped fighting this there would be passion, but the animalistic way we reacted to each other left me winded, yet begging for more.

His breath was hard, his eyes focused as he thrust into me again. He looked into my eyes, as if I was the one thing he wanted most in this world. That he would live for me, die for me, protect me. Then his hands trailed up and down my body, and I arched my back.

He moved again, this time slower, gentler, and I lifted my hips, forcing my body downward, pushing myself harder against him.

The way he made love was raw, open, exposed. He eased his way out then pushed inside me again. Watching me, taking me, in so many more ways than one. I sat up, needing his body closer to mine.

He wrapped his arms around my shoulders, supporting my weight when I curved my legs around his waist, taking every delicious stroke as his body moved with mine. We were one, rocking, moving, grinding until I pulled in one last breath, and let my body shatter to a million tiny pieces in his arms.

He rocked with me a few more times, faster and faster until I felt his release. We both collapsed back on the desk, my body taking all of his weight.

"Wow." My breaths came hard and broken.

He only nodded, pressing his forehead into the crook of my neck. The room was a thousand degrees but I didn't care. I looped my arms around his chest, squeezing him tighter as my body continued to roll with release. We stayed like that for a few minutes, just breathing, skin to skin... nothing else between us.

He kissed me one last time then pushed from the desk and excused himself to the restroom.

I rolled to my side, watching him pick up his clothes from the floor. My brows furrowed, and I sat on the edge of the desk when he closed the door. I wasn't sure what I should do now. Normally after sleeping with a man, we were in a bed. We'd cuddle for an hour and maybe go for round two, but he'd taken his clothes to the bathroom with him.

I found my top in the middle of the room and pulled it over my head. In the heat of the moment, I never once thought about how awkward this moment would be. The immediate after-sex awkwardness we were in now. I pulled the rest of my clothes over my body, picked up the stack of invoices from the ground, and began piling them neatly on the desk.

He'd been honest with me from the beginning, so why was I so nervous?

The office door creaked open a moment later, and I knew it was him, but I wasn't sure what to say. Thank you? That was great? Nothing sounded right, so I decided not to say anything at all.

He came to stand behind me then brushed my hair from my shoulders and kissed my neck. "You okay?"

I nodded, his touch taking my breath again, giving me back a bit of the confidence I'd had only a moment before. "You?" I turned around to face him.

His brow creased, and he shoved his hands into the front pockets of his jeans. "I'm fine. Better than fine." His eyes shifted to the desk and his lips lifted at the corner. "I was thinking, maybe we should keep this between us. Not tell the guys about what's going on."

My stomach twisted a little, even though it made perfect sense. They were his employees and didn't need to know about our *whatever this was* relationship. No one needed to know. But his request still stung.

I cleared my throat and forced a smile I didn't feel like giving. "Yeah, that sounds fine."

His brows furrowed. "I didn't mean it like that." He gripped the back of his neck and shook his head.

I turned to straighten the papers again and swallowed. "No, it's a good idea. No one should know. It makes total sense." I picked my bag up off the floor.

"I just thought it would be easier if they didn't know. That's all." He looked over his shoulder, clearly as uncomfortable as I was. "Do you need anything else before we go?"

I cleared my throat again, not sure how we'd gone from wild sex in the middle of my office to this awkward exchange. "Oh no. That was it." I chewed my inner cheek and looked down to his injured hand. "How does it feel?"

He made a fist then clenched and unclenched a few times before answering. "Fine." His eyes met mine again. "Thanks."

A minute later, we both stood outside Simply Tuesday's and I locked the front door. I twisted the keys around my fingers then turned to face him.

His hands were shoved deep into his pockets, and he was frowning again. "I had a good time tonight, Tuesday."

I nodded and hitched my bag higher on my shoulder. "Me too." I licked my lips, and looked toward my truck. He made me feel like I was in eighth grade and he was the boy I had a crush on. Not the grown up woman who should know that this was a bad idea...

He stepped toward me, making my heart jump to my throat. He lifted one hand and ran it along my cheek. "I'm not leaving until your truck starts. That's the most I can offer you and still sleep at night."

His hand wrapped around the back of my neck, urging me forward until our lips touched. It was a simple kiss. One with no pressure, no expectations; just soft lips that I had to close my eyes to feel better.

He let me go again, and I stepped away, my feet moving on muscle memory alone until I opened the driver's side of my cab.

My truck started on the first try, and I waved to him out the window as I pulled out of the parking lot, silently kicking myself the whole way home for not asking him to follow me.

CHAPTER NINETEEN

tuesday

* * *

I arrived at the shop extra early the next day. Not because of work, nor because I needed to get things done, but because I hardly slept a minute and couldn't stand my own thoughts any longer.

The only thing that distracted me, that ever calmed me, was work. It was something I could do without thinking, something I could get lost in, and I needed that today.

I don't know what I was thinking last night. That I could have sex with a man after a night like that and *not* fall in love a little bit? It was the best date I'd had in a long time—possibly ever. No, I was one hundred percent positive it was the best date I'd ever had in my life... The best sex I ever had in my life, and now I was supposed to go back to work and pretend nothing happened.

The crew's trucks were lined up in the parking lot like they always were, and like always, John's was the first. In the exact spot where we'd had our impromptu picnic last night.

I pulled in a breath, took the box of donuts from the front seat, and hopped down from my cab. I had to get through today. The next would be easier. And the next easier after that.

When I opened the door, John was standing at the register, his tool belt low on his hips as he examined one of my shelves. My heart leapt to my throat at the sight of him. I knew he shouldn't affect me so much, but he held a bottle of lotion in his hands, playing with it between his large fingers. "I was just looking at all your products."

He wasn't smiling now, and I wondered how long he'd been there, checking out my products and invading my space. I bit my lip, placed the box of donuts on the counter, and ran my hand through my hair. I wasn't sure what bothered me about him looking through my things. It was something I invited thousands of strangers to do on a daily basis, but somehow with John, I didn't like it. It made me feel exposed, as if he was seeing a part of me I wasn't ready to show him. Because he already took a piece of me last night, and I wasn't sure I could part with anything else just yet.

"They're named from song titles, book titles... Aren't they?"

I nodded, wondering how he'd figured that out so quickly.

His brow furrowed and he picked another bottle off the shelf. "Blister in the Sun. That's what you wear."

My throat constricted and I nodded. I wasn't sure why it mattered so much that he knew what scent I wore, but nevertheless... it did.

He moved closer, stopping at the counter to lift the lid on the donuts but didn't take one. "You okay?"

It was such a simple question, one that if asked by any other person would have meant nothing, but coming from him...

I closed my eyes and nodded. I knew exactly what he meant. He wanted to know if I regretted last night, if I wanted to take it back. But what was crazy, even though things had become awkward between us, even though I was worried my heart would break at the end of all this, I wouldn't take it back for the world. Not one second of it. I smiled a little. "I'm fine."

His lips lifted at one corner, but it was just enough—I knew he didn't regret it either. His eyes met mine again, and he took a donut out of the box. "Well, I better get to work."

I nodded, my throat tightening from the seductive way he looked at me. "Me too."

He opened the door to the back room and looked over his shoulder one last time before he pulled it closed again behind him. I placed my hand at my throat, drew in a deep breath, then took a glazed donut from the box. I bit into it, savoring the sweet, buttery texture, begrudgingly realizing he'd ruined me for life.

* * *

It was quarter to three when my last interview left for the day. Though it was as much an interview of me as it was for the vendors. I was the person they were entrusting with their products. The face to represent them, and my shoulders had been tense all day. It was a big decision, who I chose to consign at the shop. The decision could make or break me. Yet, I couldn't think clearly enough to focus on business...

I looked to the door leading to the back room, knowing John was only a hundred feet away, through a piece of wood that couldn't have been more than three inches thick. And somehow, even though I knew it wasn't possible, I could feel his energy surrounding me, wrapping around my body, and pulling me in his direction by the hips.

I picked up a locket off the counter, a sample that one of the local vendors had left for me, and began playing with it between my fingers. Flipping it open then clicking it closed. Over and over.

Becky was supposed to come in today, but she'd picked

up a last minute freelance job with a comic convention. I'd be lying if I told myself I wasn't relieved, because even though I was able to convince myself I could handle this, Becky would be harder to convince.

I was the girl who didn't just have a crush on Bobby Peterson in fourth grade like everybody else; I loved him. I loved his blond hair, his blue eyes, and the scar on his left knee. I was ruled by my emotions, and she knew it. Which was why she'd know, without me saying a word, that things had moved in a direction with John that would only lead to trouble. But I couldn't stop it... I didn't even want to. I was caught in the tide, and I didn't even want to fight my way out.

I clicked the locket closed and left it on the counter. I'd been avoiding the back room all day, but I couldn't let this craziness between us interfere with my shop. I may be willing to lose my heart in all this, but my shop was something that was far too precious to me.

His eyes locked with mine the second I walked through the door. He was working with a power saw, sweat glistening on his forehead and down his nose. His arm flexed as he held the heavy machinery, and we both paused as if years had passed since we'd last seen each other, instead of just hours.

I took a deep breath, recovering myself enough to move across the room and open the supply closet door. I needed shipping supplies, and I also needed distance from *him*. All he did was stand there and I was already breathless. *You'll give yourself away if you don't get this under control.*

I began gathering my supplies, cursing myself under my breath, and taking far longer than necessary—because I needed my heart to slow. I needed my breath even, so I could go out there again. I spotted a large box of padded envelopes on a high shelf, and I stood up on my tiptoes trying to reach them. I only touched them with my finger before the light shifted behind me; fading out, and then in again. I swallowed and lowered to my heels. I knew it was him even before I turned around.

He didn't say a word as he stood there, leaning against the door with his arms draped on the frame above him. I could have stared at him all day. Not just because he was the most beautiful man I'd ever seen in my life, but also because he looked at me like I was the most beautiful woman he'd seen in his.

He stepped toward me, slowly, without a care in the world, then both of his hands gripped the straps of my overalls, pulling me slowly but firmly toward him, until our bodies were pressed together. He lifted my chin with one finger and kissed me. But it wasn't just a kiss; our lips molded together and his tongue forced into my mouth. It was a kiss that made me feel needed, possibly more needed than I'd ever been in my entire life. My whole body melted, and his arm wrapped around my back, holding me tighter. He kissed me as if I were oxygen and he needed air, like he needed me for his own survival.

We both stumbled backward until I was pressed against the wall. He lifted me up, suspending me with the weight of his body as his kiss deepened. I couldn't stop it, nor did I want to. I didn't care that the crew was just outside the door. I didn't care if the whole world saw us, or if I ever breathed again because all I wanted was John. All I wanted was his mouth on mine, to feel his touch, to just be.

He pulled away a minute later, forcing space between us and lowering my feet to the ground. His head fell back to his shoulders and he groaned. "I've wanted to kiss you since you walked in that door this morning."

I swallowed, pulling in shallow, ragged breaths. His admission made my heart constrict. "Then why didn't you? This morning."

He looked at me and placed one finger on the tip of my nose, then trailed it down to my lips until he gripped my chin gently between thumb and forefinger. "Because I was trying to resist you. It's not working."

I smiled a little, and he dipped his head down one last

time to kiss my lips, though this time was softer, and I closed my eyes so I could feel it better.

Too soon he pulled away. He shook his head slightly then backed toward the door. His lips curved in a slight smile as he walked out of the closet.

"Get back to work!" I heard him yell a moment later.

I pressed my back against the wall, licked my lips, and played the scene over and over in my mind. Because this was a kiss I wanted to hold onto forever and ever.

* * *

I didn't come out of my office the rest of the afternoon, though purposefully I left the door open, just in case he wanted to kiss me again—but he didn't. He stayed busy renovating the back room, which was exactly what I *hired him* to do.

This was something I had to keep reminding myself. He was here because I'd hired him, he was here because I needed a workstation for making products, but I really, really wanted him to kiss me again.

Somehow, I was able to stay focused and get my work done for the night, but as the back room became quiet, my whole body tensed with anticipation.

He usually stayed behind to lock up with me. He or sometimes Eddie. But when he left, he always gave me a report of their progress. Every day. But today was quiet. Today I began to worry he'd left without saying goodbye.

Just as I pushed myself from my chair to go check, his large frame filled the doorway of my office. He was filthy from work, his tool belt still rested on his narrow hips. His arms stretched above his head holding onto the frame, which lifted his shirt just enough to show off his stomach. A smudge of dirt swept across his left cheek, and somehow, it made him look perfect. I don't know why the sight of him dirty, sweaty, and exhausted was such a turn on, but it totally was.

159

He looked me up and down without saying a word, without a smile, but his eyes penetrated my soul, speaking a kind of language only my heart knew how to speak. It caused my chest to swell with emotion and my palms to itch with the need to touch him.

I knew he wanted me. I could see it in his eyes. I hit save on the computer then rose to my feet and walked in front of my desk, but I didn't move closer. I didn't fully trust my legs to get me that far.

He looked over his shoulder then grinned a little. "It's been less than twenty-four hours, but I want you again. I've gone months without sex without having problem, but I sleep with you once, and I can't stop thinking about it. Why is that?"

His admission caused me to smile. "I don't know."

He frowned and moved a little closer. "But I want you in my bed. I want you slow, and maybe more than once. You okay with that?"

I bit my lip and looked down to my feet. He looked so serious, as if he were negotiating a business deal. But then I frowned because maybe he was. Actually, I knew that's what this was. A business deal. A no-strings relationship where my heart was held as collateral.

I could say no... I *should* say no... but I found myself looking him in the eyes and nodding in agreement in spite of my better judgment. I didn't care what this was. I wanted it. It was reckless, but I wanted it. I'd never been reckless before in my life. I did the safe things, the well thought out things, and for once in my life, I was feeling the need to take risks. Maybe it was because I'd already put my whole savings on the line with this shop. Or maybe it was because I couldn't bear the thought of ending it just yet. Yes, my heart was on the line, but I didn't care.

He pushed himself from the doorway, his brows furrowed, and I realized everything I'd just thought must have run over my face.

"Or we can go to your place if you want?"

I took a deep breath and shook my head. "Yours is good." I forced a smile and walked a little closer, worrying my lip with my teeth.

Somehow, his place seemed the safer option. Going to mine was giving him too much, and he already held a piece of the little girl heart that still hoped he'd fall for me too.

CHAPTER TWENTY

tuesday

* * *

I followed him to his condo, which was only about five miles from the shop, though in the opposite direction of my house. He directed me to guest parking thirty feet away, then pulled into his space in the garage. When he met me halfway through the parking lot, he took hold of my hand. He didn't smile, which I was becoming used to, but his expression wasn't angry either.

He looked as if he had as many reservations as me; he wasn't sure he should be doing this—that *we* should be doing this. But before long he nodded, as though silently making up his mind, and turned back to the building. He led me up the concrete steps, going faster than my short legs could keep up with. I would think he was in a hurry if it wasn't for the fact he'd led me through the zoo the very same way.

We finally stopped at the third floor, where he hesitated at the door. He turned to face me and cringed. "I have to warn you, she can be extremely jealous."

I looked into his dark, stormy eyes and swallowed, suddenly wanting to forget the whole thing. Wondering why he'd bring me here when his roommate was inside.

He pushed the door open and a ball of golden fur

immediately rushed toward us. She was wagging her tail, prancing and panting, and John fell to a squat before looking back up at me. "This is Ginger."

I smiled and let out a breath. Both in relief his roommate was an dog, and because Ginger obviously missed him a lot. It was adorable really, something that made him even more human, more real. "Is she a golden retriever?" I asked.

He nodded, but then Ginger, who was ignoring me until this point, started to bark. She was loud and intimidating for such pretty dog, and although she looked scared at the same time, she still stood in front of John like she would protect him with her life.

I shook my head and squatted down, holding my hand out so she could smell me. "Don't worry Ginger, I won't hurt him."

She came toward me, sniffing the air apprehensively, then walked closer until her nose touched my hand. She gave it a quick lick, then after a few moments, her tail began to wag and her stance softened. She licked me once more, and I reached out to scratch her behind the ears. When I finally looked over at John again, he was watching me with an unreadable expression on his face.

He stood up and grabbed her leash from the top of the banister before turning back to me. "I need to walk her or she won't leave us alone all night. You can wait here if you'd like."

But it didn't sound like a question. I nodded, only because it seemed like that was what he wanted me to do, and I walked farther into his condo.

Ginger began prancing at his feet, and he lifted his chin to gesture down the hall toward the kitchen. "I don't have much, but whatever's in the fridge, you're welcome to."

I smiled, nodded, then watched as Ginger led him out of the apartment. He closed the door behind them.

I found the braid of feathers in my hair and started twirling This was awkward. Being in his house alone. Being here at all. I turned around to the door again, wondering if I should have gone along with him, but he really looked like he hadn't wanted me to, and I wanted to respect his space. Walking a dog together was something a couple would do. Although I didn't know what to call what we were doing, a couple was definitely not it.

I shook my head, trying to figure out how I got myself into this mess, then turned toward the kitchen. His home was cleaner than I'd expected. I didn't think he'd be a slob or anything because he and his crew were pretty clean, but the dark wood floors were actually shining. There was also a faint smell of lemon, mixed with the telltale fragrance of John's intoxicating masculinity, floating in the air. I inhaled deeply, relishing the smell I couldn't get enough of.

The kitchen was simple. Stainless steel appliances, white cabinets, black counters. I opened the fridge out of curiosity but quickly closed it. There wasn't much in there besides old pizza and orange juice. I hadn't eaten all day, but I wasn't the least bit hungry. I was alone in his house, nervous as hell, plus, I really had to pee.

I headed in the opposite direction, looking for the bathroom. Searching for a glimpse of anything that would tell me a little more about him. A photo, a poster, a football jersey, but there was nothing. Nothing but a spotless house and a home decorated in a way that looked to have been done by a professional. Large prints on each wall—modern, abstract, nothing that reminded me of him. I don't know why, but it bothered me a little bit.

I walked past the bedroom that was furnished with a king-sized bed, an office with one desk, a laptop, and a pile of papers perfectly stacked and found the bathroom at the end of the hall.

By the time I was done with the bathroom, I was nervous again. I was sitting on the edge of the couch, trying to keep my leg from shaking, when I heard ringing. A landline phone that sat in the middle of the coffee table. I didn't have a landline myself, and for some reason, it surprised the hell out of me that John did.

Then I heard his voice blare through the speaker and realized that not only did he have a landline, he also had an answering machine.

"Hey, this is John, you know what to do."

BEEEEEEEP

"Shit!" I whispered to myself. Who the hell has a freaking answering machine? Then a woman's voice came through the speaker and I froze.

"Get off your lazy butt and answer the phone, John!"

My eyes widened, and I didn't know what to do. There was a pause, and I guessed she was waiting for him to answer, but there was no way in hell I was picking up that phone.

"Fine. Be that way."

I leaned forward to find the off button, but then she started talking again.

"I let Suzy in like you asked. Your house was a pigsty by the way, so I hope you're paying her well..."

The door opened and John walked in. I looked over, swallowing hard as blood instantly rushed into my face.

"...I was thinking about your little problem, and I think you should go for it. You only live once, and you just never know. Oh yeah, and I bought you underwear, which is probably a weird thing for your sister to do, but I was buying some for Tom, and well... It's time you started wearing them. Anyway, that's it. Call me back when you get home."

Click.

John unfastened the leash from Ginger's collar and looped

it around the banister. She pranced off in the direction of the kitchen, where I could hear her taking a drink of water, but I couldn't take my eyes off John, where he stood watching me but hadn't said a thing.

I pointed to the coffee table and cleared my throat again. "You have an answering machine."

He grinned and stuffed his hands into the front pockets of his jeans. "I like to screen my calls."

"Oh." I bit my lip to hide my smile. "Do you really not wear underwear?"

His eyes narrowed and he tilted his head. "You didn't notice?"

I pushed my hair behind my ear and stood. "You're avoiding the question."

He walked toward me and shrugged. "My boys like to fly free."

"Boys?"

He nodded. "We're kinda close."

I couldn't believe we were having this conversation—or that I was enjoying it so much, but I found myself enjoying everything I did with John, talking, touching, breathing.

"Did you notice, Tuesday?"

I shook my head, feeling the blood rush to my cheeks once more. "Well, it all happened so fast."

He nodded, stepping closer, and took my hand. "I think we'll go slower tonight."

He threaded his fingers through mine, turned around, and started walking down the hall.

"You *think*?" I laughed.

He pulled me into the bedroom and closed the door.

"Yeah. I'm afraid that's all I can promise right now. I've never wanted anything more in my life, and I don't know how this is going to go."

The way he said it made my stomach flutter. He was so stinking adorable; I couldn't help myself from grinning like an idiot. He looked at me like he was a little boy in a candy store, and I was his favorite variety.

He pulled his shirt over his head and threw it in the hamper. "If I was patient, I'd take a shower, offer you dinner, and make you a drink, but I've never been a patient man, and I've already reached my limit today." He stepped closer, wrapped his arms around my waist, and pressed his lips to my neck. "I hope you like it dirty."

My knees went weak. Oh my God. He had barely touched me but my panties were already soaked. My back fell against the wall, he closed the gap between us, pinning my hands above my head, and I wanted to scream. *Yes! I like things dirty! Hard, sloppy, anything—as long as you're the one doing it.* But his lips were moving down my throat, stealing my breath, and all the thoughts slipped right out of my head.

His hands came to the bib of my overalls, unfastened each clasp, and let them drop to the floor. Without removing his lips from my body, he lifted me in his arms, carried me over to the bed, and lowered me to the mattress. "God, you're beautiful." He unfastened the button of his jeans, and I pulled my shirt over my head.

He said he'd lost patience, but I was worse. Never in my life had I wanted sex as badly as I wanted it now. I wanted him to touch me, to have him on top of me, to have him inside me.

He discarded his pants on the floor, sans underwear, and I lifted my eyebrows to let him know I noticed. And boy did I notice. He pulled a condom from the top drawer of his nightstand, grinning as he crawled up the mattress. He was perfect. Sexy as hell, funny, and even though the lights were still on, he made me feel so comfortable I didn't try to shield my body even once. I felt beautiful when he looked at me.

He climbed over me, pushed my panties down my legs so nothing but skin was between us. Warm, dirty, delicious skin. I opened my legs, allowing his hips to settle between my thighs, and his expression hardened a bit. "I was wrong, Tuesday. I can't go slow."

His mouth found mine again, and his tongue plunged inside with an urgency that made me cry out.

His hand wedged between our bodies, and his fingers moved down, slowly, until he found me wet, slick, and ready. He groaned into my mouth then lifted his hips, positioned himself at my entrance, and pushed inside.

I arched my back, determined to take all of him. His head came to rest on my shoulder, and I grabbed his arms, kissed his neck, tasting the sweat, his salty skin, and him. The him I couldn't get enough of. The him I would take any way I could. I didn't even care that he hadn't taken a shower, that we were both dirty from a long day of work. In some way, it made things hotter, sexier, knowing that he wanted me so much that even a shower was too much time to ask.

He slammed into me, making me cry out from the force of it. He did it again, over and over, ravaging me, causing waves of pleasure to echo from the walls of my body. His fingers came between us, massaging me, adding more pressure, pushing me closer to the edge of a crazy, primal release. His thumb found the nub at my center, adding the perfect amount of pressure to my clit. His teeth sunk into my shoulder, and his body stiffened—and—and—I lost it.

Everything shattered inside me, my legs began to shake, but I forced them to hold on just a second longer. He pressed into me one last time then stilled, heavy, warm, dirty, and perfect...

I pulled in a breath, then another, and my shoulders

relaxed into the mattress a little more with each wave of my orgasm. Until my body became...thoroughly, completely, and utterly...limp.

CHAPTER TWENTY-ONE

tuesday

* * *

An hour later, exhausted and sore—in the most perfect way possible—we lay in bed. My chest to his, his arms around my back, my ear pressed to his skin, listening to his heart beating. He'd made love to me two more times. Once in the shower, where I almost reluctantly washed the dirt from his skin, and again back in his bed. But this time he did go slowly, just as he promised.

If I was asked to pick a favorite of the three, I don't think I could. Because each time showed a different side of him. The side that was young, eager, and maybe a bit too excited, and the other that was controlled, deliberate, and made me believe there was more to this thing than what we were both acknowledging. Something deep rooted, raw, that had the potential to hurt and leave scars.

But I didn't want to think about that now. All I wanted to do was let him hold me, to enjoy the feeling of my chest lifting with each of his breaths, and our bodies fitting more perfectly than if we were made as one.

He trailed his fingers up and down my spine, so softly I wondered if he realized he was doing it. I lifted my head to look up at him, to find him watching me. He smiled, a slow, easy smile that only came after a night like this. From being satisfied in the most primal way.

I looked into his eyes, deep brown and slightly droopy from exhaustion, to his straight nose that fit his face perfectly, and his lips. I didn't know if I'd ever get the chance to examine him this closely again, and I wanted to memorize every part of him. My eyes settled on the scar I'd noticed the first time I met him—the one wedged in the crease between his lip and chin, and I lifted my hand to touch it.

"How'd you get this?"

He closed his eyes, as if remembering, and I wasn't sure if it was exhaustion that made him look so somber, or something else. My body stiffened, and I instantly regretted having asked the question.

"You wouldn't believe me if I told you," he said then, and his lips curved a little. But it was a genuine smile, and my body relaxed a bit.

"Try me." I folded my hands on his chest, turned my head, and pressed my ear against his heart.

He paused for a long time, and I wondered if I was being too personal, but then he blew out a breath and adjusted his pillows. "Well, you remember I have sisters, and they're all older."

I nodded, remembering, and smiled at the deep rumble of his voice as I snuggled in deep.

"And I don't know if you're aware, but around twelve, boys tend to go through a temporary bout of insanity where girls are concerned."

I smiled, already enjoying this story way too much. My fingers trailed up down his chest as he continued to speak.

"Well, when *I* was twelve, two of my sisters made the high school dance team. One freshman, one senior. Penny was the team captain and invited the whole team up to our family cabin as a sort of *bonding* sleepover. I never really understood what the hell that meant. All I knew was that fifteen tight-bodied women were about to be sleeping right above my bedroom in the upstairs loft.

"Well, my buddy Joey, who lived down the hill, heard the news and tried to invite himself over, but my mom was too wise for that and nixed those plans before they even started. And that's where we got inventive. Joey lent me his father's video camera, and we rigged a pulley system that would go from our backyard tree over to the roof of the adjacent loft window. It consisted of rope, a bucket, and a bunch of knots we learned in Boy Scouts that year. To our amazement, it actually worked. We ran across it all day, had it perfectly fitted, even planted a few night lights in their room so I'd always have enough light to film."

He laughed and shook his head against the pillows. "I snuck out of my room that night about eleven, climbed the tree, somehow not dropping the camera, and then got in the bucket and started to pull."

I laughed. "Did you see anything?"

He nodded and bit his lip. "Oh, yeah. I don't know what you guys do at sleepovers, but everyone was in skimpy, little night things, dancing around. It was amazing... well... until the rope gave out. I was a big kid, and Joey and I weren't the best Boy Scouts. The rope must have loosened from us testing it all day. It slipped from the beam and I went plummeting to the ground.

"I must have called out, because when I stood up, Lisa was standing over me. She was so mad—she's the youngest of my sisters and always the one to get me in trouble. Didn't even care that my chin was busted open."

He flicked his thumb over the scar then looked down at me. "She erased the tape and made me go up to the loft to say I was sorry. She promised never to tell our parents, so I agreed."

My eyes widened and I grinned at him. "What did the girls say when you apologized?"

"They lectured me. Told me they should call the cops,

made me promise never to do it again."

"Did you?"

"Nah." He shook his head. "One of the freshman girls actually snuck into my room that night. That's when I realized all I had to do was ask."

I pushed myself up on his chest, appalled. "What?"

He laughed. "I was in eighth grade, almost thirteen, and she was in ninth, just fourteen. There wasn't that big of a gap between us—plus, I was big for my age."

"Wow." I lay my head back on his chest and grinned, knowing I probably would have snuck into his bedroom too. Actually, the me *then* wouldn't have. The me *then* was too scared of breaking rules to do things I wasn't supposed to do. But now, for some reason, I felt rebellious for the first time in my life.

We were both silent for a few minutes before I spoke again. "Do you have any brothers?"

His chin brushed against my hair as he shook his head. "No. But I always wanted one."

I frowned slightly and looked up again. "Me too. Though I really just wanted a sibling. You're lucky to have your sisters."

He grinned and closed his eyes, obviously tired. "They're okay." Though the way he said it, the softness in his voice, made me realize they were so much more than that to him... He loved them.

"Becky's kind of like my sister," I said into the dark. I don't know why I said it. Maybe because he'd just told me so much about himself, or maybe because I wanted to share a piece of me too.

He lifted his chin and looked at me. "Yeah?"

I nodded.

He scrunched his face and smiled. "Jake's like that for me."

I closed my eyes, and my stomach twisted slightly. Jake, his boss. More than once I thought about how our relationship would affect theirs. More than once I wanted to ask the question... "What would he think☐" I stopped, not knowing what to call what we were doing. "Of this?"

He folded his arms behind his head and frowned slightly. "He wouldn't like it."

His tone was slightly distant, and I shouldn't have been surprised by his answer, but for some reason, I could suddenly feel my heart beating—not hard or wild, just beating. It was in perfect unison with his, steady and rhythmic, but even so, it wasn't comfortable.

He lifted my chin and touched the side of my face, obviously noticing a change in me. "Don't worry about Jake, Tuesday. He has nothing to do with this."

Tears pooled in my eyes, and I blinked a couple of times to clear them. My chest flooded with relief, and my little girl heart grew a little more hopeful.

"I don't kiss and tell," he said then. "He'll never find out."

I forced a smile and nodded, but quickly looked away so he wouldn't see how badly his last statement hurt. I rested my head on his chest and waited for the panic that invaded my chest to dissipate, but it didn't.

I knew I was being irrational. In two weeks, the job would be over and he'd be gone. I understood when I agreed to this, but for some reason, it felt different now. Maybe because talking like this made everything feel like so much more. Lying in his arms didn't feel like we were just sleeping together. It felt like he was making love to me, and I wasn't sure I'd never been made love to in my whole life until now.

We lay there a few more minutes, while I tried to convince myself I could handle it, but things had changed after tonight. It was different—somehow tainted by the fact that I knew it was almost over. I rolled over on the bed and pushed off the edge to collect my things from the floor.

He was quiet a moment as he watched me, then he finally sat up and arched a brow. "Are you leaving?" he asked, his words coming in such a casual way it made my heart hitch.

"Yeah."

I found my overalls in the corner and pulled them on, not even fazed by the fact I hadn't found my panties. "My cat's going to be pissed at me."

He threw his legs over the side of the bed, his brow furrowed as he pushed himself to stand. "I'll walk you out."

I laughed, even though what I wanted to do was cry, and shook my head. "Nah, it's late, I'll be fine." I pulled my top over my head, slipped my sneakers on without bothering to tie them, then walked over to him and gave him one last kiss to say goodbye.

I intended for it to be just a peck so he wouldn't worry and ask questions, but when my lips met his, he grabbed the back of my neck and held me captive. His mouth worked over mine, achingly slow, as if he were memorizing my taste.

He groaned in the back of his throat, sending tingles to my belly, then he finally pulling away. He ran his thumb one last time over my bottom lip and I closed my eyes. Allowing myself just a few seconds to collect myself before I grabbed my bag from the floor and made my way to the front door. Knowing this had to be the last time I allowed myself to be this weak.

CHAPTER TWENTY-TWO

tuesday

* * *

The next morning, I convinced myself I needed to end it. This thing between us wasn't good for me, wasn't good for him, and we needed to stop whatever this was before someone got hurt. Though even as I told myself this, I knew it was a lie. Because I would already be hurt by this ending. I knew that even if I got out now, it would hurt, but it would be a little hurt, a manageable one. If I waited, it would be a big, gaping artery of a hurt I may not be able to recover from.

When I pulled into the parking lot, I still wasn't exactly sure *how* to end it... or if I needed to end it at all. Last night he said he wanted me again, wanted me more than once, but we'd done that. Multiple times. Maybe he'd gotten his fill, maybe we could move forward like mature adults, knowing it happened, but pretending it didn't.

The guys were already busy in the back room, so I sat at the register and picked up the phone to call potential vendors. I didn't realize until I got there, but I hadn't bought the donuts today. A piece of me panicked when I realized it was the first time I'd forgotten in a month, but no one came to check for them, so I eventually let it go.

When I was done with my call list, I immediately began doing research for a summer line. The more I did, the less

I thought about him, and that was exactly what I needed right now. To not think about him.

My nose was deep into one of my herbal magazines when my phone rang for my regular "Tuesday" conversation with my mother.

"Hey, sweet pea," she said when I answered. "How's the store coming along?"

I sat back on the stool and closed the magazine on the counter. "It's good." But my words were lifeless in a way I could even hear myself. Yes, the shop was going great—had turned out more beautiful than I had ever imagined. I was getting so many inquiries from vendors it was hard to keep up, but what was happening between John and me made those words feel like a lie. Because somewhere along the way, he'd become more than just my contractor. He'd become a part of *this, a part of me.*

I pulled in a deep breath and resolved to change the subject, wanting to talk about anything but myself. "How are things in Crescent City?"

"Good." She sighed breathily. "It's beautiful here. Things grow like it's the Garden of Eden. I have a fresh organic salad every day, and all I have to do to is walk out the back door."

She went on to tell me about the local scenery, about getting a part-time job at a vegan eatery, where she quickly became famous for the date-nut-candy roll she'd been making since I was a child. It all sounded amazing, and I found myself smiling for the first time all morning.

"I wish you'd come up here, sweet pea. It would be good for your soul."

She was right; an escape from everything so dauntingly heavy *would* be good for my soul. It would be good for my heart too. Because even though John was at least ten yards away through a closed door, my heart still felt his presence. It would be good to get away today, to clear my head, to leave all this frustration behind. "Maybe once things settle down here," I said, closing my eyes and gripping the bridge of my nose.

She was quiet a moment before she whispered, "Sounds good, honey." But I knew she sensed there was more I wasn't saying, but she was good that way. She didn't press.

"Well, I have to go eat something before my break is up. I'll call you again next week?"

I smiled sadly. "Sounds great."

"I love you, sweet pea," she whispered.

"I love you too," I whispered back.

I waited for her to hang up, just as I always did, before putting the phone back on the counter. It was half past noon, time for lunch, but I couldn't eat. Even though I'd only finished half my smoothie before pouring the rest down the sink this morning.

A few minutes later, the door to the back room opened, and I sat up as the whole crew walked through the product floor. John was the last, and he only acknowledged my presence by tilting his chin up while he took a drink from his stainless steel mug.

"We're breaking for lunch. Can we get you anything?" Leo asked, stopping by the register to wait for my reply. All I could do was shake my head, because my focus was on John as he walked out to the parking lot without saying a word.

"Suit yourself," Leo said, grinning. I forced a smile and rose to my feet. "You guys have fun."

He nodded, lifted an imaginary cap with his hand, and turned toward the exit.

I didn't wait for them to pull out of the lot before heading back to my office. I sat on my couch and stretched my legs out in front of me. I wanted to scream, but at the same time, I had my confirmation. The time John and I spent together was one of the most earth-shattering nights of my life, but to him it was nothing. I was just another girl he had *asked*.

Those were the last thoughts in my head before my eyelids grew heavy, and I fell asleep.

* * *

The sound of an electric saw woke me hours later. I bolted up on my elbows and pushed myself to sit on the edge of the couch to right my glasses. The room was fuzzy, and I strained to clear my vision. I glanced at my desk to check the time and cringed. Five after five, which meant I'd slept over three hours. I hadn't fallen asleep like that in years, but with all that had been on my mind lately, I doubt I'd gotten three hours of rest all week. I gripped my skull, trying to clear my head from the fog that always settled after a nap. I still felt exhausted.

I pushed myself to stand, hoping that if I got to work I'd start to feel better, and I opened my laptop.

Before I could process even half a dozen orders, there was a quick knock at my door. John stuck his head in and lifted his chin. "We're taking off. Need anything before we go?"

I gazed at him, searching for any fleck of emotion to cross his features, but he looked normal. He didn't raise his brows, or give any indication his words meant more than his question, and I couldn't help wondering if this was his way of letting me know this was over.

The guys could still be heard in the back room packing up, and I shook my head, stuffing a bar of soap into a box without checking to see if it even belonged there. Then I took a handful of lip balms and stuffed them in too, because I couldn't understand how John and I could share the same moments, from which my heart ended up like a pulverized piece of meat, and his remained so closed, as hard as a diamond yet black as coal.

179

I knew I'd have to start the shipment over again when he left, but I needed to appear as though the casual way he spoke to me didn't affect me. That I wasn't breaking inside because he was leaving without a word of acknowledgment about what happened. I managed to shake my head, but no words could be forced from my tongue.

He nodded, and Eddie appeared behind him. "You have a good night, Ms. Patil."

I forced a smile. "You too."

They both left, and I took a deep breath before dumping out the contents of my last order. I should have been relieved. I'd worried about how to end things all day... and now I didn't have to. It appeared that the only person I should have been worrying about was myself. He was fine... Could sleep with me and be completely unaffected the next day. He was an adult, pretending nothing happened, even though it did.

Things did happen.

Big things.

Deep down, vulnerable things—things I wasn't prepared for—and now I was paying the price.

I pushed myself back from my desk and closed my eyes. I'd convinced myself I could sleep with him with no emotional investment, that we could have this short affair and go our separate ways. But somehow, in a short amount of time, a part of me had fallen in love with him.

I let my head fall back to my shoulders with the realization. "How did you let this happen?"

* * *

I continued to process the rest of the orders in tears, adding them to the crate scheduled to be picked up by the postman in the morning. I cried for a good fifteen minutes, allowing myself to mourn his loss, even though he was never mine in the first place.

I took the box to the front room and placed it by the door. Then I grabbed the notes I made for a summer line from the top of the register and headed again for the back room. Instead of crying like I wanted to, I was determined to be productive, to push John from my mind like he'd done with me the moment I'd walked out of his room last night.

When I reached the supply closet, I loaded my arms with oils, herbs, and butters. I carried them to the kitchen, disregarding the fact it was under construction, and set them up on the dust-filled counter. The debris of sawdust, scraps of wood, and nails was at least a quarter-inch thick.

I placed my whole arm on the counter and pushed it all to the floor, not caring about the mess I would leave behind. I hadn't made anything new in weeks, and even though the conditions weren't ideal, these products weree just for me. I would run them over and over again a dozen times before perfecting them, but I always felt so much better when creating.

I needed that now. I needed to clear my head and focus on something that filled my heart with joy, so some of the cracks would fill up, and I wouldn't feel so empty anymore.

I ran to my office and got my cleaning supplies, then spent ten minutes clearing off enough space to work. When I was finally ready, I took three deep breaths, allowing my mind to go blank so I didn't give too much thought to what I was doing.

I always allowed myself to make mistakes when I worked. I realized long ago that closing myself off to the idea of perfection only made for boring products, things that weren't unique or special in any way. But when I cleared my mind and allowed my nose to guide me, allowed my heart and soul to express themselves in the form of a lotion of body butter, magic happened.

I scooped a good portion of shea butter into my bowl,

added some coconut oil and vitamin E, then I started the electric mixer and began blending. This was my base for all my butters. From here, I just let things go. A little of this, a little of that, until it was done.

My arm tingled with the rhythmic hum of the mixer as I beat the formula into a substance that resembled a bowl of thick whipped cream. The door to the back room opened, and I didn't even have to turn around to know it was John. I could feel his presence, because the piece of my heart he owned began beating. Soon he was behind me, brushing my hair from my shoulder and leaning down to kiss my neck.

"What are you doing?" His voice was low, happy, and caused my stomach to clench with the memories of last night.

I pushed them away, closed my eyes, and added a couple drops of Bergamot to the mixture. The room filled with the clean, seductive scent that always reminded me of a cool, citrus drink on a warm, summer day.

I cleared my throat, trying to ignore his lips that were placing feather light kisses along my neck. "I'm working on a new body butter."

The heat from his body sent little surges of warmth to my belly.

He smiled against my skin and came closer, until the fabric of my skirt tangled around his legs. "It smells good."

I took a deep breath, because what he was doing felt so good. I tilted my head to the side, allowing him better access, even though only minutes ago I had resolved to never let him do this again. "I thought you left."

He shook his head then wrapped his arms around my middle and pulled me closer. "The guys were getting suspicious. I had to make sure they left before I came back. It took forever for Eddie and Marco to leave the lot."

I swallowed. His words made me cringe. They confirmed

once again how he felt about us. We were a secret, an affair that would end whether I wanted it to or not. I turned around, knowing I had to face him, knowing I had to say something, but not knowing what.

I was met with his face, his beautiful face that was both rugged and raw. Even though he wasn't smiling, I knew he was happy—his eyes, big and brown, danced with joy at the sight of me. Eyes just for me. I swallowed. "What happens if they find out?" I asked in a whisper.

He shook his head. "They won't."

I took a breath, needing air. "But what if they do?"

He bit his lip then placed a hand on either side of me on the counter. "Then I fire them."

I frowned, shaking my head slightly. "I'm serious. I don't want you to get in trouble. With Jake—or... or with anyone." It was such a sad attempt at ending things, but he was standing so close, his kisses still burning the skin at my neck, and I wasn't sure I wanted to end it anymore. I knew I was being irrational, stupid, because the smart thing to do would be to push him away and tell him it was over. But I couldn't.

He stepped closer until his body was flush with mine. "I like trouble." His eyes traveled to my mouth. "I like trouble a whole lot."

I nodded because the way he said it made me like trouble too. A lot.

He lifted me to the counter and spread my thighs until he fit between them. Then he kissed me so hard, so desperately, that I had to grip his shoulders to keep from falling backward. He kissed me with a hunger that shocked me; it was a kiss that held nothing back, a raw, teeth-clashing, tongue-plunging kiss that made me wrap my arms and legs around his body.

He pulled me tight against him, his erection pressed into my belly, and his hands gripped my backside. I could feel the emotion of the day bubbling out of me. I wanted this so much, but I was still angry.

"You ignored me all day," I said against his mouth, my words so full of emotion that he pulled back again.

He looked into my eyes, eyes I was sure showed every vulnerability I'd ever felt, and he shook his head. "I wasn't ignoring you because I don't want you." He brushed a lone tear from my cheek and kissed it from this thumb. "I was ignoring you because every time I look at you, every time I get too close, this happens. Because I have no self-control when it comes to you, and I didn't want the guys to see that."

My lips began to quiver and he came closer again, resting his forehead on mine. "What's wrong?"

"Don't ignore me, John, I don't like it."

His lips lifted in a sad smile and he kissed me again. "Never again." His kiss was sweet, tender, and made me emotional all over again. "Never again."

He lifted me for a second time and turned around to head for the office. I held on to him with arms and legs, completely trusting him not to drop me as he walked with me across the floor. Our mouths never parted the whole way, and when he kicked the office door open with his foot, I completely surrendered.

He laid me down on the couch, kneeled in between my thighs, and lifted my skirt. My fingers worked at the fastening of his belt, while he tore a foil packet open with his teeth. He rolled the condom over his erection and pulled down my panties. He yanked them the rest of the way down my legs, threw them to the floor, and we both called out at the same time when he entered me.

It had been less than twenty-four hours since he'd filled me in his bedroom, but now, right now, I felt like I was eating for the first time in a week.

He rocked with me, filled me, stretched me in the way I

needed to be stretched, and loved me the way I needed to be loved. He plunged inside me, deep and hard, then slow and deliberate. He pulled out of me until only the tip remained before slamming inside of me again, over and over, again and again, but it wasn't enough. I needed more of him; I needed to be closer. I found the edge of his shirt and pulled it up, sighing when my fingers found the skin of his back. I gripped him to me, savoring the flex of each muscle as it constricted with each thrust into my body.

His head rested in the crook of my neck while our bodies moved as one. I kissed his ear, nipping at any skin with my teeth, filling my mouth with every bit of him I could get my lips on.

He groaned in the back of his throat then plunged inside me again, making love to me in a way that felt like dancing. He was leading me in a waltz, so perfectly it was as if we'd practiced a thousand times. It was a dance that was raw, passionate, and hungry—so, so hungry.

In that moment, with my back pressed into the green upholstered couch, the edge of my skirt pushed up to my throat, and my arms wrapped around this solid man, I resolved not to care what happened in the future. I didn't care if I ended up crushed into a million vulnerable pieces on the floor, because each moment with John was worth the risk, worth the hurt.

And that's when I shattered, my heart open, my legs shaking as the man I was falling in love with collapsed on top of me with his pants still pushed down around his ankles. I wrapped my arms around him, panting, feeling his heavy breath against my neck, cooling the perspiration that had settled on my skin.

I was in for the long haul with John, because not in a million years could I force my legs to walk away from him. The only way this would end was if he walked away from *me*.

CHAPTER TWENTY THREE

tuesday

* * *

I smothered a cry into the side of the couch as John inched his way up my thighs. He had his tool belt still on, grinning like the devil as he kissed, licked, and bit his way up my legs. It was broad daylight out, the guys were on the other side of the closed door, and this wasn't a good idea. I shook my head in protest. "We can't do this, John, they'll hear us."

His grin only widened, and he kept coming, kissing his way up my body until his mouth settled on the thin cotton underwear that was the only thing separating his tongue from devouring me.

I grabbed his shoulders, halfheartedly trying to push him off, but he pinned my arms at my sides. "Shhh... Be quiet, Tuesday, or they'll hear you." Then he bit his lip, knowing *quiet* was an impossibility for me. His head dipped down again, and he pushed my panties to the side with his nose.

Oh God, I surrender.

My head fell back to the corduroy cushions, and I found the pillow behind my head and covered my face to muffle my cries. He was so good at this, his tongue warm, wet, and soft. His fingers plunged inside me, curling up to add the perfect amount of pressure. Then his mouth started doing magical things, sucking, blowing, licking, and making love to me in a way that was completely selfless.

I wasn't sure what spurred this delicious form of torture this afternoon, but I wasn't complaining. Five minutes earlier, I'd been stocking the shelves in the front of the store when he came from the back room to tell me he needed to talk to me about the new project I'd asked him about.

A lot of extra things seemed to be popping up lately. Projects were taking longer than originally expected, and I kept finding little additions I was convinced needed to be done. But we both knew what we were doing. We were trying to prolong this thing for as long as we could, avoiding the conversation that was too difficult to face— the conversation where we talked about what this would become when the shop opened, when his job was over.

As soon as I walked into the office, he closed the door and started kissing me, which was the first time he'd done that with the guys around. We'd made love every night that week, but it was always after the guys went home, always... Until now.

I could feel myself climbing as he made love to me with his mouth. I alternated between gripping the cushion with both hands and pressing the pillow to my face to muffle my screams, and that's when the knock sounded at the door. I pushed him away so hard he hit his lip on my knee, but I was barely able to pull my skirt back down before the door opened and Eddie's head poked into my office.

He cleared his throat and looked down to the wood floor, but not before I caught him grinning. "Jake just pulled into the lot. I thought you should know."

John licked at the blood that glistened on his bottom lip and nodded. "Thanks, Eddie."

Eddie closed the door without saying another word, and I

stood, pulled my panties up, and turned around to face John.

"Oh my God." I smoothed my hands over my face then began patting down my hair, because I was sure it looked as crazy as I felt right now.

John took a tissue from my desk and dabbed his lip as another knock sounded at the door. I looked over at him, feeling guilty, panicked, and so many other things I didn't have a name for.

He nodded, silently telling me to let him in. I swallowed before answering the door. "Come in."

Guilty. That was exactly what my voice sounded like. Like I'd just gotten caught with my hand in the cookie jar, only it was John's tongue, and it was in my...

Jake poked his head in then pushed the door open and entered the room. He looked from me to John, brows furrowed and suspicious. "Am I interrupting something?"

I smoothed my hand over my hair and shook my head. "No... no, we were just going over the plans for the back room." I gave him my best smile, but Jake didn't look convinced.

I went on. "Did John tell you about the new addition? I know it's last minute, but I think it's going to be great. I've always wanted to teach classes, and then it hit me. I have all that space we didn't know what to do with, and then John came up with the idea of the big table, and it all just went from there. So yeah, that's what we were doing." I took a deep breath, realizing I hadn't taken in oxygen for a very long time, and I found the strand of feathers in my hair. "What are you doing here?

Jake frowned, then nodded to me before turning to look at John again.

John grinned, then pinched the space at the bridge of his nose and shook his head. "Ah, fuck it." He threw the tissue in the trash, crossed the room, took my face in his hands, and kissed me. Right there, in front of his boss and best friend, not hiding *anything*. He pulled away a second later, and my fingers covered my lips. I hadn't expected that at all, and I was sure my shock was plastered all over my face.

Jake gripped the back of his head and nodded. "That's what I thought." He turned around and walked back out to the kitchen. "I'll give you guys a moment to collect yourselves." He closed the door again behind him, but he wasn't angry like I feared, and I could almost swear I saw him smile before I heard the door click.

I picked the pillow up off the couch and whacked John in the arm. "I told you it was a bad idea."

He bit his lip and pulled me into his arms. "Sex with you is never a bad idea."

I laughed and pulled in a deep breath. "Do you think he's okay with this?" My throat constricted with the question, but I needed to know.

Ne nodded. "He'll be fine."

"Are *you* okay with this?" I told him only a week ago I didn't need all the answers, but I needed them now. I needed them so desperately.

He nodded again, pulling me closer. "Are you?"

I closed my eyes and nodded into his chest. "Yes."

* * *

That evening, I invited John back to my house for the first time. It felt like the natural progression to our relationship, but even so, it seemed like such a big deal, inviting him into my home, my life... everything.

This afternoon, when he kissed me like that in front of Jake, it was as though he was screaming to the world that he'd claimed me. It filled me with a confidence I didn't even realize was missing until then.

His arms were filled with brown paper bags as he followed behind me up the steps to my apartment. Mrs. Sanders peeked her head out of her screen door and gave me the thumbs up sign to tell me she approved, but I couldn't imagine anyone *not* approving of John. He was handsome, funny, and had one of the most giving hearts I'd ever been witness to... and I couldn't believe he was mine.

The plan was for me to make dinner. My famous vegan tacos that even my meat-eating friends like Becky loved. We'd stopped by the store on the way over and purchased all the ingredients to make them, plus a bottle of organic wine too. We'd had dinner together plenty of times in the bed of his truck, or the floor of my office, even huddled up in a blanket on his patio. But now, today, it felt different, almost like we were celebrating.

When I pushed open my apartment door, Whiskers took one look at him before turning around and making a run for my bedroom. He always did that when strangers came over—ran for my closet, which was his safe haven at times like this. But John wasn't a stranger anymore, wouldn't be leaving anytime soon, and Whiskers better get used to it.

John placed the groceries on the island and took a look around. Unlike his home, mine reflected so much of the person I was. Inviting him inside was like cutting open my chest and handing over my heart, red, vulnerable, and raw.

My walls were covered with things I'd picked up in my travels. Things that spoke to me, things that no one else had because they were handmade and one of a kind. The tree rubbing from a two-hundred-year-old redwood, a tapestry from a tribe we stayed with for six months in Oklahoma. But the things that were the hardest to let him see were the things that were out of my own soul. Paintings that reflected everything I wanted in life. Like the baby suckling at her mother's breast, the family walking hand-in-hand down the beach, and the man with arms so large he could wrap them around the entire world.

I didn't realize, until standing there next to him, how transparent it all was. Seeing them through his eyes, they looked almost desperate.

He didn't speak for a moment, just looked from one to the other, to the abstract paintings of reds, oranges, and violets. All the colors of a sunset, because to me they all represented beginnings. Because every day was a chance to start over, to live the life of your dreams, and I guess I'd always been a dreamer.

I took a deep breath, and my shoulders lifted and fell with the hugeness of it all. He took me by the hips and pulled me closer. "So this is you?"

I nodded, rationally knowing he was talking about my place, emotionally thinking he was talking about so much more than that. That he was seeing all of me for the first time, all my secret parts, and he was asking if they were true.

He looked around again, to each painting, then back to me. "It's perfect."

I nodded again then bit my lip because his words made me so happy. "So are you."

He grinned but pulled his chest back so he could look at me better. "I don't think anyone has ever described me that way." He looked up to the ceiling as if trying to recall. "No... Sexy as hell, yes. Witty, all the time. But perfect? I'll have to add it to my list."

I grinned at him then turned out of his arms and started unloading the ingredients from the bag. "You should add cocky, too. That one definitely needs to be there."

He came up behind me, pressing his body against mine and caging me in against the counter with his arms. "I'll show you cocky."

"Mmmmmm..." I leaned back against him. "You need to stop," I whispered, "or we won't eat, and then I'll get cranky."

191

He bit my ear, making me groan, then pushed himself off the counter. "We wouldn't want that." He grabbed the bottle of wine from the counter then walked to the other side of the island.

I pulled the cilantro and walnuts out of the bag. "The opener is in the top drawer by the refrigerator."

We spent the rest of the evening making dinner, drinking wine, and talking. Like a normal couple. About life, places we'd been, books we'd read, and then finally we made it back to my bedroom, where he finished what he started that afternoon in the office.

We took a shower afterward, where he opened every bottle of soap in my shower and tested them on my skin. He told me it was for product knowledge, but I knew this was just part of him. He was like a little boy concocting a potion, and I thoroughly enjoyed being part of his experiment. After he washed every nook and cranny, he carried me back to bed and made love to me one last time.

I lay there now, my head on his chest, listening to him breathing.

"Are you going to go home tonight?" I asked. It was already midnight, and the question had been aching in my chest for over an hour.

He lifted his head, shifting slightly so he could look at me better. "Do you want me to?"

I swallowed, my heart suddenly picking up speed. "I was just wondering about Ginger."

His forehead creased slightly, and he shook his head. "She's with my sister." But he didn't look away. "Do you want me to stay, Tuesday?"

It was such a simple question, but one that was so hard for me to answer, because it was admitting that I wanted this, telling him I wanted him, saying it out loud for the first time. Something I'd said a million different ways in the last week and a half, but I'd never actually verbalized.

"Yes," I whispered. "I want that very much."

"Do you want me?" His question surprised me. So did his vulnerability I'd never seen him like this before.

I bit my lip and shifted my eyes downward. "Again?"

He lifted my chin, his face serious as he shook his head. "That's not what I meant."

I cupped the sides of his face, feeling tears fill the back of my throat, but knowing he deserved my honesty. I trusted him. Trusted him with my heart, even though it was so hard to give. I nodded. "Very much." My voice held all the emotions I felt inside.

He smiled then and traced my lips with his finger. "Me too."

I lowered my head back to his chest and hugged him so hard. He hugged me back, and we fell asleep, completely nude, nothing between us but a future I couldn't wait to begin.

CHAPTER TWENTY-FOUR

tuesday

* * *

A week later, sitting on the stool behind the register, I passed the sales ad across to Becky. She snatched it out of my hand, turning it twice before resting her back on the counter. She smiled so wide I could see all of her perfectly white teeth practically sparkle with pride.

"Damn this looks good." She flipped through each page, reading each description, even though she knew them by heart. She'd helped me write every one.

She was even here when Jake's wife, Katie, sent someone to take product photos. But still, Becky looked over each page as if she was seeing it all for the first time. She turned around with tears brimming her eyes and pulled in a breath. "I'm so happy for you."

I nodded, feeling extra emotional too. The ad wouldn't go live until next Tuesday, yet we were both already crying. Tuesday was my lucky day, the day I was born, the day I met John, and it would be the day I opened my shop to the world. But Becky wasn't just talking about the ad or the store. She was talking about John too; she was happy about all of it.

John came out from the back room, and Becky and I both straightened and wiped at our eyes.

He glanced between Becky and me as he came closer. "Everything okay?"

Becky held the paper out to him and sniffed loudly. "Oh you know, looking at an ad for an awesome store that just happens to open next Tuesday."

He grinned slightly, took the paper from her hand, and flipped it over. I could tell he was happy, but there was something hard there, too. The store opening was a beginning in so many ways, but it was also an end. And end of the relationship as we both knew it. We both felt it, and it was something that was heavy on my mind.

As he flipped through the pages, examining each breathtaking photo, I could tell it was heavy on his mind, too.

Over the past three weeks, we'd spent almost every moment together. Even when he was deep in work in the back room, I knew he was there, but now we only had four more days of this. John already had another job lined up to start on Monday. All the way across town.

We'd stay together of course, but it would be different. It scared me a little because things were still new, exciting, and even though I trusted him completely, I still feared it wouldn't be enough.

Becky excused herself, moving to the back room to make a phone call, and John handed me the paper. "You should frame that. Add it to your wall."

I grinned a little because in such a short amount of time, he knew me so well. "I just might."

He looked over his shoulder to make sure we were alone. "I was wondering,"—he took a deep breath and faced me again—"what are you doing this Saturday?"

I inched my body closer, concerned by the hush in his voice. I wasn't used to seeing him so nervous. "Nothing. Why?"

He pushed my legs open so he could stand between my thighs. "I wanted to know if you'd spend the day with me, to celebrate." He tipped his chin to the ad on the counter, and I found myself smiling with relief.

"I'd like that," I whispered. "I'd like that very much."

"Good."

He placed his hand on the side of my jaw and traced my bottom lip with his thumb. "I'm going to miss kissing you every morning."

"Me too." It was the first time we'd acknowledged he'd no longer be here, and it was more painful than I thought.

He pressed his forehead to mine, and I swallowed back a ball of tears. "But I promise," he continued, "no matter how late it is, I'll always kiss you goodnight."

I gripped the back of his neck and pulled him closer. "Good."

The door to the back room opened again, and Becky walked onto the product floor. She put her hands on her hips and frowned. "You guys are so cute, it's sickening."

John's smile widened, but his eyes remained on me. "We are cute, aren't we?"

I nodded. "Very."

He bent down farther, kissing me briefly before pushing away from the counter. He turned around and sighed. "I fucking hate work."

I laughed, knowing exactly what he meant. "You're mine for four more days, John Eaton, and I'm going to get my money out of you."

He winked over his shoulder, obviously not intimidated. "You girls stay out of trouble." Then he walked to the back room, in the relaxed way he did everything, and closed the door.

I bit my lip, wanting so desperately to follow after him, but knowing we both had work to do.

Becky came to stand beside me and stared at the closed door. "Does he have a brother?"

"No," I said with a sigh.

"A friend?"

I shook my head. "Married."

"Damn." She bumped me with her shoulder, the way she always did before saying something meaningful. "He better be good to you, Tuesday, or I'll kick his ass. He knows that, right?"

I laughed, burying my face in my hands because I was suddenly feeling emotional again. Being with John was making all my hopes and dreams come true. Actually, he was more than what I'd hoped for. He brought things out of me I didn't even know were there, and it scared the crap out of me. I turned to face her, tears brimming my eyes. "Becky, I think I may be in love with him."

She took my hands, a serious expression on her face. "That's a good thing, right?"

I shrugged then lifted my glasses and wiped my eyes with the heel of my hand. "I think so. But it scares me."

"Is that why you're crying?"

"I don't know. I feel like I'm at the top of an emotional rollercoaster, and I'm about to fall."

She paused a second then looked me in the eye. "Maybe you're pregnant."

I frowned and cleared my throat. "Don't even joke about that." I turned away, but a sick feeling grabbed my stomach. I stared at her.

"What?"

My nose burned with unshed tears. "I don't remember when my last period was."

"Ha-ha. Okay, I know, it wasn't funny, but I've never seen you like this before."

I grabbed her arm, my heart constricting. "I'm serious. I don't remember. I don't remember, Becky." My chest grew heavy, and the air thickened around me. Becky sat on the stool opposite me and put her hands on my knees.

"Have you been using protection?"

"Yes."

"Okay, then things are probably fine. You've been under a lot of stress lately, and that can affect your cycle, trust me."

I nodded, desperately wanting to believe her, but knowing in the pit of my stomach it wasn't true. I could almost feel the life inside me. No movement, just a glow of something that wasn't there before.

She stood. "I'll go get a test."

I looked to the closed door. "I'm going with you."

* * *

I didn't tell John I was leaving, didn't even bother going back to my apartment before taking the test. I took it right there, in the drugstore bathroom. The very pink, very bright two lines showed up immediately. The sight of them took the strength from my knees, and I crumbled to the ceramic tile. I turned to Becky, choking. "Do you think it could be a mistake?"

She squatted down beside me, the test in her hand, her face white as she smoothed the hair from my face. "I don't know, sweetie."

I closed my eyes, wanting desperately not to face this, to pretend it wasn't real and to go back to John at the store.

"Maybe we should go to the doctor?"

But I *did* know, and running away wouldn't make this untrue. I shakily pushed myself from the floor and somehow made it to the parking lot without falling over. Becky had a friend who worked at an OB's office, and she was able to call in a favor and have the doctor see me before the office opened again after lunch.

I peed in a plastic cup, gave blood a short while later, and then Becky and I moved to a tiny room where I changed into a paper gown and sat on a table to wait for the doctor.

The moments that followed were excruciating. All I kept thinking was how I would tell John. We'd only been together for three weeks, and babies hadn't even been a whisper on either of our minds. We'd only just come out of the relationship closet, and now a little life, had changed everything in the blink of an eye, . I knew so little about John. What he wanted for his future, what he'd done in his past.

"I don't know if I can do this, Becky."

She shook her head. "Do what?"

"Be a mother. Tell John he's going to be a father."

"You can do *anything.*"

My chin sucked in involuntarily. "But what if he doesn't want a baby?"

"What if he does?" She sat down beside me on the table, causing my paper gown to crinkle as she squeezed in closer. "I've seen the way he looks at you, Tuesday. If you're pregnant, he'll be there."

I wanted to believe her so much, and a part of me began to have hope. He was a good man. This wasn't ideal, but I couldn't imagine him turning his back on his own child. I couldn't see him walking out on us the way my father had done, but at the same time...

"I never thought this would happen to me."

Becky tucked my hair behind my ear. "I don't think anyone ever does, sweetie."

There was a quick tap on the door a while later, and we both looked up.

A petite woman with dark brown hair peeked into the room. "Hi, I'm Dr. Kim." Her smile was bright, cheerful, and easy on the nerves. She entered the room and walked across the floor to wash her hands. She dried them slowly then sat on the rolling stool in front of me, as though purposefully allowing me time to collect my emotions.

"I have a feeling this news was unexpected," she said softly, but the tone of her voice only confirmed my fears. What I discovered in the drugstore bathroom was true: I was pregnant.

I nodded, fighting back tears.

"When was your last period?" the doctor asked.

I looked to Becky, as if expecting her to know the answer. "Umm... Six weeks ago? I don't remember exactly."

I faced her again, not able to control my fluster. This was something every woman should know, especially while sexually active, but I hadn't been in a relationship for over a year. I'd been too... busy to pay enough attention.

The doctor nodded, not seeming to judge me in any way, and asked me to lie back on the table so she could conduct an internal ultrasound.

Becky moved from the table to stand by my side, holding my hand and telling me everything would be okay. I was trying to stay positive, but the reality of what was happening overwhelmed me.

I closed my eyes, trying to focus on my breathing, but then the room filled with a loud swishing sound that reminded me of a million tiny horses. I let out an audible gasp and turned toward the monitor. Tears filled my eyes, so thick they were almost blinding.

There, on the twelve inch black and white monitor, was my baby. Curled up like a tiny pea, hands and arms perfectly formed, heart beating even faster than my own.

"Oh, my God." I looked to Becky, who may have been crying harder than me. "I'm going to have a baby."

She nodded. "You're having a baby."

The doctor continued to move the ultrasound around, clicking buttons before turning to me. "It looks like..." She hit one more button. "You're about ten weeks. Maybe eleven."

My chest tightened, and all the air expelled from my lungs. I wiped my eyes with the back of my hand and shook my head. "That's not possible." I could feel the walls coming in around me at the possibility of this not being John's baby. "I've had my period. I know I have."

I looked over at Becky again, needing to convince her, because maybe if I did, I could make this nightmare untrue. That I could make this baby John's, instead of a man I barely remembered.

I looked at Becky's face; it was drained of all color, her eyes filled with a pain I knew she was feeling for me. "Remember when you came to my apartment to help with invoices? I had it then, I know it."

Dr. Kim's brows furrowed, and she rested one hand on my knee. "It's common to bleed in your first trimester," she stated. "But you are in fact, close to your second."

A sob fell from my lips, and I covered my face with my hands. This couldn't be.

This couldn't be true.

Dr. Kim squeezed my knee then stood and crossed the room, where she tossed her rubber gloves to the trash and collected a handful of brochures. "I know this is a lot to take in all at once, but these will help." She handed them over then put her hand on my shoulder. "Do you have any questions for me?"

I looked to Becky again, my lips frozen. "I've had alcohol. Beer, wine." Becky shook her head, tears welling in her eyes as I looked back at Dr. Kim.

Her smile was kind. "It happens all the time. If you're concerned, we can run some tests, but many women consume alcohol before finding out they're pregnant. It will be okay." She looked from me to Becky, silently waiting for more questions, but I could only stare into space.

Becky turned to her and smiled. "Thank you so much for seeing us today. I think she's good. Just needs some time to process."

Dr. Kim nodded. "Of course." She smiled one last time before leaving the room and pulling the door softly closed behind her.

I turned to Becky, hardly able to contain my emotions. "You have to find him. You have to find Austin."

She sat beside me again, knowing exactly whom I was talking about. "You don't have to tell him, Tuesday. He walked out on you. What kind of father would he make?"

I shook my head. "It doesn't matter what I want..." I played with the edge of my paper gown. "I spent my whole life desperate to know my own father, not caring how good or bad he was. I just wanted to *know* him. To know what he looked like, to know if he looked like me." I grabbed a handful of my hair. "To know if he's where *I got this*."

I squeezed my eyes shut and let my hands fall to my lap. "I won't deny my child that. Even if the thought of telling Austin makes me uncomfortable."

Becky laughed a little, not in a humorous way, but in a way that admitted I was right. "Are you going to tell

John?"

My throat tightened, and I looked her in the eye. "I have to."

She nodded, because really, there was no other option. I had to tell him, I just had no idea how I would bear it.

She pulled in a breath, as though this news was as difficult for her as it was for me. "What do you think he'll say?"

I pinched the bridge of my nose, unable to answer. My heart was already splitting in two at the thought.

If my biological father wouldn't stay, why on earth would he?

CHAPTER TWENTY-FIVE

tuesday

* * *

It was quarter to six when I finally made it back to the shop. Becky and I had spent the afternoon drinking tea and talking, but so few words came about my situation. We were both in shock, which was strange, considering I was the one who was pregnant. But things that affected me had always affected her just as much, no matter how far apart we were at the time—ever since we were little girls.

Before I left though, she promised, without a shadow of a doubt, that she would find my baby's father. She would find Austin, and I believed her.

I opened the door to the back room, where the guys were already packing up for the day. This was how I planned it. Because I couldn't bear to face John while the guys were here.

He was in the far corner of the room talking to Leo, and I fought to keep my breath even. I didn't know how to do this. Tell the man I loved, loved more deeply than I ever thought possible, that I was pregnant with another man's baby. But I had no choice.

He looked over at me out of the corner of his eye, but his lips curved in that crooked smile I loved. He was excited to see me, which would normally fill my stomach with butterflies and excitement but crushed me so much now. Because I knew after tonight, he'd never smile at me like that again. After I told him, he wouldn't look at me like that anymore. It would be different, and I wouldn't blame him even a tiny bit.

The guys gathered the rest of their equipment, eager to be gone. There were only a few days left of work, and they didn't want to be here as much as I wanted them gone. Though the closer they got to leaving, the higher my anxiety climbed.

"Night, Ms. Patil," Leo said, as he made his way to the parking lot.

I nodded like always. "Night." But tonight was so much different. Because instead of being excited to finally have John to myself, I was filled with fear, panic, and regret. So much regret.

I wrapped my arms around my belly, to the baby that had been growing there without my knowing, and swallowed back the bitter bile that was clawing up my throat.

John leaned against the new stainless steel counter and beckoned me with his finger. It was a game we played, the christening of every single surface of the shop. Every table, floor, chair, and tonight would be the new counters. I walked toward him, my lip between my teeth, but words trapped in my throat.

"Where'd you go?"

I stopped in front of him, shaking my head, and I pulled in a deep breath. I wanted to spit it out, to get it over with, to just say the damn words. *I'm pregnant John, and you're not the father.* But I couldn't. My eyes brimmed with tears, and my chest grew heavy with the words that were trapped inside me. As if my body was trying to protect my heart by incapacitating my vocal chords.

His brows furrowed, and his hand came up to touch my jaw. My head leaned into his palm involuntarily, and I took a deep breath. God, I loved this. I loved the way he touched me, loved his rough hands that were so gentle at the same time.

"Is everything okay?"

I closed my eyes, trying to force back tears that threatened to spill over. He pulled me into his chest, encompassing me with his arms, and surrounding me with his heat. It wasn't even cold out, but I hadn't been warm since I heard the news.

"Shit." He hugged me tighter. "What's wrong, Tuesday?"

I could feel my heart ripping in two, but I wrapped my arms around him, pressing my ear to his chest to feel his heart beating, and trying to memorize all of it. He was a man who didn't run from a conversation. He confronted things head on, eyes open, but how could I tell him I was pregnant with another man's child? How could I face him every day afterward?

I took in a deep, shaky breath and opened my eyes, forcing myself back just enough so I could look at him. He was watching me, jaws tight but eyes soft.

He touched my face again, then his other hand came up so he cradled my head in both hands. He looked into my eyes without words, telling me I could say anything, that *it was okay to be vulnerable because he would protect me.*

"What's wrong?" he asked again.

I shook my head, fighting an internal battle between pushing him away and squeezing him tighter and never letting go. I tried to think of the words that wouldn't be misunderstood. Because if I said I was pregnant, he would think the baby was his, and I'd have to explain. If I said I was pregnant with another man's baby, he would think I'd been unfaithful. Been with other men when we were together. But this situation was far more complicated than that, and I couldn't stand either option. Even for the split second before I got to explain.

I looked to the floor then, knowing I couldn't bear to see what he looked like when I said the words. I wanted the last memory of John to be the way he looked at me when I walked into the room.

"John, I—" I pulled in a deep breath, unable to force the words from my lips. I needed him to know this time between us wasn't nothing. That being with him made me realize I'd been selling myself short for a long time. I took another breath and started again. "I need you to know something... These last weeks have been the most amazing of my life."

A tear fell down my face, and he pulled me closer, crushing me against his chest as he let out an audible breath. "Nothing's going to change, baby."

I shook my head, more tears welling in my eyes and spilling down my cheeks. I wished he were right, that we could go on like this forever. But he was wrong. So wrong.

He pushed me back at my shoulders, just enough so he could look at me. Then he lifted my chin with his finger. "Just because I won't be working here any longer doesn't mean I won't be here every day."

His eyes were penetrating mine, honest, and I choked on a sob because I wished, so desperately, that that was what this was about. More than anything in my life. His brows pulled together, and he brushed a tear away from my cheek with his thumb. He searched my eyes then shook his head slightly, as though realizing it was more than that.

My breath slowed, and his lips pressed against my forehead, my nose, on each cheek, kissing the tears away. My chest heaved and I forced my eyes open. In four more days, this job would over. Four more days, so why tell him now?

His jaw flexed, as though preparing himself for what I was about to say, knowing it would be something huge.

My chest tightened as I looked into his eyes. "I love you."

It wasn't how I expected to tell him, but I needed him to know. I'd never felt for anyone the way I felt for him, and spending my whole life not having said those words was more than I could take. His eyes bored into mine, never wavering, never a hint of uncertainty, and he cupped the side of my jaw. "I love you too."

I cried harder because I knew it was selfish to take his love. To take his trust, when I held this secret. When I knew it would end our love story the moment he knew. But as selfish as it was, I was somehow able to convince myself it would be easier if I waited.

Easier for him, because when I told him he could walk away, and never have to see me again. Easier for me, because I wouldn't have to relive his disappointment every day when he came to work.

He pressed his lips to mine, lifted me in his arms, and turned around to set me on the counter. He kissed me harder, standing between my legs and pulling me against his chest. Heart to heart. "I love you," he whispered against my mouth. As though he'd held the words for just as long as me.

"I love you, too," I said again, vowing to say it a million times in the next four days. Because I had a lifetime of *I love you*'s I'd never get to say to him. "I love you." A lifetime of *I love you*'s I'd never get to hear.

He lifted me again, but this time he cradled me and carried me to the front door.

"What are you doing?"

He grabbed my bag from the register without breaking his hold, then pushed the door open with his back. He lowered me to my feet, took my keys from my bag. "I'm taking you to dinner." He locked the door then turned around and shook his head. "No, that's a lie." He grinned again, stepping toward me in a way that filled my stomach with butterflies. "We're going to pick up dinner. Then I'm going to strip you naked and take you right there in my living room. 'Cause I need you, Tuesday. I've needed you my whole life."

CHAPTER TWENTY-SIX

tuesday

* * *

Becky was true to her word. I got the call Friday afternoon that Austin would meet me in the cafe across the street from Parker Studios. It was terrifying. Knowing I had to tell someone I barely knew that he was going to be a father. That I was pregnant with his child.

I sat across from him now, tapping my foot under the table as I passed the paper cup back and forth in my hands. He wore dark-wash jeans, a black t-shirt, cowboy boots, and was more attractive than I remembered. His hair was blond, though I could barely tell because it was cut so short, and his eyes were blue and framed with dark lashes that would make most women jealous. *The exact opposite of John.* I couldn't help wondering how our baby would turn out—if she'd have a wild mane like me or the light features like him.

"So you wanted to talk to me?" He spoke with a Texas accent, which didn't quite surprise me from the way he was dressed, but it made me sad nevertheless. Because I realized I didn't know him at all. He was the father of my child, and I barely knew him. A man I would be connected to for life, yet all I kept wishing was that he was John.

Austin took a sip of his flat white latte then leaned forward and rested his elbows on the table. "I feel like I need to say something." He tilted his head to the side to crack his neck, clearly having as hard a time with the situation as I. "About the first time we met."

I inwardly cringed, because by *met* he meant *slept together*. If we'd just met, I wouldn't be here right now. Pregnant with his baby, and deeply in love with another man. I shook my head. "That's not why I'm here☐"

"Ya see," he cut me off. "I had a modeling job that morning and woke up twenty minutes late. I tried to find you, but I couldn't... It was only later I thought to leave a note." He scratched the back of his head, and I actually felt bad for him. I also felt relieved in a sense. He was my baby's father, the man who would mean the most in her life, and deep down, I wanted him to be a good guy. I wanted him to be so good for *her. (Or him. Whatever this baby turned out to be.)*

I nodded and forced a little smile. Even though it didn't change our situation in the slightest, it was warming to know he'd looked for me. Because it said something about the type of person he was. And that fact eased my heart because I wanted my baby's father to be kind. I wanted him to be everything I never had.

My palms began to sweat under the table, and I knew it was my turn to talk. To tell him the reason why Becky had hunted him down and made him come here today. I had no idea how he'd react, but I'd prepared myself for the worst. I had brochures for DNA testing and a phone number in my purse. I was even prepared to fund the whole thing with my American Express. There was no doubt in my mind he was my baby's father; I only needed to convince him of that.

But in the pit of my stomach, I wasn't sure I'd use any of it. If he didn't want this baby, that was his choice. I was here because he deserved to know, because my baby deserved the opportunity to have a father. My mistakes were my own, and I wouldn't let embarrassment stop me from trying to provide that for her. But I wouldn't force him to be there either.

I didn't need his money; I could support this baby on my own. But there was one thing I couldn't do—and that was fill his shoes. My mother had tried. God knows, she'd tried so hard... but there's something deep down inside that longs for a daddy. To have the thing that everyone on earth had... but me.

He rested his hand on the table, obviously in tune with my distress as I tried to figure out what to say.

I cleared my dry throat then took one last deep breath. "There's something I need to tell you." I forced my eyes upward, and he leaned back in his chair. I knew a whirlwind of ideas must be going through his head. I took pity, knowing this must be terrifying, and I pushed the words out. "I'm pregnant. Eleven weeks. It's yours, I'm sure of it."

His brows creased, and I wasn't sure if it was from anger or confusion. He looked down at the table as if calculating the weeks. Then his eyes shifted even lower, to where my belly still masked the fact that cells were multiplying under my skin.

He pushed himself to stand and threaded his hands behind his neck. "Wow." He looked to the window, and I could see an array of emotions pass over his features in an instant. "Wow." But he didn't leave as I feared he would. He pulled out another seat closer to me and sat back down at the table. His eyes locked on my belly the whole time, his face intense, but nothing more.

We were both silent a moment, and even though it was terrifying not knowing what was going on in his head, I gave him time. This was a shock to me, one I'd been crying over for the last forty-eight hours, and I knew it must be a lot for him to process as well.

He sat forward then and looked me in the eyes. "Can I touch it?"

Tears clogged my throat, and I let out a gasp. I hadn't expected this reaction. The fact that he was interested

212

sent a gush of emotion to spill from every pore of my body. He didn't doubt that what I said was true. He knew me just as well as I knew him, and still he trusted my words without question. I almost opened my mouth to ask why, but I pushed my chair back to give him better access to my belly instead.

He took both hands and placed them on my stomach. We were both quiet, his face intense, as if he was waiting for the baby to kick, but it was too soon for that, and I almost said so.

"I wasn't expecting this." His voice was deeper, though maybe a bit gentler. "I thought you wanted to yell at me, tell me I had an STD or something." He looked up, meeting my eyes. "I never expected this." My heart constricted as his big blue eyes met mine. "I had cancer when I was three years old—I was told it was a real possibility I could never have kids."

A big fat tear ran down my cheek, and I covered my mouth. His statement shocked me, made all the blood leave my face, and sent a tingle up my spine. As though it was fate we were brought together that night. That this baby, who wasn't planned, had forced her way into my belly. I wiped the tears away with the back of my hand, trying to pull myself together.

He closed his eyes and kneeled in front of me. "I had leukemia," he continued. "I always expected the worst. Grew up thinking I was sterile. To me, this baby is a gift from heaven."

My mouth fell open, and I took in a shuddering breath. I'd come here prepared for the worst. Prepared for denial, hatred, and blame. To be faced with a man who didn't want to be a father. And I could have taken all of it. But the fact that this man, who barely knew me, thought our baby was a gift from heaven?

My body began to shake with emotion. It hadn't been my intention to get pregnant, but I had, and out of sheer luck, I did it with a man whose reaction told me he'd be there for everything. His eyes lowered to my belly again where his hand still rested.

"Is it a boy or a girl?"

I shook my head and pulled in another breath, trying to take in enough oxygen to keep from passing out. "We won't know for another nine weeks, but I keep having dreams it's a girl."

He nodded but didn't move from his spot on the floor, as if he was afraid to do so or possibly too shocked. We sat like that a few moments, his hands on my belly like a scene from a movie, but unlike a movie, it wasn't me he loved. He loved our baby—he was holding our baby, not me.

He looked up then, his face soft but intense. "I'll marry you." He nodded. "My mama raised me right, and I won't run away from my responsibilities."

My nose burned and I blinked back the tears that threatened to spill over. I'd almost hoped he would be a jerk, but with each passing moment, he proved more and more that he wasn't. There was a part of me who hated him for that. For putting me in this situation. To be in a place where I'd found the love my life but couldn't keep him. And here this other man was on his knees at my belly, telling me he'd do right by me.

I shook my head and squeezed my eyes shut. He'd given me something I'd prayed for every day of my life, but taken something I never knew possible at the same time.

When I opened my eyes again, his brows were knit together, and he was sitting back in his seat. "You don't have to answer now. I just needed you to know that."

I nodded and placed my hands on my belly, feeling a little calmer with the distance between us.

"I hate to do this." He looked over his shoulder to the front door. "But I was supposed to be back on set fifteen minutes ago. Can I call you later?"

I nodded my head and waved away his concern. "Go. I totally understand."

He pulled out his phone. "I guess we should exchange numbers." He gripped the bridge of his nose and winced. "This is embarrassing, but what was your name again?"

Our eyes locked, as if both in shock by the situation, then I buried my face in my hands as a mixture of laughter and tears bubbled from inside me.

I looked up at him, overwhelmed with all of it. "Tuesday. Tuesday Patil." I reached across the table to shake his hand. "Nice to meet you."

His grin never faltered as he took my hand in his. Strong and firm. "Austin Stratton." He pushed himself to stand and pulled me out of my seat. "Ahh hell." He wrapped his arms around me and pulled me against his chest. "We're having a baby. The least we can do is hug."

I nodded, my cheek rubbing against the thin cotton of his t-shirt. "We're having a baby."

I looked up again, meeting the brightest smile I'd ever seen. He looked over my head to the couple that watched us from the corner. "We're having a baby," he stated, then he looked around the whole cafe, to the twenty plus people who sat all around us. "We're having a baby!" he shouted.

His reaction caused my heart to fill up and *break* at the same time.

* * *

A short time later, I wiped at my face as I ran across the lot of Parker Studios. Becky was back on set and waiting for me to fill her in on my meeting with Austin.

I slipped through the familiar door that led me to her station, pushed past the lighting crew, PAs, and extras who lined the long hall on the west end of Parker Studios. I found Becky in the corner, her long black hair hanging loose as she touched up someone's makeup.

She looked up when I got closer, examined my tear-streaked face, and then tilted her head to a nearby chair. "Have a seat. I'll be right with you."

It was the way we always behaved when I came to see her. That I was her next client, instead of her pregnant basket-case best friend.

I hopped up in the chair and grabbed a magazine, but I couldn't really look at it. All I could do was replay the meeting at the cafe over and over in my mind.

Becky continued chatting with her client, but I could tell by her expression that she was concerned. I needed to relax, to calm my mind, but all I could do was think about Austin's proposal. Think about John, who was the last person I needed to tell.

These past days I tried to push it from my mind. To enjoy his love, which he gave freely and abundantly. We spent each day flirting in the shop, and each night wrapped in each other's arms until we fell asleep. Tomorrow, we would go out on our date and I'd tell him. And I was pretty sure it would all end there.

Becky took out a large Kabuki brush and ran it over her client's face to set the foundation, then nodded for me to take the seat as soon as the woman left. She wrapped the silky black drape around my shoulders and turned me around to face the mirror. "So what happened?"

My throat thickened, and I took a deep breath to push back the threatening tears. "He asked me to marry him."

Her eyes widened, and her mouth fell open.

"Actually, he said 'I'll marry you', which is different but means the same thing. He was nice. He said he believed the baby was a gift from heaven." My chin began to quiver, and I pulled my glasses from my face.

"Oh, honey." She handed me a tissue. "What did you say?"

"I didn't say anything."

There was a long pause before she spoke again. "Have you told John?"

I shook my head, my lip quivering again. "Tomorrow."

She put down her brush then sat in the chair beside me. "Do you know what you're going to say?"

My shoulders rose and fell as I took a big breath. "Not in the slightest."

CHAPTER TWENTY-SEVEN

tuesday

* * *

I took in John's reflection in the bathroom mirror, his bare chest, clean wet skin after our shower, and his still sleepy eyes as we brushed our teeth. It was something we'd done at least a dozen times over the past four weeks, but an act I tried to memorize now. The way his muscles shifted with each tiny movement of the brush, the way he looked right now with his hair damp, doing the simple things I wanted to do with him for the next fifty years. But today would be the last I'd see of those things. Because today I promised myself I would tell him.

Last night, the guys had finished all the last minute details of the shop then packed away every bit of their equipment. My shop was empty of any trace that he'd ever been there, but my heart would never be. It would be broken, shattered, but the pieces that remained would forever be filled with our days together.

My chest grew increasingly heavy as I watched him. I knew I should tell him about the baby. Right now. To not wait until later, to not spend another second deceiving him into loving me, because he deserved so much more.

He spit into the sink then rinsed his mouth with water

before wrapping his arms around my waist. "I'm going to go back to my house to change. I'll pick you up in an hour?"

The toothbrush was still my mouth, which gave me an excuse not to speak. I nodded, but the pit of my stomach was turning in disgust with my cowardice.

He smiled against my neck, kissing up to my ear and causing goose bumps to rise on every bit of my skin.

"Wear something comfortable," he said in my ear, his mouth lingering on the patch of skin at the edge of my jaw. I closed my eyes to feel it better, inhaling the warm minty scent of his breath. "Panties optional," he whispered.

I grinned in spite of my somber mood, rinsed my mouth, and wiped over my lips with a towel. "Where are we going?"

He shook his head, his eyes meeting mine in the mirror. "It's a surprise."

I swallowed, my tongue heavy with the words I needed to say, but I only nodded, allowing myself one more moment, one more goodbye, one more hello before it all ended.

* * *

True to his word, he picked me up an hour later. We sat quietly in the cab of his truck, watching out the windshield as the city came and went. Even though I still had no clue where we were going, I didn't ask, because where we went didn't matter anyway—we wouldn't make it.

My secret rolled in my stomach, fighting a battle where I knew there could be no victory. Because part of me wanted to stuff it down and forget it even existed, and the other wanted it over with, to do it quickly so it would hurt less—but I couldn't. He was my captive audience; there was nothing to distract him, but still, I said nothing.

219

I rested my head on the window and took a breath. The weather report had predicted rain, and the dark, ominous sky off in the horizon told me it was true. But for now, the sun was still shining bright and beautiful, causing a rainbow to peek out from the clouds. A prism of colors, a promise of better days. But for me, it would always represent the day I lost the love of my life.

John's fingers wrapped around my hand, grabbing my attention. I looked up, meeting his soft smile.

"You okay?"

He looked exactly how I wanted to remember him. His face still shadowed with whiskers from the night before. Comfortable, messy... mine. Moisture filled my eyes and I nodded. "Tired."

His mouth lifted in a slight smile, and he turned back to the road. "Me too."

We pulled off the freeway and onto a two-lane highway. I sat up a little, forcing myself away from the cool window, realizing we'd gone farther than I ever intended to go. I cleared my throat, trying to dislodge the tight, constricting feeling around my vocal cords, but it wouldn't go away. It was my subconscious telling me not to say anything, to keep this secret... just a little bit longer.

But I couldn't.

I turned to face him, drawing my foot onto the seat and hugging my leg to my chest. Pastures framed both sides of the road, leaving us isolated except for the cows grazing on their lush green foliage.

I wished I'd written a letter, so I could hand it over, and he could pull over and read it on the side of the road. But I didn't have that much foresight, and deep down I knew it should come from my lips, from my heart, and not from a perfect list of words that were rehearsed so many times they lost their meaning.

We turned off to a little dirt road, and I could feel us

approaching our destination. We had driven for over an hour now, and I was filled with regret that I let us get this far.

I grabbed the strand of feathers in my hair and twirled them between my fingers. "John, I▢" I closed my eyes, my throat full of tears as I grasped for every bit of courage I had. "I have something I need to tell you."

I kept my eyes shut, concentrating on the sound of gravel beneath our tires as we came to a full stop. I imagined us pulling to the side of the road, and any smile that had been there only moments ago gone from his face. I opened my eyes again and found his body turned toward me. His brows pulled together, and I knew, knew in every crevice of my heart that he already knew what I was going to say.

"I don't know how to say this." I clasped my hands together and twisted my fingers. "I should have told you so long ago."

The soft purr of the engine stopped, a feeling that would normally go unnoticed, but I had to concentrate on something so the excruciating quiet didn't tear me up inside.

TAP TAP TAP.

I jumped a foot at the sound.

Pulling in a ragged breath, I whipped around toward the window, where a little girl stood on the other side of the closed door, watching us.

"There you are!" Her head barely reached the edge of the window; her honey blonde hair was pulled into two high pigtails.

I turned back to John, my chest heavy with the words I'd left unsaid. He didn't seem fazed by the little girl standing there. His eyes narrowed, and he shook his head, telling me to continue.

"Uncle John, you're late!" The little girl's small voice

continued, seeping into the truck and interrupting us. She was tiny and innocent, having no clue of the tension that was building inside the cab. "Hurry up, Uncle John! I've been waiting for *years!*"

John rolled down the window, and I tried to calm my breaths. "I'll be there in a minute, Shelly. Run along now, my friend has something to say."

She frowned, her eyes meeting mine for a second before she turned around and skipped away toward a large redwood cabin thirty yards away. I recognized the house from the stories he told me about his childhood. And that's when I noticed the other people sitting on the porch and leaning over the banister. They waved to us, causing nausea to roll through my entire body.

I turned to face him, finding him stone-faced and distant. "Where are we?" I asked almost whispering. "Is that your family out there?" My chest tightened, making each breath more painful.

He only nodded. "What did you want to tell me, Tuesday?"

I forced my gaze up to his deep reflective eyes, knowing I couldn't possibly tell him now. Not with his entire family only feet away to witness what my words would do to him. If there was one thing I learned about John over our time together, it was that he had a heart as big as the ocean, but he didn't like others to see it. He deserved privacy at a time like this, to not hear this news when a whole audience of people waited for us to come inside.

As hard as it was for me to play along, I needed to. Because this was my fault. I had spent four days taking his love, and when I said the words, I needed for him to be able to yell if he wanted to, to walk away and never turn back, for him to be able to cry... and I knew he wouldn't do that here.

I pushed my glasses up the bridge of my nose and stuffed down the scream that was building in my chest. "I'm allergic to bees." My words were tight, as though my heart was trying to hold back the words. Even though it was the truth, the lie that twisted in my gut was so painful.

His brows knit together and he shook his head slightly. "What?"

I forced a smile and nodded over my shoulder. "I saw a hive a few miles back and realized I should tell you." I pulled my bag from the floor and took my epi-pen from its pocket. "Just in case you need it."

He studied me a second, then leaned forward to grip the back of my neck. He pulled me closer, until our foreheads touched and our breath mingled. "You scared me."

I closed my eyes, my skin heating from the rush of adrenaline that surged through my veins. "Why?" I whispered.

He was quiet a second before answering. "I don't know. I saw the fear in your eyes and thought you were going to tell me something horrible."

I swallowed back tears, knowing his fears were true. "No. Just bees."

His lips hovered over mine, and his grip tightened on the back of my neck. "Bees I can handle."

The little girl yelled from up on the porch again. "Uncle John, are you coming?"

He smiled against my mouth then lifted his head to look into my eyes. "Are you ready to meet my family?"

I pulled in a deep breath, knowing this was the biggest mistake of my life.

Never.

"I'd love to."

CHAPTER TWENTY-EIGHT

tuesday

* * *

John took me by the hand and guided me up the long walkway toward the cabin. The essence of *family* practically oozed from the large wooden logs that held the two-story home together. It was bigger than any cabin I'd ever been to, surrounded by a redwood porch that was filled with at least a dozen people.

I gripped the strap of my bag as we walked toward them. Enormous oak trees framed the path on either side of us, reminding me of the places my mom and I stayed at when I was a child. The area felt majestic in a sense, the gaps in the trees casting bits of filtered light through their huge extending branches. This was the place John had told me stories about. His family cabin. The place he stayed every summer as a child.

"Why are we here?" I whispered, suddenly quite aware of what I was wearing. When he said comfortable, I took him literally, but now I was about to meet his parents with wild hair, big glasses, and overalls that were two sizes too large. My only saving grace was that unlike his request, I had opted for panties.

He squeezed my hand, taking his normal long strides that were twice the length of my own. "It's my mom's birthday."

I hurried my steps to keep up. "Is *everyone here*?"

He shook his head. "The others are probably inside."

I groaned. "Oh God…"

He laughed. "Don't worry, they'll love you."

His tone was so amused, so sure of himself that it made me look up. "Why do you think that?"

He squeezed my hand and pulled me so close our legs brushed. "Because I do."

It was a simple statement, said without any speck of humor, and it filled my chest with excitement and guilt at the same time. They were two emotions I never thought would go together, but they did, whirling around, moving toward my stomach and making me sick.

Soon we were climbing the six steps to the covered porch, and I tried to stuff down all of the feelings. The guilt, my heartache, and especially the nausea. I was almost twelve weeks into my pregnancy, and the whole Internet was in agreement I should be feeling better, but since hearing the news four days ago, my stomach hadn't felt settled for even a second.

A woman with dark blond hair was waiting for us at the top of the landing. Her smile was large and bright, and deep creases framed the corners of her light blue eyes. "I'm so glad you could make it." She took my hands and smiled at me. "My name's Lucy Eaton. I'm John's mother."

"Tuesday," I said, having a hard time not withering in a puddle on the floor. For the first time in my life, I could relate to being a mother. And if I were her, I would hate me. I would hate me with every bone in my body. But her eyes were warm and told me she didn't hate me in the slightest.

She moved to John next, pulling him into a big hug that showed how close they were. Her tiny frame was completely encompassed by his.

"Happy Birthday, Mama," he said.

She squeezed him tighter, closing her eyes briefly before opening them again. "I'm so glad you made it—and I like her already," she whispered, though her tone wasn't hushed enough to be private, and she winked at me, making it obvious she meant for me to overhear.

She pulled away a moment later, and a cluster of people waited for us on the deck. There were his two sisters, Penny and Margaret, a whole handful of cousins whose names all came so fast I couldn't catch any of them, their spouses, and six other children. The smallest one was Shelly, who belonged to Penny, and who immediately put a death grip on John's leg. Her little three-year-old arms didn't appear to be letting go anytime soon.

She turned to face me, her face turning in a horrible frown. "Who are you?" she asked in an accusatory tone.

"I'm Tuesday," I said softly, meeting her tiny face.

Her head bobbed up and down with each step as John moved across the deck to the entrance of the house. "She's my girlfriend, Shell." He laughed a little and squeezed my hand as if to assure me she didn't bite.

Shelly turned her head away with a pout, sniffed loudly, and rubbed her nose on the leg of his jeans. I imagined myself in her situation, faced with another woman honing in on the man I loved. I think I would have felt the same, possibly even down to the nose bit.

"I thought I was your girlfriend," she stated after a long pause.

"You're my niece, baby girl."

"Aaaaand your friend."

"Yes. And my friend," he agreed.

"Aaaannd a gull."

He laughed. "And a girl."

She giggled a little and squeezed his leg tighter. "I misseded you, Uncle John."

He grinned. "I missed you too, Shelly."

Someone pulled open the door, and one by one, we all entered the kitchen. The smell of warm cake and fresh cut strawberries hit my nose, making the already homey feel of the place feel even homier.

It was then that all my emotions hit me, and I had to turn away slightly to wipe the tears from my eyes. If this had come only a week earlier, I would have been elated... but now, it felt like a sick joke. A dangling carrot to someone who hadn't eaten for a long time.

No one seemed to notice me crumbling, not even John, because I was only one person in more than a dozen. I'd just met them, but already I was part of this huge, boisterous family as they laughed and joked with each other in the kitchen.

Hugs spread from person to person, and I took the time to calm my heart. To breathe and settle in for the next few hours. This was exactly what I'd wanted my whole life. Siblings and cousins, grandparents and grandchildren; I'd dreamt of it all for as long as I could remember, and now I was here. But now there was a baby in my womb, and I knew I could only keep both for today. Because as sad as it was, only the baby would still be in my life tomorrow.

My hand fell to my belly, under the bib of my overalls so no one could see—I'd already made my choice. I just wished I could feel her, so I knew it was the right one.

My eyes locked on a pregnant woman who stood at the sink, wiping her hands on a gingham rag. I couldn't help but be jealous of her because she had everything I wanted. When there was a break in the crowd, they came toward me, the tall brunette extending her hand with a warm smile. "Hi, I'm Katie Johnson, Jake's wife," she stated.

I looked into her eyes then down to her belly and shook my head. "I thought—"

"We're out of the danger zone now." She smiled and rested her hand on her stomach. "The placenta moved up and everything's good to go. Four more weeks."

I nodded, wishing for the hundredth time that things were different. She looked kind, and if things were different, maybe we could have been friends.

I swallowed back more tears and turned to a petite, blonde women who'd come to stand beside me.

"Lisa," she said brightly. "John's favorite sister."

I smiled, my head swimming with all the names I'd learned in the past few minutes. I stuck out my hand. "It's nice to meet you."

John came to stand by my side, little Shelly hanging from his arm as he bent over to whisper in my ear. "The guys are all outside. Do you mind if I leave you?"

My eyes widened and I glanced over at him. He looked so happy, in his element, and I couldn't stop myself from nodding. "Go ahead."

* * *

Katie and Lisa both stayed in the kitchen, talking to me as they assembled what had to have been the most mouth-watering strawberry shortcake I'd ever seen in my life. They asked where I was from, how John and I had met, and all the other typical questions that came when you met someone's family for the first time.

Katie excused herself to the restroom when they were done, and Lisa gestured to a room on the other side of the house where it was quiet. "Follow me."

We passed through the dining room, where older children sat at the large table playing Monopoly, and the smaller children were coloring on the floor. They barely looked up, barely noticed us, and my heart was pounding as if we were climbing a tall mountain.

I didn't want to be here. Meeting his family, having them hug me, smile, and wrap me in warmth. I was already in love with John; I didn't want to fall in love with his family, too.

We stopped at an oak bar in the living room, and Lisa gestured for me to take a seat as she walked behind it.

"We have beer, wine, or I can make you a margarita if you'd prefer." She took a deep breath. "You're going to need it. You've only met half of them so far."

I turned toward the barstool and inwardly cringed. I couldn't think of a lie, so I just nodded, knowing I would dump it later. "Wine, please." I sat down, folded my hands in my lap, and smiled. "Can I have some ice water too?"

She nodded over her shoulder. "Of course." Then she pulled a bottle from the fridge and twisted the cap before sliding it across the bar. "How was your drive?"

I cleared my throat and took a deep breath before answering. "It was good. Went by quickly."

She grinned, taking the corkscrew from the top drawer and opening the wine. "Good." After pulling the cork from the bottle, she poured chilled chardonnay into two bulbous glasses and passed one to me. She rested her hip on the counter and looked around the large room. Her face transformed into an expression of nostalgia, as she gazed out the large picture windows.

"We don't come up here very often anymore." Her eyes met mine again. "We used to practically live here in the summers. It's hard to believe they're going to sell it."

I frowned, taking in the room that smelled of cedar and earth. This was the first time I'd been here, but it didn't feel like it. John had told me about this place. I'd laughed with him over memories of his childhood, and my shoulders slumped at hearing it was for sale. I took a sip of water before turning back to her.

"Why are you selling it?"

She shrugged. "Dad's getting older, doesn't want to keep up the property anymore."

My brows furrowed. I looked out the window again, where I could see John laughing with a group of other men. Old and young, all laughing and joking in a way I'd never seen before. "He told me about this place. He told me about all the trouble he used to get into here."

She smiled over the rim of her glass and leaned forward on the bar. "Oh God. John's full of stories. Which ones did he tell you?"

I laughed and looked to the large window where a giant oak tree was spreading its branches like a large welcome sign. "He told me about falling out of that tree. About the scar on his chin." I grinned, even though my insides were crying. I turned around to face her, but her expression wasn't lighthearted like I'd expected. Like it was only a second ago. It had changed, transforming her features from something happy to something very sad.

She looked to the door that John had exited through only moments before and cleared her throat. "I've never heard him talk about that before." She met my eyes again, but hers were glassy as if holding back tears. "He doesn't tell many people about his life before us. In truth, I wasn't sure he even remembered it."

Before us? I frowned, not knowing what she meant.

"He must really trust you."

I looked down, unable to meet her eyes any longer, because her words hit me in the most vulnerable place. "Yeah." He trusted me, and I was about to break his heart.

"We're only a few months apart, John and I☐" Her voice was distant as she continued to speak. "He was always so much bigger than me, but I felt like I had to protect him

230

like my baby brother. Because the day he came to us forever changed me. Before that day, I didn't realize people could be so cruel."

She took another long sip of wine before meeting my eyes again. Hers were light blue, almost clear, so much different from John's. *He was adopted.* I didn't know why, but the fact he'd kept such an intimate detail from me made my heart constrict. It broke me.

"I'm sorry." She closed her eyes and shook her head. "I didn't mean for this to get depressing—it's just been on my mind a lot with the letter." She pursed her lips and shook her head again.

I pulled in a breath, feeling my hands tremble in my lap. "What letter?"

She held her breath, finally realizing I had no idea what she was talking about. She looked to the window, where John could still be seen smiling and laughing in the group of men, then to me. "I'm sorry—I thought ." She looked down to her hands. "Did John warn you I was the sister with the big mouth?"

I laughed slightly, more to fill the space than because of humor. "That's okay... You don't have to tell me."

She nodded, though her eyebrows scrunched and she took a deep breath. She bit her lip then raised her chin to the back door. "Come on." She came from around the bar. "Grab your drink. I'll introduce you to everyone on the porch."

CHAPTER TWENTY-NINE

tuesday

* * *

I rested my head on John's shoulder, letting my face bask in the last rays of sunlight before the clouds covered every bit of the blue sky. John's mother had laid out a half dozen quilts under one of the large oaks, allowing us some time alone for the first time in two hours.

The afternoon had been filled with stories and laughter, except for my conversation with Lisa. Her words still swarmed in my mind, causing a million questions to linger on my tongue. The thought of anyone hurting him—especially as a young boy—caused my chest to harden with pain.

His family was amazing, and although I would be gone from his life tomorrow, I knew he had others to take care of him. To take the heart I would crush and make it whole again.

They told me I was the first girlfriend he'd brought home since high school. And every story, every warm hug or smile that showed how happy they were to have me, made the anxiety in my stomach grow. I tried to stuff it down, to breathe in the crisp, clean air and forget about the baby, but it was impossible. This little life was all I thought about. Every second, every breath, I thought about her, or him, even more. Trying to forget felt like a betrayal to the child I'd already started to love.

"You okay?" John whispered in my ear. His arms wrapped around my chest as we sat together. I nestled between his legs, my back to his chest as he surrounded me with his body.

"Yeah," I sighed, though it couldn't have been farther from the truth. "Everyone's been really nice."

His lips brushed my ear, and he hugged me tighter. "They better. I'm paying them enough."

I laughed slightly and jabbed him in the ribs with my elbow.

"Easy." But he pulled me closer, smiling against my cheek. "They love you, just like I said they would."

My eyes closed at the words because hearing the words felt like a hot iron poker straight to my stomach. Tears welled behind my lids as I felt him bury his nose in my hair.

When I opened my eyes a moment later, little Shelly was coming toward us across the lawn. She'd been stuck to John's side almost the whole afternoon, and now her little limbs picked up speed as she spotted him again. Two feet before the blanket, she flung her arms into the air, causing her tiny body to fly, crash into us, and knock us over.

"Dare you are!" she said, grabbing hold of his neck. "I've been wooking for you everywhere!"

John laughed, falling back against the blanket. "Did you find the treasure?" he asked her.

She scrunched up her nose and frowned as she squeezed in between us to take a seat on top of his chest.

"No." She pulled a crumpled up piece of paper from her

pocket, taking extra care to unfold it just so.

Various lines were drawn upon it: a few squiggles, something that looked like a bush, and a stick figure house drawn in the very center. She leaned down, examining the paper with intense concentration. "Are you *sure* there's treasure there?" Her chubby finger pointed to the X in the far corner.

John folded his hands behind his head and grinned. "Course I am." Then he lifted his head and pointed to his ear. "See that hole there?"

Shelly came in closer, taking his lobe between her chubby fingers. "Yes, I see it."

"That's from back in my pirating days." He nodded once.

Her eyes widened. "Did you get shot?"

He laughed then pinched her nose. "No, silly. It's from my earring. All pirates wear earrings. It's part of the uniform."

Her eyes widened and she stretched her legs out in back of her. "Were you really a pirate, Uncle John?"

"Yep."

She folded her hands on his chest and grinned. "Is that where the treasure came from? Is that why you had the map?"

"Sure is." He nodded. "I buried it under one of those trees out back."

She bunched up her shoulders and suppressed a giggle. "Will you tell me a story? About when you were a pirate?"

"Don't you want to find the treasure?"

"Not yet. I want a story first."

He narrowed his eyes at her. "If I tell you a story, will you run along so I can spend some time with my lady?"

She looked over her shoulder, her eyes meeting mine for just a second before she turned back to John. "Are you going to kiss her again?" she whispered.

His brow lifted as he looked at her. "What do *you* know about kissing?" he whispered back.

She scrunched her shoulders and squeezed her eyes shut.

"Ahhh... Well, I might," he said, leaning back on the blanket again.

"Yuck. I'm *never* going to kiss a boy."

He laughed. "That's good. Boys are gross." He took a deep breath then closed his eyes. "So you want a pirate story, do ya?"

She smiled and laid her head on his chest, nestling in. "Yes, but it has to be your *best* pirate story ever."

"No guarantees." But his face transformed into a content grin, and he started talking.

The next fifteen minutes were filled with the most elaborate tale I'd ever heard in my whole life. Filled with mermaids, crocodiles, and sword fights, but as the story went on, Shelly's little body became more and more relaxed, and John's words slowed, becoming softer and softer until they completely faded.

I couldn't help but watch them. How they fit together like two peas in the same pod, and how she'd completely pushed me out of their whole garden. He would make such a good daddy. He didn't just pay attention to her because she loved him; he loved her too, and I could see that from a mile away, both resting peacefully under the large oak tree.

Her little head was nestled right under his chin, and his hand rested on the small of her back, their breathing deep and even, in complete sync with one another. I could feel my emotion building again, and tucked my feet under my body to push myself from the ground.

I looked to the house, where the sounds of laughter and merriment filtered through the cool air, then turned around and began walking in the opposite direction to the woods. I didn't know where I was going, just that I needed a few moments alone to find peace with myself.

CHAPTER THIRTY

john

* * *

I tucked my legs under my body and pressed my ear to the floor. The tile was sticky and cool beneath my cheek, but I closed my eyes and practiced my ABC's inside my head like he told me to. Maybe he wouldn't find me here. Maybe he would forget about me and finally get so tired he'd fall asleep.

SLAM!

The sounds of something shattering against the wall jolted my body. It was so close I could feel the impact through the floor. I pulled my legs in tighter, wanting so badly to disappear. But as hard as I prayed, it never happened. God never came to save me when my daddy behaved like this. I cracked my eyes open and peered through the gap between the couch and floor.

Maybe that lady would come back, she could find his keys, and he would be happy again. Or maybe they would go into the bedroom, and he'd forget about me. Sometimes, if I was quiet enough, he would forget he was so thirsty, forget he was mad at me for all the things I did. I squeezed my eyes harder, pretending glue had stuck them together like two pieces of paper.

More slams echoed through the walls, and even though

237

my arms and legs were shaking, I didn't cry like I wanted to. I couldn't. *Shhh... Be quiet. Be quiet or he'll hear you.*

"JOHNNY! Where are you?" His angry voice growled like a monster, echoing against the walls and through the floor. The couch shifted as he sat on the cushions, squeezing my bones as his weight pressed on my hiding place. A small sound came out of my mouth, and I quickly covered it with my hand. But it was too late.

"JOHNNY! Is that you?"

I squeezed my eyes shut as tears fell to my cheeks, sneaking past the imaginary layer of glue. The couch shifted again, and I wrapped my hand around the welt on my arm still burning from the last time he was mad at me.

He looked down at me, swaying slightly with his hands on his hips. "I've found you Johnny, and now you're going to find my keys."

CHAPTER THIRTY-ONE

tuesday

* * *

I pressed my back against a giant oak tree and let my head lull, until the hard, rocky bark could be felt against my scalp. *What the hell am I doing?*

I closed my eyes, filling my lungs with cool, moisture-laden air, wishing so badly that this day was over. Because the words I needed to say were still heavy on my chest, suffocating me, filling my veins with trepidation, and I needed them out. I needed to be able to breathe again, and somehow putting the distance between us made that easier. Somehow, alone in the woods, I could breathe.

The lights of the cabin glowed faintly in the distance, but I couldn't see the blankets any longer, nor John and Shelly, who I was sure were still resting peacefully under the large tree. I didn't know how far I'd gone; all I knew was that it wasn't far enough. But no distance or time could separate me from what I needed to do. Running would only prolong the inevitable and cause more pain. That was the last thing I wanted to do.

I lowered myself to the ground, digging my fingers into the earth and pulling in deep slow breaths. It was dusk now, and off on the horizon, the sun was making its descent into the dark, stormy night. The combination of darkness and light was breathtakingly beautiful. The sky held me captive with a vibrant show of magenta, violet, and orange, a show just for me.

I knew I should go back because I'd been gone at least fifteen minutes, and I hadn't told anyone where I was going. But I needed this. I needed to ground myself for a few minutes longer. To go back to my roots where things weren't so complicated and set my mind free.

I thought about Lisa's words in the cabin, about the glimpse of a wounded man I'd seen so many times but couldn't place. It all fit now. The scar on his chin wasn't from a fall from a tree; it came from a darker place. A place I wasn't sure I wanted to know about and was sure I didn't deserve to hear.

My hands played with the moistened soil of the forest floor, crunching bits of fallen leaves with my fingers. Somewhere along the way fate, had brought him here. To this family, whose love and warmth could be felt even from so far away. I placed my hand on my belly, feeling the slight curve that told me my baby was growing.

The first roll of thunder sounded off in the distance, breaking my mind free. I opened my eyes, and there, not five feet in front of me I saw John's name, carved into the trunk of a tree. It was drawn by a child, darkened by time and weather, and I pulled myself to my knees and crawled toward it, my breaths coming faster.

I traced each letter with my finger, as a sense of something bigger than myself ran over my body. Out of all the trees in the entire forest, I had stopped at the one that led me back to him. To the man I loved so deeply it hurt.

For the last four days, I never once considered that he might want this baby. That he'd be able to see past the fact that it wasn't his, that he would listen to me, hear my answer, and be able to love me anyway. My chin quivered. The thought was terrifying, but maybe it was possible.

Another crash of thunder boomed closer, and I knew I had to go back. I flattened my hand on his name, feeling the scars of his boyhood scrawled beneath my palm. I pushed myself from the ground, and using the cabin's lights as a beacon, I trudged through the leafy ground back to the house. I only made it a few feet before a fat drop of rain landed on my cheek like a tear. I pushed a branch away from my face and picked up my pace, knowing it wouldn't be long before the storm was directly overhead.

A sliver of light was all that remained of the sun on the hilltops, making it increasingly hard to see, but I had lots of practice running through the wilderness. When the clouds opened up, releasing all the rain they had been storing up all day, I only ran faster until I pushed my way through to the clearing.

I found the blankets John and Shelly had been sleeping on empty and made my way to the back porch. My hair was completely drenched and stuck to my skin, but for some reason, it felt wonderful, almost cleansing, washing me of the guilt I'd been carrying around for the past four days.

"TUESDAY!" The sound of John's voice boomed as the first crack of lightning appeared in the sky.

"John, I'm here!" I hurried up the steps, turning in the direction of his voice but stopped as he came into view around the corner. He was still twenty feet away, but I could see the relief on his face, the largeness of his body, and took it all in.

"Where were you?" he yelled across to me.

I grinned, suddenly filled with joy at the sight of his face. "Watching the sunset!" My foot slipped on the top step, causing both of my feet to jet out in front of me, and my bottom to land hard on the wood step.

He ran toward me, sinking to his knees in a puddle of rain. "Oh my God, are you okay?"

"I'm fine." I laughed, taking hold of his arms as he pulled

me to stand. "Just wet."

I found my feet again, and he grabbed me around my waist and lifted me up. I slipped again.

He caught me under my arms, laughing, and lifted me up for the second time. "I got you."

My face was plastered to his chest and I smiled up at him. "Why is it so slippery?"

He grinned then guided me a couple of steps to the left and pushed my hair from my face. "It's just that spot. It's been like that as long as I can remember."

I looked down at the floor, holding onto the banister to test my traction before letting go. "My God, it's like ice." I smiled up at him, gathering my hair to the side of my neck to wring the water from it with both hands. His face was relaxed, but there was something there I'd never seen before. "What?" I asked, shaking my head.

"When I woke up you were gone. I got worried."

I breathed in, taking in the sight of him every bit as drenched as me.

"Where'd you go?" he asked.

I looked over my shoulder, in the direction of the woods, where the sun was now completely gone. "I just wanted to see where you grew up."

He took my glasses from my face and dried them as best he could before replacing them. "Did you find anything interesting?"

I nodded. "I found *you.*"

His forehead wrinkled with confusion, and I shook my head. "I found your name. Out there. On a tree trunk."

He smiled then. "You did?" His nose wrinkled, and a content expression softened his face. "That was the year

Grandpa gave me my first pocket knife. I think I carved it into every surface I could get my hands on."

I smiled at him, even though I was shivering, and I never wanted this conversation to end. I wanted to stand here with him all night and learn about his past. I wanted to ask him why he lied to me about his scar, and what happened to him that landed him here with this family. But at the same time, I didn't want to ruin this moment.

I wanted to stay just like this, the storm blocking out the others inside the cabin, leaving us in seclusion, and never having to face tomorrow. "Did you see the sunset?" I asked, not wanting to let him go.

He shook his head and tucked my hair behind my ear. "No."

"It was beautiful."

His hand moved along my neck, and he lowered down until his lips hovered just above mine. "I bet I know something prettier." His face came lower still, until his soft lips touched mine. It wasn't a passionate kiss. It was gentle and sweet, but it told me how much he cared for me, and I never wanted to forget it.

He took my hand then and pulled me in the direction of the back door. "Come on, we need to get back, everyone's waiting."

"Oh God, are you serious?"

He looked over his shoulder and nodded to me. "Yes."

"Why didn't you tell me?"

He dropped my hand just outside the front door and began removing his jacket. "Because I was having too much fun." He took the jacket and looped it over my shoulders, pulling it snug around my chest. "Here, wear this."

My brows furrowed. "Why? It's just as wet as I am."

He bent down low, whispering softly in my ear. "'Cause your t-shirt's white."

My eyes went wide and he turned around to open the front door.

"I found her!" John yelled, causing cheers to sound from inside the cabin. My cheeks flooded with warmth as I stepped inside, clutching the jacket to my chest— mortified, but at the same time, content because I was with John.

CHAPTER THIRTY-TWO

tuesday

* * *

"Here, I think this should fit." Lucy, John's mother held up a pair of drawstring sweatpants and a matching sweatshirt that had a picture of a crockpot on the front. She made a face then handed them over. "Sorry, they were my mother's. Unfortunately, it's all the clothing we have up here anymore."

I smiled and clutched them to my chest, already loving John's grandmother for her eccentric taste in clothing. "Thank you, they're perfect."

"Hardly," she said, looking over at John with a grin. "What were you two up to, anyway? It's crazy out there." She shook her head, not waiting for an answer before she turned around and continued looking through the closet.

John turned to me and raised his eyebrows suggestively, making me hyper-aware of my still see-through t-shirt.

I clutched the neck of his jacket tighter and gave him a look. "Well, I'm just glad you have something for me to change into. Anything's better than this wet mess."

But John started shaking his head slowly, making it very clear that he didn't agree.

His mom opened the other side of the closet, completely unaware of our silent conversation. She looked back to John again. "Now *you,* on the other hand, are going to be the difficult one."

He laughed, reaching out to pull me against his side. "Don't worry about me, Mom, I'll be fine."

"Nonsense," she muttered, continuing to push more clothing down the long rack.

John's hand inched up the small of my back as we watched his mother pass one sweater after another down the closet, and before I knew what he was doing, his hand had found its way into the gap in my overalls, and was making its descent down toward my underwear. I turned to face him, widening my eyes to silently tell him to knock it off, but he only gave me the most mischievous smile I'd ever seen and hooked his thumb in the elastic of my panties.

I stepped away, moving a good foot to the side, but he pulled me right back and bent down to whisper in my ear. "If she doesn't leave soon, I'm going to have to take you in the bathroom and have my way with you. I don't even care that my whole family is right downstairs."

I stomped on his foot, letting him know I didn't think this was funny at all. He then looked down to his wrist, as if checking the time on his imaginary watch and mouthed the words. "Thirty seconds."

I swallowed and turned back to the closet, feeling like a giddy teenager who was about to do the naughtiest thing of her life.

His mom finally stopped at a dark, gray sweater with the initials UCLA written on the front, and pulled it out of the closet. "Here," she said. "I think this is yours anyway." She clutched her chin, thinking. "I don't think I have any pants, though."

His thumb gave a slight tug on my underwear. "I don't need pants," he said, and I closed my eyes as tight as I could.

"Okay, well, I'll leave you two to change then."

I opened my eyes again, finding her grinning as she closed the closet. "I have to go get the pies out of the oven, but you guys come down and eat when you're done."

I nodded then grabbed a pillow off the bed and hit him with it. He bit his lip, grabbed me by the hips, and pulled me forward until our bodies collided, and his lips pressed into my hair. "You're adorable when you're angry, you know that?"

I laughed and shook my head. "You're horrible!"

He grinned and lifted his eyebrows. "You're freaking hot when you're wet, too. I don't think I can stand it any longer." He pushed me backward until the tops of my thighs hit the mattress of the bed.

"Whose room is this?" I asked, looking over my shoulder to the four-poster bed.

"My parents'."

I shook my head, pushing at his chest. "I'm *not* having sex with you in your parents' bedroom."

"It's okay. They won't mind."

I laughed, letting him push me back on the bed. "Your whole family is downstairs," I whispered.

"It's raining," he stated, before dipping his head down again to kiss my neck. As if that was all the answer I needed.

"So?"

He continued kissing me. "They won't hear a thing. Trust me." Then he handed me a pillow. "On second thought. Use this."

I laughed out loud, pulling at his drenched clothing so I could feel his skin. "What are you trying to say?"

He laughed. "You're loud." He kissed my neck. "Hot." He kissed my collarbone. "And sexy as hell."

I grinned from ear to ear then pushed at his shoulders until he rolled to his back. "I'm still not having sex with you in your parents' bedroom."

He groaned, letting his head fall back to the mattress as I climbed off the bed.

"Where are you going?" he asked as I walked across the room.

"To the bathroom. To change."

"Change here. I want to watch you."

I shook my head, grinning. "Not a chance."

He stuck his bottom lip out and sat up on the edge of the bed, sulking like a little boy who was just told he couldn't play with his favorite toy any longer. "Why?"

"'Cause I don't think I'd be able to resist you when I'm naked." I looked at the pillow beside him on the bed. "And that's not enough insulation."

I slipped into the bathroom, grinning before I shut the door behind me. The sound of John's groans could be heard through the walls.

One more night. Just one more night and then I'd tell him. One more night to play with him, and love him, and *make* love with him.

I set the powder blue sweats on the vanity, removed his soaking jacket, and hung it up on the towel rack. Then I took a seat on the toilet and unsnapped my overalls. So wet and heavy, they were completely plastered to my legs. I began tugging at the fabric, inching them slowly down my legs. Deciding to take my panties too, I pushed them down to my ankles then stopped.

My breath caught, and I covered my mouth to suppress a scream. On my panties was blood. Bright red and unmistakable.

I blinked, hoping it was just my imagination that the light was funny, that I was seeing things, but it didn't go away. My eyes filled with tears and I blinked harder, taking longer and longer before opening them again, but every time, it was still there. I was bleeding. I was pregnant and I was bleeding. I remembered the words Dr. Kim spoke when she'd told me the news: that some women bled early in pregnancy. But it did nothing to comfort me. I hadn't bled in nearly seven weeks; why would I start bleeding again now?

I wrapped my arms around my belly and began to rock back and forth, prayed to God to let me wake up. Then my mind flashed to earlier that evening, to me running through the forest back to the house, to climbing up the steps and falling. My lips began to quiver, and I shook my head. I fell so hard. I didn't even think about the baby when I did it. I was irresponsible, and I fell, and I hurt my baby.

I pulled at my overalls, but they were stuck to my ankles, heavy and soaking, so I kicked them to the side and pulled on the pale blue sweat pants. I pushed myself to stand, holding onto the vanity because the room had started to spin. I opened the bathroom door and found John right where I left him, sitting on the edge of the bed.

He stood up as soon as he saw me, his face drained of color as he shook his head. "Are you okay?"

My lips began to quiver, and I looked him in the eyes. "I'm bleeding." I pulled in a deep breath, hearing my heart break and everything inside me crumble with an exhale. "And I'm pregnant."

CHAPTER THIRTY-THREE

tuesday

* * *

"How far along are you, Miss Patil?"

The doctor moved the ultrasound on my belly, the question echoing through the room like a violent alarm. My baby was safe, its heart beating fast and strong on the monitor, but I still couldn't breathe. I was out of days, out of hours, out of minutes. I was out of time with John.

The doctor's hands moved to palpate my belly, checking for pain, but his words kept rolling around in my head. *How far along are you?* It was the question that when answered would reveal everything, and my heart was screaming for me to run away. Because when I answered it, my time would be over. My eyes shifted to John, to his legs braced apart and his face hard with worry. I didn't want him to find out this way. I wanted time to explain, to convince him it was an accident, to beg him to believe me, but I didn't have that now. I was looking into his eyes, knowing it was the end, and yet he was holding my hand, telling me everything would be okay.

The doctor asked the question again, and I shook my head and started to cry. John's eyes narrowed slightly, as though reading something on my face. His expression hardened, and he tilted his head toward the doctor, silently telling me to answer the question.

"Twelve weeks," I whispered, but the sound was so quiet, said between heart-wrenching sobs, that the doctor asked me to say it again.

"Twelve weeks," I said as clearly as I could.

The doctor nodded, scribbled notes in my chart, but all I could do was look at John. To the expression on his face that was filled with confusion. But there was pain there too. Pain that I put there. He took his hand from mine and stepped backward, just as I knew he would. He was leaving me. This was the end. He was leaving me, and I deserved it.

I sat up, my eyes welling with tears as I tried to get off the bed. I needed him to listen to me. I needed him to know this wasn't what he was thinking. I needed to explain. But the doctor urged me back on the bed, telling me I needed to stay settled, and John moved farther and farther away from me.

"John," I whispered. "Listen to me." I needed him to look at me, to *see* me, to know that I wouldn't purposely do this to him. "I love you." And although my words were almost so quiet I couldn't hear them, his face twisted in pain at the sound of them.

The doctor continued to ask me questions, but I couldn't focus enough to answer. Because my heart was dying as I watched John turn around and walk out the door.

* * *

An hour later, I lay in bed watching the rain fall, spattering against the large window of my hospital room. Giant, thudding drops, telling me the storm wasn't close to being over. I wrapped my arms around my abdomen and closed my eyes. I was trying to block out the chill that had settled in the dim room, fiercely wanting to protect the baby I'd only just found out about, but was already terrified of losing.

There was desperation in my heart that was foreign to me. A gut-wrenching, heartbreaking desire to wake up—but my eyes had been open for a long time now, and everything that had happened over the past eight weeks was mine to own.

"I'm prescribing light bed rest until you can get in to see your primary doctor."

I nodded, turning to watch the doctor scribble something on my chart before I looked out of the window again. John hadn't come back yet, but his truck was still in the parking lot. I could see it from my bed, and the sight of it gave me hope.

"The ultrasound was clear, and I don't see any signs of bleeding inside the uterus. But just as a precaution, no sex, no exercise, no shopping. Just stay off your feet for a few days, and if the bleeding continues, come back in. Do you have any questions?"

I wrapped my arms around my belly and shook my head. "Why am I bleeding? Is it because of the fall?"

He scrunched his shoulders and lowered his clipboard. "It could be anything. Possibly your fall." He lowered his pen and looked at me. "Blood volume increases during pregnancy. Tissue becomes more delicate. There could be any number of reasons. But I don't want you to worry. Twenty-five percent of women bleed during pregnancy for completely benign reasons. Your baby looks strong and healthy. You're over twelve weeks, which means you're out of the danger zone. Chances are this will be a one-time event. Follow up next week with your primary doctor. It was likely just a vaginal tear and this will be the end of it."

I pulled in a breath, looked out the window again, and nodded. He closed the folder and patted me on the knee. "You're free to go whenever you're ready."

"Thank you," I whispered, then turned back to the window and continued to watch the rain.

A tap sounded at my hospital door a short time later, and

the door opened just as I looked up. John walked into the room, his head covered by a drenched hoodie, his eyes hollow, but possibly looking more beautiful than I'd ever seen him before.

I swallowed, sat up a little straighter and folded my hands in my lap.

I'm not ready for this.

I knew when I saw his truck he'd be back, that I couldn't avoid this conversation forever, but I wasn't ready. I wasn't sure if I'd ever be.

I pressed my fingers hard against my lips, trying to prevent the sob, but it was too late. I hated seeing him like this—hated knowing I was the cause of it. "John, I□"

But he held up his hand, stopping my words, and sat down in the chair beside my bed. His head sagged from his strong shoulders, defeated in a way I'd never witnessed in him before. Then he sat forward, bracing his arms on his knees as he looked at the floor. "Is the baby okay?"

I pulled in a jagged, painful breath. "Yes."

He looked to the window where the rain had softened, but the sky was as menacing as ever. Then his eyes met mine for the first time, the deepest, darkest brown that bared a thousand souls. He shifted his gaze to my belly and pressed his fingers to his lips. "How long have you known?" His face contorted with pain.

My chin began to quiver, but I wouldn't look down. "Five days." The admission of truth caused my stomach to roll in disgust, but I welcomed the discomfort. I deserved it.

His eyes never wavered. "Did you know?"

I looked away then, not able to make myself answer, but his words came again.

"Did you know the baby wasn't mine?"

Tears spilled from my eyes, down my cheeks, and into the corner of my mouth. "Yes." I sobbed. "Yes, and I'm so sorry. I'm so, so sorry."

He squeezed the bridge of his nose, turning to face the window again. This rock of a man was trying not to cry, and it was tearing me apart.

john

* * *

I squeezed the bridge of my nose, my head pounding, my throat so tight it was suffocating—because I finally got the confirmation I'd come back for. She knew she was pregnant, she knew the baby wasn't mine, but she didn't tell me. My heart felt like it had been rolled by a semi-truck, pounding the muscle into the black earth over and over. "Whose is it?"

I looked back at her, into her puffy eyes that were vibrant green but showed her devastation.

"His name's Austin," she stated. Her voice was small, defeated, and shaking. "Austin Stratton."

I swallowed. "Does he know?"

She hesitated a moment then nodded. I pushed my head back to my shoulders and gripped my forehead; her answer clawing at my heart. "You told him, but not me?"

"John, he's my baby's father□"

"And who am I, Tuesday? Who the fuck am I?"

"John!" she cried. "Don't do this."

"Does he know about me?"

She shook her head. "It's not what you think□"

"Does he know about me?" I asked again.

254

She shook her head and her lips began to tremble. "N-no."

I sat forward and pressed my fingers to my mouth. "What does he think of the baby? What does he think of *this*?"

She looked to the window, where the rain was softly beating against the dark glass. "He wants to marry me."

A surge of adrenaline ran through my body and I stood up. Hearing those words twisted my gut so painfully I couldn't see straight. "Is that what you want?" I pushed the tray table away from her bed, needing there to be nothing between us. Nothing but her and me, me and Tuesday.

She shook her head, and tears ran down her cheeks as she clutched her stomach. "John, you're scaring me," she whispered.

"That's bullshit!" I yelled at her. "You know what you want. Just tell me! Tell me what you want!"

"I want you!" she yelled. "And I want my baby to have its father!"

I shook my head, my throat constricting so tight I wasn't sure I'd be able to get the words out. "What the fuck does that mean?"

Her face contorted with hurt and sorrow, and she looked down to her lap. "You can't ask me to choose between you, John. You can't do that." Her voice was soft, almost a whisper.

"Why not?"

"Because it's not my choice to make!" She looked up, her voice stronger. "Because my baby deserves a father. I never had one, he left before I was even born, and I won't take that away from her. I won't take that away from *him*. I can't."

I nodded, meeting her eyes one last time before backing up a step. "Then you've made your choice."

She sobbed, but no words came from her lips any longer. I looked to the bedside table and saw her discharge papers already there. "I'll take you home."

Her body was shaking so hard it was difficult for me to watch. I'd never seen anyone cry like that before, as though her whole body, inside and out, was feeling every part of her pain. But she did everything like that. She kissed like that, with her whole body. And she made love like that.

I rubbed my hands over my face, needing to leave, needing to think—even though every part of me wanted to crawl in beside her and hold her so tight that she would stop shaking. To kiss her and tell her everything would be okay. But I couldn't let myself. I didn't know if I believed it. I couldn't share her with anyone, and the fact that she was asking me to, proved she didn't know me as well as I thought she did.

"Tuesday, it's time to go."

She turned to me then, her face red and streaked with tears. "Will you come with me?" she asked. "Will you take me home and will you come inside? Will you hold me? Because that's what I need right now. I need you to hold me. I need you to love me. I need you to be with me. Will you be with me, even though I'm pregnant with another man's child?"

I only stood there shaking my head, because even though she needed me to do all those things, I couldn't.

"Then go," she screamed. "Leave me!"

I shook my head again, my chest heavy from the sight of her. "I'm not leaving you like this. I'm taking you home."

"No. You're not! Leave me! Just do it! Please... please just do it!" She pulled in a breath and looked me in the eyes. "I need this pain to be over. Please," she whispered. "Becky is already on her way."

I looked to the closed door, everything hurting so badly I

could hardly see straight. She continued to cry, filling my head with sounds that would never leave me because the sound of her tears mirrored the tearing apart of my heart. I gripped the back of my neck, squeezing so hard I knew I would leave a bruise, then I forced my feet forward, making myself walk away.

I pulled the door open, filling my lungs with the same air she breathed for the very last time, and left—just as she asked me to, and I didn't look back. I would never look back.

CHAPTER THIRTY-FOUR

john

* * *

The road was black and dark, like everything else around me. Like my life, drained of all color since the moment I walked out of that room. I tried to breathe, although my chest was so tight I could hardly manage, but I did. Just enough to keep living. Just enough to feel the pain that was spreading like poison through my veins.

The yellow lines were dashing by on the road in front of me, the wipers swishing from side to side, clearing the rain from my windshield as I sped down the highway. I knew I should slow down, but I couldn't. I needed to be far away from her; so far away, I wasn't tempted to go back again.

Her cries rang like a blaring scream in my head, growing louder and louder with each second. And soon all I could see was her face. Visions of the day we met, kissing her against the display in the hardware store, finding her in the back room in tears because she was so tired, the way she melted in my arms like warm honey, and her hair, her wild and crazy hair framing her face when she sat on top of me as we made love.

The screams kept coming, louder and louder, filling every part of me with memories, taking every bit of life I had left. The sound grew louder, but I welcomed it, surrendering my heart to all of it.

My phone began to ring in the passenger seat, and I glanced over. Lisa's name flashed across the screen. I turned away, knowing I couldn't bear to explain why we'd left. My hands tightened on the steering wheel as I looked back to the road. But it wasn't black anymore; it was bright and blinding. The screams weren't my memories of Tuesday; they were the blaring sound of a semi-truck.

I swerved to the side, causing my tires to skid and spin. I gripped the steering wheel, not even fighting it anymore because my life had ended the moment I walked out of that hospital room. My truck continued to turn, round and round, and just when I thought it wouldn't stop, my whole life went still.

The darkness filled my truck again and I slumped over in my seat. Silence took over the dark night as I replayed the events of the last few seconds. Then my shoulders began to shake, hard and uncontrollably, and for the first time since I was five years old, I let myself cry.

* * *

"Why didn't you answer your *phone*?" Lisa's voice called through the empty living room as I closed the door behind me. It was past one in the morning, six hours since our panicked departure from the party, two hours since I left Tuesday at the hospital. Ginger was asleep at her feet and barely glanced up when I came inside.

"Everyone is worried sick about you."

I threw my keys on the table and ignored her, not caring when they slid off the surface and hit the floor.

She stood up, looking to the closed door. "Where's Tuesday?" she whispered. "What happened?"

None of your fucking business.

It was what I wanted to say, but I didn't. I was numb, and all I wanted was to sleep and forget about everything that had happened over the past eight weeks. Forget about everything that had happened since the night she walked into that *fucking* bar.

Lisa covered her mouth with her hand and followed me to my bedroom. "John, you're scaring me. Why did you leave like that? What's wrong? Talk to me. What happened?"

I sat on the edge of the bed, leaning forward to grip my skull because it hurt so fucking bad. But not just my head. Everything hurt. My body, my heart, every fucking crevice of it.

I rubbed my hands down my face and turned to face her, knowing she wouldn't leave until I explained. "Tuesday's pregnant," I said. "She fell out in the rain and started bleeding. We left because I took her to the hospital."

"Oh, my God." She sat down beside me and touched my arm. "Is everything okay?"

I nodded, knowing it was the baby she was asking about, then I shook my head and met her eyes. "The baby's not mine, Lisa."

Her brows knit together. "What?" Her breathing slowed, as though she couldn't quite understand what I was trying to tell her.

"It's not my baby. She's pregnant with another man's child."

She covered her lips and shook her head. "How do you know?"

I stood up, raking my hands through my hair. "Because she's twelve weeks along and I only met her eight weeks ago. That's how I fucking know!"

Lisa didn't deserve my anger, but I couldn't hold it in any longer. I was so mad I could hardly see straight. So broken I didn't know if I'd ever be whole again. The scene at the hospital played in my head over and over, shredding me further than I ever thought possible.

"I asked her what she wanted, and she said she wouldn't choose. I didn't even care that it wasn't my baby, Lisa. I didn't even care."

I heard her sob behind me but I couldn't turn around. I couldn't handle seeing her cry when I was so close to losing it myself.

"What did she say?" she whispered.

Tuesday's words ran through my mind for the thousandth time. *You can't ask me to do that, John. That's not fair.*

"She said she couldn't choose."

"Is she still seeing him? The father?"

I squeezed my eyes shut, the thought of her with another man turning my stomach. "I don't know," I said in a low, distant voice. "I didn't ask."

She put her hand on my shoulder and pressed her forehead against my arm. "Don't you think you should find out?"

"No."

"Why?" she asked between tears.

"Because she needed to choose."

tuesday

* * *

Becky stood behind the couch, gripping my shoulders as dozens of new customers filled the shop. She softly kneaded, trying to ease the tension in my muscles that hadn't felt normal since she picked me up from the hospital two days ago.

"You okay? Feeling good?" Becky asked.

I pulled in a breath, knowing she was asking about the baby, and I nodded. "I'm fine." The baby was fine. There had been no more bleeding since that night at the cabin, but I still couldn't breathe. I couldn't sit in my own shop without missing him, without something, everything filling me with memories of our time together.

Becky had insisted on setting up the grand opening so I could rest. She even pulled the couch out of my office to the very middle of the product floor so I could interact with the customers during the party. But it hurt so bad to be here, to remember, and all I wanted to do was go home.

My eyes shifted to the entrance as I tried to swallow the lump in my throat. John promised me he'd be here, that he'd stand by my side, hold my hand. The door had opened hundreds of times in the last few hours, but none of them had been him. Not that I expected him to, but I was prolonging my hurt with hope. I needed to explain, I needed him to know the truth. I wanted him to know that what we had wasn't a lie. I loved him. And I would never stop.

A little old lady stepped into my line of vision, blocking my view of the entrance and pulling me from my thoughts. I looked up to her kind face, her hair so white that it glowed from the sun streaming through the windows behind her.

"Hi dear," she began, her voice quiet and hoarse as she twisted a tin of dried herbs between her crooked fingers. "I was wondering if you could help me. I don't see very well. Would you tell me how much this is?"

I smiled and nodded. "Of course." I took the tin from her hand.

Her eyes were soft, but there was something in them that made me feel uncomfortable as if she recognized me, although I was certain I'd never met her before in my life. I quickly took the tin and flipped it over. "Um, nine dollars and ninety-nine cents." I met her eyes again as I handed it back. "They're very good. Grown locally by a farmer, not thirty miles away."

She smiled back and took the herbs from my hand. "Is this your shop, dear?"

I nodded, curious as to why she was asking the question, but there was something about her I didn't like. I could almost see my own fear when I looked into her eyes. Normally, I loved meeting people like this, the eccentric ones, the ones who knew *more* than the rest of us did. But not today. I couldn't handle it today; I was too vulnerable.

She smiled and met my eyes again. "Are you married, dear?"

"No," I said, shaking my head.

"Divorced?"

"No," I whispered.

She frowned, as though I'd given her an answer she wasn't expecting. "Ahh, well... I just felt something here when I walked through the door. I thought it might have been because of *you*."

She turned away from me to walk in the opposite direction, but I sat forward and touched her arm. I knew I should just let her go, but I couldn't. "Ma'am, what did you see?"

She turned to face me again, looking from ceiling to floor before meeting my eyes. "There was love here once." She shook her head. "It was very strong, not something you find every day." She looked into my eyes again. "It was given up on too easily. Like it was nothing. Such a shame." She tsked.

My eyes brimmed with tears, but I wiped them away before she addressed me again. "Do you know who owned it before you?"

"No." I pushed myself from the couch. Goose bumps covered my body as I headed to the back room. I barely made it through the door before my shoulders began to shake. Becky was right behind me, as she always was, closing the door before turning me around.

"She's just a crazy old lady, Tuesday. You're okay. Don't let her words get to you."

I shook my head and looked her in the eyes. "You think she's crazy?" I cried. "Becky, she knew things! She said there was love here, and there was. She said something happened, and it did. She said it was given up too easily... and maybe that's true too! Don't you believe in fate, Becky? Maybe she was meant to come in here and bring me that message. Maybe I'm giving up too easily."

"Tuesday," Becky began, shaking my shoulders. "Those words could be true for anyone. To you, to me, to everyone out there in your shop. Because we've all loved and lost, don't you see that?"

"No." I shook my head. "This was different. This was so different."

She gripped my shoulders and spun me around before opening the door a crack so we could peek back into the store. "She's crazy, Tuesday, look at her. Look at her socks—who wears socks like that?"

I found her in the corner of the shop by the lotions, opening jars and sniffing them before putting them back on the shelf. She wore knee high socks, visible beneath her yellow sack-like dress, and little red capes were flying off the backs of her calves: Wonder Woman.

I blew my nose on a tissue, not knowing what to think. She did look crazy, but the same argument could be used for me most days. Then the door chimed at the front entrance, and I looked in its direction. A large bouquet of roses was all I saw, and my heart slammed in my chest.

I tried to see who it was, but the crowd was too large for me to see beyond, even when I went up on my toes. I held my breath, waiting for the crowd to clear, holding Becky's hand and praying that he had come back to find me. Then Austin stepped out from a group of people and began looking around the shop.

His hair was combed back, and he wore fitted jeans that showed off his muscular thighs. The sight of him initiated a hush of whispers to roll over the entire store, but all the air expelled from my lungs as I turned around. I should've been happy he was here to see me, that he wasn't running away like my own father, but I wasn't. I was disappointed he wasn't John. All I wanted was him.

Becky opened the door, and Austin slipped into the back room. "Wow, it's standing room only in there. You must be so happy."

I forced a smile and took the flowers from his outstretched hand. A full dozen long-stemmed red roses. "You didn't have to do this."

He shook his head slightly, looking at the floor then up to me. His jaw tightened and he didn't look so happy anymore. "There's been talk around the studio that you were in the hospital because of the baby."

I looked to Becky, wondering where he'd heard the news, then turned toward the kitchen and placed the roses on the counter. I could hear the frustration in his voice and knew it wasn't invalid. He should have been the first person I called, but I hadn't even thought about it.

"I'm sorry," I began, turning around to face him. "I slipped in the rain, but the doctor assured me it was nothing, so I never thought to call you. I'm not used to having to report back to anyone... about anything."

His expression softened and he nodded. As though he understood completely. "We have a lot to figure out in the next few months..." He walked toward me and rested his hip on the counter. We were both quiet a second, awkwardly looking at the counter, then he swallowed.

"There's also something else." He looked over his shoulder to Becky, as though looking for her support. She looked down at her feet, and right away, I knew she was responsible for this. For all of it.

"When I asked you to marry me," he began, "I hadn't even

considered there was another guy."

I squared my shoulders and inhaled a breath. I looked to Becky, but she only gestured for me to listen. I met Austin's eyes again and nodded my head, urging for him to continue.

"I wanted to say I'm sorry. I'm sorry you're facing this difficult situation. I'm sorry I got you pregnant when you didn't want to be. If there's anything you need me to do☐" He stopped and looked to the ground before meeting my eyes. "I know something happened and I'm sorry. If you need me to talk to him, to straighten things out for you, you just let me know, and I'll do anything."

Tears were streaming down my face by now, and I shook my head. "It's not your fault, Austin. You don't need to be sorry."

He opened his arms to me, not crying, but I could see he was close to it too. I stepped into his chest and let him hold me. He wasn't John, and he would never be, but I could tell he would be a friend to me. And he'd make an excellent father.

CHAPTER THIRTY-FIVE

john

FIVE DAYS LATER
* * *

I threw Ginger's leash to the coffee table, knocking over the basket and causing its contents to spill out all over the floor. I didn't care. I didn't bother to pick it up, and pulled my shirt over my head as I headed for the bathroom.

I needed a shower. To wash away this crap of a day and forget about *her*, but I couldn't. I couldn't stop thinking about her because her name was everywhere. Because her fucking name would forever be stuck in the middle of each fucking week! For the rest of my life, I'd have to see it every time I looked at the fucking calendar.

I sat on the side of the bed, my body heavy with exhaustion as I began to unlace my boots. A knock sounded at the door, but I ignored it, wanting whoever it was to go away. I wasn't in the mood for unexpected guests, and I sure as hell wasn't going to be nice if I answered it. But the sound only came louder.

"Fucking shit." I pulled off one boot, just as Ginger began to bark at the door. I pushed myself from the bed, Ginger's bark increasing in volume, as I stormed down the hallway and yanked the door open.

Tuesday stood at the landing. She stepped back at the sight of me, her chest visibly rising and falling as she breathed. Ginger rushed out to greet her, sniffing and licking her hand like a week hadn't gone by since she'd seen her last, but Tuesday never looked down. She only stood there, wearing overalls with one of my big flannel work shirts over the top, her face streaked from tears.

"You didn't come," she said after a moment. Her voice was low and winded, as if she had run the whole way here.

I looked to the ground and pulled in a breath. The sight of her was still too painful to bear. "You honestly expected me to?"

"You promised."

I gripped my forehead, letting out a slight laugh that held no humor. "Well, a lot has changed since I made that promise." I glanced up, but my eyes locked on her hands, fisted at her sides as though she was afraid of me. I hated it. I was mad as hell about what happened, but I hated every damn second of her fear. "What do you want, Tuesday?" I asked in the softest voice possible.

She didn't answer.

I opened the door wider and stepped to the side to let her in. "Come in. You're supposed to be resting."

She shook her head, but her body became more rigid. "This will only take a second." She looked down briefly. "Becky's waiting for me in the parking lot."

I rested my shoulders in the doorway and nodded. Her body was shaking so badly, I knew whatever she planned to say was hard for her, and I wanted to make it as easy as possible so she could go.

She wrapped her arms around her belly and met my eyes. "Thirteen weeks ago I got drunk at a party and woke up with a man in my bed. I was so drunk I don't even remember a single thing we did that night. I'm not proud of it, but it happened. I never saw him again after that, but I knew who he was. He worked at Parker Studios with Becky."

She took a deep breath then closed her eyes briefly before continuing. "I didn't know it then, but I got pregnant that night—then a few weeks later construction began and everything was busy. I didn't even notice when my period was different, but I had it, John. I swear."

She was crying between each word, and my chest was heavy from the sound of it. I wanted to grab her and hold her, but I stayed where I was, needing to hear what she came to say.

"And then I met *you*." Her eyes lifted to mine. "I hated you at first... and I was pretty sure you hated me too. I never meant to fall in love with you—but I did. I never meant to get pregnant, but I did. And I found myself in a position of finally finding the love of my life, and discovering I was pregnant by a different man."

She wiped at her eyes with the backs of her hands.

"I should have told you right away, but it was so hard. I know that's a crappy excuse, but I convinced myself it would be easier once the job was over. Because then you could walk away like you deserved to do." Her hand covered her mouth, muffling a sob. "I never meant for you to find out the way you did, and it's killing me that you think things about me that aren't true."

I stepped toward her, wanting to hold her and take away her pain, but she held up her hand and stepped backward.

"I lied to you, and I shouldn't have, but you lied to me too."

I shook my head, looking into her eyes. "What did I lie to you about?"

"You lied about your scar. You didn't tell me you were adopted."

269

I gripped the back of my neck. "That's hardly the same thing."

She stared at me. Her green eyes burned with passion, heat, and heartbreak. "We both lied, John. But I came to tell you the truth. The truth is I fell in love with you, not knowing I was pregnant. But I also fell in love with this baby. I realize it's not an ideal situation, because no matter what happens, Austin will always be my baby's father. He will always be a part of my life."

I stepped toward her, shaking my head. "You think DNA makes him a father? You think he'll be there because his blood is in that baby?" I shook my head. "Well that's bullshit, Tuesday! My *father* is the man who gave me this scar." I flicked my thumb over my chin. "The man you met at the cabin, that was my *dad*. He was the man who was there at every one of my baseball games, the man who put me through college, and still calls me to talk about the Dodgers when I really know it's because he wants to hear my voice. Just because that other guy got you pregnant doesn't make him that baby's father. Don't even pretend they're the same thing."

My jaw tightened with anger as I looked at her. "You want to know what the truth is? I don't give a shit that baby isn't mine. I know what makes a father, and it has nothing to do with blood."

I turned around, pressing my thumb and forefingers against my eyes, trying to calm myself.

"I'm so sorry that happened to you," she whispered. "And I'm sorry I didn't tell you about the baby as soon as I found out. But never once have I compared the two. My father walked out on me before I was even born. Austin is this baby's father, and he wants to be a dad. I know this is hard for you, and I'm so sorry, and I know you want me to choose, but I can't. This baby didn't choose this life, and I'm not going to take away her father because I fell in love with you."

She turned around then, and I pressed the back of my

head against the wall. "Tuesday..."

But she was already running down the steps away from me. I pushed myself from the wall to go after her, but she was already at the bottom of the stairs. "Tuesday!"

Ginger ran halfway down the steps then turned and looked up at me, as if telling me to go after her, but I didn't. I watched as she ran around the side of Becky's red sports car and yanked open the door.

She looked up for a brief moment, meeting my eyes, her face red and streaked but stunning, then she ducked into the car and disappeared from view. She slammed the car door, and I watched as they pulled out of the parking lot and turned the corner. I fought the urge to go after her, because I needed time to process all she had said. I needed to figure out what was going on inside my head.

Ginger followed me back into the house, where I slammed the door. I didn't know what to think anymore. I didn't know what to do. I looked around the room, trying to find my cell phone because I needed to call someone. Lisa or Em, or someone who could help me sort this out. I walked over to the couch, sat down, and ran my hands through my hair. My eyes locked on a letter on the coffee table. I picked it up, my finger running across the name I'd hated since the day he gave me up.

Gabriel Mucci.

My father.

TWENTY-THREE YEARS EARLIER.

* * *

"He's here!" I shouted over my shoulder. It was the first time I'd seen my daddy in days and days and there he was, right outside the window. He was standing big and tall because my daddy was *so* strong, and his face was nice and friendly, so I knew he'd kept his promise. He wasn't talking like a monster anymore. Not like the day he had to take me to the hospital.

271

Lisa was holding my hand, and I couldn't wait for her to meet him. She would like him. Because when my daddy didn't drink from the brown bottles, he was the best daddy in the world. He took care of me, and he read me stories, and we made big tents in the middle of the living room, and he bought me rainbow cereal and let me eat it right out of the box.

The lady was asking him questions though, and I was scared he was in trouble. Everyone was frowning and looking at me, but I knew my daddy was being good. He told me at our last visit. He told me he was going to be good so he could get me back. He told me he would get me back, and he would buy me a big box of Legos so we could build a whole house.

I looked over to Mr. and Mrs. Eaton because I was pretty sure I saw Mrs. Eaton crying. I hadn't seen her cry since she came to pick me up at the other foster home, when Em cried and we had to leave her behind. Mrs. Eaton was always so happy, and I wasn't sure what was making her so sad. She wrapped her arms around me and whispered that she was sorry, but I didn't know why. Why did she want to hug me so hard?

Then my dad turned around so I could just see his face, and he looked like he was crying too. My daddy never cried. Why was my daddy crying?

A lady pulled a sheet of paper out of her bag, and he looked over at the house before he bent to sign it. He looked at me, but I didn't think he really saw me, 'cause he didn't smile like he normally did.

"Daddy!" I called out, but he wouldn't look at me anymore. He picked his things off the top of her car then started walking down the sidewalk away from me.

"DADDY!"

Lisa squeezed my hand in hers, and Mrs. Eaton hugged me from behind, and everyone was crying. Then my daddy disappeared from view, and I started kicking and screaming.

"DADDY! Where's my daddy going?"

Mrs. Eaton shook her head and pulled me into her arms, squishing my face against her shoulder. "It's okay, baby, everything will be okay…"

I shook my head, fighting against her arms and kicking my legs to get away. "Daddy! You said you would take me to the park! You promised!"

The door closed again, and I couldn't see my daddy anymore. Mrs. Eaton hugged me tighter, and I realized my daddy was gone.

* * *

The tortured screams of a little boy played in my head as I sat down heavily on the couch. It was midnight, the screams still vivid in my head from my nightmare as I leaned over to pick up the envelope. The weight of the letter felt like a thousand pounds in my hands. A thousands pounds covered by the piles of dirt I'd piled on top of it trying to forget.

I tore open the envelope open, took out the folded yellow paper gingerly with my fingers, and spread it out on the table. In my mind, I'd read it a thousand times. A thousand letters from him that never came. I wanted so desperately to know he hadn't forgotten me. I looked down at his handwriting, elegant and beautiful, just as I remembered it.

Dear John,

I've written this letter a thousand times, but there are no words good enough to express how sorry I am.

You were my little boy, and there hasn't been a day that has gone by that I haven't thought of you. I'm writing this letter to ask for the chance to explain myself. Please give me the chance.

273

TAYLOR SULLIVAN

Love always,

Your daddy – Gabriel Mucci

I squeezed my eyes shut. The pain and rejection experienced by a five-year-old boy surged through my blood. I gripped the letter tightly in my hand. A phone number, written in the handwriting I could still remember, followed his words. Elegant, structured penmanship that was so different from the drunk I remembered him to be.

I didn't know if I had it in me to see him again, but I didn't know if I had it in me not to. Tuesday's eyes flashed into my mind. Bright, green, and heartbroken... I put the letter on the coffee table, smoothed it out on the surface, and picked up my phone, not caring what time it was.

"Hello?" A gruff voice answered.

"Gabriel?"

"Yes?"

"This is John Eaton. I got your letter. When would you like to meet?"

274

CHAPTER THIRTY-SIX

john

* * *

The park was empty as I sat across the table from my father. He looked the same. It had been nearly twenty-three years since I'd seen him, yet he was just as I remembered. Broad shoulders, full head of dark hair, good-looking.

I was told as a child I looked like him, but until right now, I didn't see it. We had the same eyes, so dark they were almost black, and the same chin, except mine held the mark he'd given me before I was finally taken away.

He shifted in his seat, leaning forward to brace his forearms on the table. "I feel like I'm looking in the mirror, son." He flashed me the charming smile that I used to love. The one that had women in and out of our lives all the years I could remember.

My stomach twisted. This was the man I still had nightmares about, even at twenty-eight years old, but he wasn't my father. I shook my head. "No. I'm not your son. You gave that up twenty-three years ago."

His smile fell away, and he nodded once. His gaze dropped to the table. "Fair enough."

I knew I was making him uncomfortable, but I didn't care.

He deserved it. He deserved everything that happened to him over the last twenty-three years. The DUI's, the arrests, the jail time.

I couldn't help but think of Shelly as I sat there. She was the same age now as I was when he started doing those things to me. I was a helpless boy who was just being a kid. A defenseless child who loved him so desperately, in spite of all his faults. And even when he left bruises, I still forgave him. Because I still believed he was good. I still believed, even after all of that.

He cleared his throat then pulled a tattered sweater box out of an old paper sack and set it on the table. A blue rubber band was wrapped around it, and he pulled a pocketknife from his pocket and cut it free. "I brought some old photos. I hope you don't mind."

I clenched my jaw, fighting the urge to get up and leave. But I came here for a reason. I wasn't sure exactly what it was, but after all these years, I needed to hear him explain.

An image of a woman with long, brown hair sat on top of a large stack of photos. She had big, brown eyes and stood sideways as she smiled at the camera. She was pregnant, and the sight of her stirred feelings deep in my gut.

"This was your mother."

I took the photo from his outstretched hand, breathless, my heart racing. I remembered seeing the photo before, but barely. She was so young. It was hard to believe she was my mother, but I knew she was. I could see myself in her smile. "How old was she?"

He met my eyes, as though reading my thoughts. "Eighteen." He handed me another photo, this one of her holding me in her arms. "That's you. Eight pounds, four ounces." He looked down to the stack of photos and kept flipping. "This," he said, handing me another, "was the night we'd come home from the hospital."

It was of me and my mom sitting in a rocking chair. She

was holding me in her arms, and I could see her profile as she looked down at my face. My tiny hand wrapped around her finger.

"We were so in love with you. We had our baby boy and were on top of the world." He picked up another photo and held it a moment. "We'd only been home for a few hours when she started complaining of a headache."

He grimaced. " 'Go lie down, you're just tired,' I said to her. I thought I knew everything..." He took a deep breath. "I tucked her into bed, took her a glass of water, then gave you your first bath." He met my eyes and the corner of his mouth lifted. "You didn't like it one bit." Then his expression changed, and he looked over my shoulder into the distance as if remembering. "I promised you so many things that night..."

His face grew somber, and he cleared his throat. "When I brought you into the bedroom that night, your mom was sitting on the edge of the bed, gripping her head. I laid you down, went to get her some Tylenol, but when I came back, she was talking funny. Slurring her words. That's when I knew it was something more serious.

"I should have called an ambulance. I should have known better but by the time I got us to the hospital, it was too late. She died an hour later of a brain aneurysm."

There was so much pain in his eyes I couldn't breathe. He squeezed his eyes shut, as if the memory was too painful to keep them open, and I suddenly felt empathy for my father for the first time in my life.

"It's no excuse for the way I treated you, but I was lost after that. I was twenty years old, had a baby I needed to take care of all on my own. Your mother and I didn't have family to speak of, so it was just me and you." He met my eyes. "Believe it or not, those days were some of the best of my life." He closed his eyes. "And some of the worst."

I looked away, unable to bear the pain any longer. I picked up a handful of photos and flipped through them one at a time. They were all of me. Me and my mother, me and my father, the three of us together, all taken just days after my birth. So many photos taken in such a short amount of time.

"I loved you, Johnny. She loved you. I just needed you to know that."

I stopped flipping and stared at a photo of the three of us together, huddled in in the middle of a hospital bed. "What was her name?" It was a question I'd wanted to know for as long as I could remember, but I'd had no one to ask until now.

"Kate."

I looked up at him. His face twisted in pain, and his hand gripped over his mouth. "I'm so sorry you never got to meet her."

His pain tore at me. I lowered my gaze and flipped to another photo—me at two years old, riding a wooden rocking horse. My throat grew so thick I could hardly talk. "I remember this." My gut twisted in knots. I was so confused. I'd hated this man. I hated him for twenty-three years because he was the man who had left bruises on my tiny, defenseless body. But right now, I felt sorry for him.

I turned over another photo, where yellow bruises could still be seen on both of my skinny arms as I gripped a teddy bear. "I remember a lot."

I slid the photo across the table, and he picked it up, running his hand over the picture of the little boy who still smiled because he didn't know better. "I was a drunk, Johnny. It's no excuse, but it was only then that I did it."

"Don't□"

He shook his head. "I was angry. I was angry about so many things, and I took it out on you. I was angry about trying to make it alone, losing your mother, having to take care of my boy alone. And when I drank□" He stopped talking, because there was no need to continue. We both knew our past.

He gazed at the photo a moment longer, and then turned it face down on the table before he looked back up at me. "I sobered up when you were taken from me and put in that shitty foster home. I got you out, had you placed with the Eaton's. You were all I had left, and I would do anything to get you back. I got a new job, was working sixty hours a week, I was working hard to make a life for you. For us.

"But when I saw you with that family... They had so much I could never hope to give you." He leaned forward, pushing his hands through his hair. "With them, you had a mom. And not just any mom... A mom who looked like Betty fucking Crocker. You had siblings, and a father who ran around with you on his shoulders... One who would never dream of hitting you.

"When I left you☐" He paused, gathering his words. "When I left you, it tore my heart out, but I did it for you. I did it to give you a chance. To give you the life I never had. To get you away from me."

He scrubbed his face with his hand and looked at me. "I disappeared because I was a chicken shit. I could have been there, but I was too stubborn to realize you could have had both."

My chest tightened painfully. "Why are you telling me this? Why now?"

He shook his head. "Because it's taken me this long to grow up."

* * *

The floodlights slowly flickered to life as I looked through the photos in the front seat of my truck. My father had left hours ago, yet still I sat in the same spot, looking at the same photos over and over. They were parts of my life that existed; yet, I didn't remember most of them.

Photos of my mother, barely more than a child in a

wedding dress, pregnant with me, then holding me like I was the love of her life. She died only three days after birthing me. And my father, so young, lost, and overwhelmed. A young man trying to do the best he could as a single father. He gave them all to me—insisted I take them. Said he'd had them long enough...

"Ah fuck..." I wiped over my face, feeling drained and raw. I spent most of my life hating my father, but it was evident from these photos that he spent all of his loving me. He'd been in and out of prison his whole life, yet somehow he'd managed to keep this box.

But out of all the photos, what got me the most were the ones sent to him from my mother. Every Christmas, every birthday, high school, and college graduation. And the letters. Telling him about my life... Telling him how proud they were of me, and thanking him for trusting them enough to be my parents.

I picked my cell up off the passenger seat and dialed a number I vowed to use more often after tonight.

She picked up the phone on the first ring. "Hello?" The sound of her voice was familiar and comforting.

"Hey, Mom."

"Hey," she said. The faint sound of running water played in the background before she shut it off. "I was just thinking about you. You okay?"

I nodded, gripping the bridge of my nose before answering. "I just saw my father."

She was quiet a second, and I could only imagine what was going through her mind. "How'd it go?"

I picked up a photo of me and my family. Mom, Dad, Lisa, Penny—everyone. "It was good. He gave me a whole box of photos."

"Did he?" she said, and I could hear her voice thickening with emotion.

"Yeah." I swallowed. "Some of them I'd never seen before. I was a pretty cute baby." I wiped my eyes, realizing she'd never seen me that way before. I was five years old when they took me in. They missed so much, but I felt like they'd been there my whole life. "I'll bring them on Thursday."

I could hear that she was crying now. "I'd like that."

I leaned back in my seat and closed my eyes. "Mom..." I hesitated, wanting to ask in just the right way. "Why didn't you tell me you've been sending him pictures all these years?"

She was quiet a moment. "John, I—"

"Mom, it's okay. I'm not mad."

She took a deep breath. "Because he loved you. I could see it on his face every time he came to visit you. I could see it. And he did something I don't know if I could have ever done. He gave me his son to raise. He gave me *you. My* son. I sent him photos because I wanted him to see that you were loved."

I closed my eyes and leaned my head back into the seat. "Thank you."

tuesday

* * *

Becky leaned over the counter and yawned as I pulled out the cash drawer from the register. "You should go home," I said. I climbed down from my stool and grabbed my smoothie. "I'm just going to count this, print some invoices, and go straight to bed."

She frowned at me, but I could see the bags under her eyes and knew she was exhausted. She'd been here with me all week after working her normal job. I knew she was worried, but I'd gotten the all clear from the doctor yesterday, and frankly, I could use some time to myself.

281

She started following me to the back room and I turned around, halting her. "I'm serious, Becky. If you come back here, I'm going to pour my smoothie over your head."

She grinned. "Sounds kinky."

"Ha, ha..." I smiled softly, knowing she loved me, but also how much I needed space.

She let out a sigh. "Are you sure you'll be okay?"

"Yes."

"Pinky swear?"

I grinned. "Pinky swear. Now go!"

She dropped her shoulders, and I walked her to the door before locking it and turning around to face my empty shop. It had been open for five days, but right now was the first time I'd been alone. I was still too emotional to let myself think about how I felt about that, so I headed straight to my office to work. It had gotten me through a lot in the past, and it would get me through today.

I set the drawer on my desk, leaned back in my chair, and unsnapped the bib of my overalls. My hand rested on my belly, and I closed my eyes. I'd heard the baby's heartbeat again yesterday, and it had been just as emotional as every time before that. Even though I was still less than fourteen weeks into my pregnancy, the technician said she guessed that the baby was a girl. Just like in my dreams.

This pregnancy was so surreal, nothing like I planned, but beautiful nonetheless. I blew out an exhausted breath, opened my eyes, and startled.

John was leaning against the frame of my office door, watching me.

I snatched up the bib of my overalls to cover myself. "What are you doing here? How'd you get in?"

"The back door was unlocked."

But there was something in his voice that made me look at him more deeply. His hair was a mess, which was something I'd seen a thousand times, but his eyes... They were red-rimmed, searching my face as if he could see into my soul.

"Is everything okay?" I whispered.

He pushed himself from the doorframe and walked toward me. "I met with my father today."

My brows furrowed, trying to understand why that upset him so much.

"My biological father." He pulled the other chair from beside my desk and sat down right in front of me.

I swallowed because seeing him like this made my heart jump to my throat. He looked raw, and open—and scared.

He took my hands in his and kissed my knuckles. "Things aren't always black and white, Tuesday. I realized that today. I was abused as a child, and I spent most of my adult life hating the man who did it to me... but today..." He grimaced. "I'm not saying what he did wasn't horrible... but today I forgave him. I forgave him because he was human. I forgave him because he was a man who lost the love of his life and had to figure out how to raise his son alone."

He reached into his pocket, pulled out two photos, and handed them to me. One was of a happy, young couple holding a newborn baby in a hospital bed. The next was of John, proud in a cap and gown, surrounded by his smiling family. His mom and dad and all his sisters at his high school graduation. He pointed to the first one. "That's my mom and dad," he said, his voice thick and quiet. "And that's my family. They're all my family. All of them."

I nodded, taking his face in my hands and kissing his cheek. "Yes."

He leaned his forehead against mine, shaking it slightly as he took my hands again. "I spent a lot of time thinking today. Then I called my mother. She's an amazing woman, and I know there is a God because he sent me her. And then I came here to you. Because today I got a piece of my past back, a past I'd been running from for a very long time. And the first person I wanted to share it was with you. Because I want you to be my future. Please tell me you haven't given up on me."

"Never."

CHAPTER THIRTY-SEVEN

tuesday

FIVE MONTHS LATER
* * *

I leaned back on the couch nestled in the middle of the product floor and adjusted my pillow.

"Close your eyes, Tuesday. Don't peek." Becky had surprised me with a blessingway this afternoon, and everyone was here. All of John's sisters, our mothers, little Shelly, and even the placenta encapsulation lady, who was my new friend. They had all just taken turns layering plaster over my eight-month belly, and now the cast was removed, and I was sprawled in the middle of the shop as Becky painted a henna tattoo on my stomach.

I was on display for everyone to see, but I didn't care. Women who loved me surrounded me, and even though I was only four weeks from my due date, I felt beautiful.

Becky took her intricate brushes and set them on the table. I leaned back, closed my eyes, and tried to keep from giggling. The last few months had been amazing. Filled with love, support, and life. I spent much of my time working on the shop and planning for the baby, but every night was spent with John, where he'd patiently listen as I told him about all of it.

After about twenty minutes of what I was sure was slow torture for pregnant women, there was a lull in the room, and I lifted my head. "Are you done?"

"No," Becky said, pushing my head back down to my pillow. "And keep your eyes shut or you'll ruin the surprise."

I grinned, but I did what she told me and waited until I felt the brush stop. "Are you done now? Can I look?"

There was a long pause, and I felt a tingle up my spine. "Yes," she whispered.

Slowly, I opened my eyes, seeing Becky seated at my feet, but there at my side was John. He was on one knee, and he held up a ring in a plain wooden box.

I covered my mouth, and looked around the room. "What are you doing?"

He only shook his head and smiled at me, but his face contorted with an emotion that came so rarely from him. One he usually reserved for when we were alone. I looked around the room, finding Jake, Katie, John's father, Em— everyone. Then I looked down to my belly.

Becky's design spread from my panty line to the top of my rib cage. A huge sun twisted and turned with flowers and leaves. It was like a flower blooming from my insides, full of life and filled with love. But arched over the top was John's writing—lettered upside down but unmistakable. "Will you marry me?"

I looked back to John again, my throat so full of tears I couldn't speak.

He took my hand and looked me in the eyes. "I've been through a lot in my life. Some things I want to forget, and others I wouldn't give up for the world. I have scars. Scars it's taken me twenty-three years to heal, but for some reason, knowing you for only a few months changed all that. Before you, I didn't know what I was living for. I was living day by day, not knowing what my purpose was... I spent most of my life pushing through each week just to get to the next."

He kissed my knuckles and closed his eyes. His voice grew a little huskier. "But I think all that time, all those hours, all those days, I was waiting for you to walk into that bar. I was waiting for Tuesday."

I looked into his eyes, my shoulders shaking with emotion. "I love you."

He grinned and pressed his forehead to mine. "Will you marry me, Tuesday?"

Sobs and laughter poured from my mouth, and I nodded my head. "Yes."

He pushed the ring onto my finger then lifted me off the couch and turned around. "She said yes!" he shouted to everyone in the room.

Everyone was crying, laughing, and cheering all around us, and John pressed his lips to mine, kissing me in the way that always made my knees weak, but I didn't care. I didn't care that we had an audience, or that little Shelly started laughing in the corner. All I cared about was that I'd finally found my ever after. In the man I never once thought could be my prince charming.

CHAPTER THIRTY EIGHT

john

Four weeks later
* * *

I yanked the passenger door open, my jaw tight, and my breathing out of control. Tuesday sat in the front seat of my truck, her face twisting with the pain from another contraction, and all I could do was wait. God, I hated this. Hated seeing her in pain and having nothing I could do about it. I put my hands on both sides of her hips and added pressure like we learned in class, but goddamn it, it wasn't enough. "I know baby, you're almost there. Just a little longer."

She nodded her head, her body relaxing as the tension eased from her belly. She met my eyes again, and she was as determined and fiery as the night we met. "I'm ready." She grabbed hold of my arm, and we walked slowly up the path to the birthing center.

Austin was there in the waiting room when we entered, rocking back and forth on his heels before pushing himself from the wall.

"How far apart are they?" he asked, his face hard and tense like I'd never seen before. It was obvious he was nervous. He cared for this woman, loved his baby, and I couldn't help but respect that, but adjusting to Austin hadn't been easy for me. "About four minutes. We're getting close."

Tuesday gripped my arm before transferring her weight to

the back of the couch. "You need to call Becky. I need Becky," she panted.

I nodded to the midwife in the corner, taking in the urgency of Tuesday's words, and put the bag on the counter. I began tearing out clothes, diapers, and baby things looking for the phone. The midwife took hold of Tuesday's arm and grabbed the suitcase from my hand. "I'll go get things ready. Just relax, there's still plenty of time."

I nodded, my throat still constricting with fear, hope, and adrenaline. I found the phone at the very bottom of her diaper bag, punched the buttons to locate Becky's name, and waited for her to answer. My sisters had done this a half dozen times, but for some reason, I was scared out of my mind of losing Tuesday.

"Hello," Becky answered on the third ring.

"Becky, it's John." I took a deep breath. "It's time"

I could hear her breathing, but she was quiet a moment. "You take care of her, John."

I nodded and gripped my forehead before answering. "I will." I hung up the phone, packed everything back into her bag, and turned to Austin. "Are you ready?"

He looked to the closed door where Tuesday and her midwife had gone only moments earlier and shook his head. "She doesn't need me. She needs you." He looked back at me, his face just as scared as mine, and something transferred between us. There was a mutual understanding of what we were getting into. I never imagined myself in a situation like this, becoming a father for the first time and sharing it with another man. I cupped his shoulder and nodded, thankful for this gift he was giving to me and my wife. "You're a good man, Austin."

He laughed slightly and tilted his head toward the door. "Go. She needs you."

I turned to face the birthing room, my throat so tight I could only nod. I picked up her bag from the counter and opened the door, ready to be with my wife. Ready to start our family.

tuesday

* * *

The room was finally quiet, the lights low, as I leaned back on John's chest. Every muscle in my body was sore, but I didn't care. Our beautiful girl was nestled in my arms, healthy, strong, and fully alert in spite of her only being earthside for less than an hour.

John wrapped his arms around my waist and nestled in, his bare chest to my back, his cheek next to mine as we looked down at our daughter. "I'm going to love her for as long as I live."

His voice was husky and raw in a way I had never heard before, a voice meant only for his daughter.

I nodded and choked back tears. "I know you will."

Her little finger wrapped around his pinky, squeezing tightly, showing us how strong she was, and how she wasn't going to let him go. He kissed my head, pulling in a ragged breath as one of his tears ran down the bridge of his nose and onto my skin. "I'm going to love you longer."

His mouth pressed into my temple again as I focused my attention on our daughter. To her sweet lips, her delicate nose, and her tiny body. It fit so perfectly with ours, like the completion to our perfect puzzle.

John held onto me as I nursed her for the first time, and I began to cry. For all my life, I'd wanted to be a mother. I knew it would be amazing, that my life would forever change, and that I would fall in love. But nothing—no words—could have prepared me for the emotion that hit me all at once. Tears ran down my cheeks, shaking my shoulders with the intensity of them, but John only held me tighter, silently telling me he knew exactly what I was feeling.

I didn't cry because I was sad; I cried because it was beautiful. I cried because in that moment, wrapped in a cocoon of warmth, I realized that family wasn't made of blood. It was made of harder things, deeper things. It was made of trust, devotion, hope, and unconditional love. I had them all. Had them for a long time but didn't realize it. My mom and Becky, who I would squeeze so hard the next I saw them, and now the man I loved more deeply than I ever thought possible—and our newborn daughter, the one who was not his by genetics, but who already had him wrapped around her little finger. To some, she would forever be tainted, but to him, she was perfect.

As I lay there exhausted, womb empty, and heart exploding with more love than I knew what to do with, I realized I had everything I ever wanted.

I had a family.

It was not perfect, but it was perfectly mine, and I was going to love it for always.

the end

ABOUT THE AUTHOR

Taylor is a contemporary romance author who loves writing stories about real people. Ones with hopes, dreams, fears, insecurities, and flaws. She loves to read as much as she loves to write, and is trilled to share her stories with you. When Taylor isn't writing, she can often be found with her nose in a book, her face behind a camera, or spending time with her husband and three young children.

Taylor would love to hear from you.

Website: TaylorSullivanAuthor.com

Email: Taylorsullivan.author@gmail.com

Facebook:
https://www.facebook.com/TaylorSullivanAuthor

Twitter: https://twitter.com/@AuthorTSullivan

ACKNOLEDGMENTS

Honestly, I never quite know where to start with acknowledgments, but there are three women in my life who stick out extra special in my mind.

My sister, my niece, and my best friend.

Honestly, your support means so much. Your feedback means so much. The fact that you listen to my endless musing about my fictional characters, and treat them like they're actual human beings, means SO much.

I will never be able to thank you enough.

My readers.

Lisa, Kim, Samantha, Kelly, Kishan, Nancy, Kaci, Kristen, Dana, Emma, Bobbi, Brandy, Brenda, Sha... and so many more.

Your emails, your texts, and your phone calls mean the world to me! Especially when you tell me I made you cry! I LOVE that.

My editors.

Bree and Chris. Thank you for your encouragement, your support, your attention to detail, and for helping me make my work the best it can be for my readers.

My family and friends.

You know who you are, and I would honestly run out of space if I tried to list everyone. I would be lost without your support. Both in writing, and in life. I love you all.

ALSO BY TAYLOR SULLIVAN

HOME TO YOU
STORY OF A KISS ANTHOLOGY
NEVER REGRET

94592594R00165

Made in the USA
Lexington, KY
31 July 2018